CW00865368

MAGIC GAMES

MAGIC GAMES

Dragon Born Serafina: Book 2

www.ellasummers.com/magic-games

ISBN 978-1-5197-2911-8

Copyright © 2015 by Ella Summers

All rights reserved.

Cover art by Rebecca Frank

MAGIC GAMES

Dragon Born Serafina: Book 2

Ella Summers

Books by Ella Summers

Dragon Born Serafina
1   Mercenary Magic
2   Magic Games

Dragon Born Alexandria
1   Magic Edge

Sorcery and Science
1   Enchanted
2   Wilderness
2.5   Menace
3   Machination
3.5   Revelations
4   Skybuilders
4.5   Masquerade

And more coming soon…

Read more at
www.ellasummers.com

Contents

CHAPTER ONE
Battle of the Elements

SERA HIT THE dirt, narrowly missing the fireball tearing through the air toward her. It blasted over her head and crashed into the East River. She barely had time to watch it. She was too busy rolling to avoid the second fireball. Its enraged crackle hissed in her ears as it passed. Yes, enraged. Magic was as alive as any person or monster on this earth, its song as unique as a fingerprint—or a snowflake. Especially magic from *that* mage. He stared across the field at her, an amused twitch tugging at the corner of his lip.

As though he'd heard her internal meanderings about snowflakes, he pushed his hands forward to unleash a sphere of sparkling blue light that shot at Sera like a missile. She rolled away, the ground rumbling beneath her as the ice blast hammered down. A million tiny shards shattered. They bit at her body, dissolving through her bare arms, her stretchy sport leggings, and her tank top. She sprang up from the roll, shaking off the remaining ice splinters. They sprinkled down to the grass like crystal tears.

"Sera, this would be a lot easier if you stayed on your feet," her opponent said, his lip twitch upgrading to a full-out smirk.

"Easier for you maybe. To hit me," she added in an agitated growl.

"You need to fight back," he said calmly. Before she could speak, he added quickly, "With magic. We're practicing magic, not snark. That smart mouth of yours won't help you defeat your opponents in the Magic Games."

He was right. And Sera hated it when Kai Drachenburg was right.

"Giving up already?" he called out to her.

In response, she clenched her teeth, reaching for her magic. Lightning flashed in the cloudless sky, and a bolt of crackling purple-gold energy slammed down at Kai. He moved away, calm and agile, easily sidestepping her attack. The lightning bolt crashed against the ground with a resounding boom.

"Better." He waved his hand, crystalizing the residual lightning flames to ice. "But not good enough. You're moving too slow. Instead of puffing out one spell at a time, you need to link your magic into combination attacks. Your spells need to work together, like an orchestra."

Said the man rated number one of all elemental mages in the whole world. Magic came easily to him. As for her... Well, she'd spent too many years hiding her magic. Using it was like riding an old, rusty bicycle. With a loose handlebar. And a flat tire.

And then there were those other times—the times when her magic bubbled and burned beneath the surface, longing to gush out. It was too wild for her to control.

Not that she was going to complain to Kai about that. He wouldn't understand. For him, self-control was simply part of his daily regiment, like brushing his teeth. Or stepping on werewolves.

"Ok," Sera said, refocusing.

She drew her hands together. Soft vibrations rippled across her palms. They grew stronger and spread, flooding her body with magic that tingled and pulsed and popped. Her head burned with magic fever. Her magic wanted out. Now.

But she held onto it. A sweet and tangy taste—vanilla and cherries—slid across her tongue, flooding her mouth. Her magic was breaking free. She held it back a few more seconds, letting it build up. Then, just as she thought she'd collapse from the strain, her magic burst out of her. A swirling ball of wind exploded from her hands. She hurled it at Kai.

And this time, he wasn't fast enough.

It smacked against his chest, the impact throwing him off his feet. He hit the ground hard but got up immediately. He stared at her, a challenge in his eyes.

Sera didn't wait. She dipped again into her magic, and a wind barrier burst out of the ground to swallow Kai whole. It spun like a tornado, trapping him inside. Red-orange flames sparked to life atop the lip of the spinning wind funnel. They slid down the sides like a waterfall of fire, setting the wind funnel alight.

"Let's see you get out of that," Sera said softly, more to herself than to him. She brushed off her hands in satisfaction.

An ominous crack splintered the air. A moment later, the burning wind barrier froze solid. A second crack, louder than the first, swallowed the silence. The frozen cocoon shattered, and Kai stepped forward. The icy pebbles dissolved to steam beneath his feet. The heavy vapor wafted and curled in the air around him, hugging him like a suit of armor.

Sera gaped at him. "How is this even possible?"

He gave her a smug wink, and the fog armor dissolved. "Practice. Years of practice."

"Practice?" she choked out.

Any other mage could have practiced every second of his life and never been able to do anything like *that*. Kai didn't just wield the elements; he bent them to his will. He dominated every fabric of their magic.

"It's no wonder everyone's afraid of you," she said.

A smile spread across his lips. "Not you."

"I told you before. I'm too dumb to be scared of anyone."

"That's not true, Sera. You just like to pretend that it is. You act tough and prickly so that people leave you alone."

"It didn't work with you."

"Maybe dragons like tough and prickly."

She grunted in response. In addition to being the master of the elements, Kai was one of very few mages in the world who could shift into a dragon. He was dangerous. She'd had to remind herself of that far too many times over the past several weeks. Her stupid hormones kept getting in the way of common sense.

"Could you teach me to do that with my magic?" she asked him, steering the conversation away from dangerous waters.

"Yes," he said without hesitation. "You have the power inside of you. You just need to practice controlling it."

"I *am* trying."

"Yes," he agreed. "Setting the wind barrier on fire was a good move. A combination like that will work well against most opponents you'll face."

"It didn't work on you," she grumbled.

His shoulders lifted in an easy shrug, and his fitted black t-shirt stretched taut against his chest, showcasing every dip and bulge of muscle. Not that she was looking. Or ogling.

You've been ogling at him for the past hour. That's why he's kicking your ass, the voice in her head said helpfully.

I have not been ogling at him, she told the voice.

It snorted. How many people had voices in their head who could snort? She did glare extra hard at Kai, however, just to prove she wasn't ogling.

The lift of his dark eyebrows told her he wasn't fooled either. "Like what you see, sweetheart?"

"I'll like what I see when you're flat on your back."

His smile spread wider.

Argh, not like that! She tried—and failed—to hold back the heat spreading across her cheeks.

"With my boot pinning you down," she clarified.

He walked toward her, his eyes shining like blue glass. And burning with magic.

"You know, like a wrestling match." She held her ground, resisting the urge to flee. She was a tough mercenary who killed monsters for a living. She wasn't afraid of a big, bad mage. Even if he could shift into an even bigger and badder dragon.

"You have to pin down your opponent..." Her voice trailed. She wasn't helping matters.

He stopped in front of her. "Tell me more about these boots." His deep voice buzzed against her skin, his magic electrifying the air around them. "And what else you'll be wearing."

She folded her arms across her chest and scowled at him. "That's not what I meant, and you know it. This is about fighting. You're supposed to be helping me."

"I am helping you," he replied, his voice low. He looked offended.

Ok, that was true. For three weeks, ever since that messenger from the Magic Council had showed up on her doorstep, Kai had spent every day training her. And, much as she hated to admit it, she really did need his help. She was so out of her league that it wasn't even funny.

When the council had found out she was an unregistered mage, they'd told her she would be participating in the next Magic Games to have her magic assessed. Well, maybe 'assessed' was too nice of a word. The Games weren't just about the actual fights. That would have been easy; Sera had been fighting monsters since she could walk, after all. The real fight in the Games was on a whole other front. They would try to get inside her head, to crack open her magic, dig out her secrets, and hang them out to dry. And the moment the Magic Council learned Sera's secret, they would kill her.

She couldn't tell Kai that. He was on the Magic Council himself. He knew she was hiding something, but he'd stopped asking what it was. Maybe he didn't care. Maybe he cared about her, as he claimed. She hoped...

No, she couldn't hope. The day she started hoping and dreaming was the day she started forgetting to check behind her back. Things had already spun too far out of control. The Magic Council knew she was a mage, a fact she'd managed to keep hidden from them for twenty-four years. She'd gotten sloppy.

This had all started when the guild sent her to do a job for Kai. Well, she'd made a mighty mess of that. She'd allowed her feelings for him—hell, she shouldn't even be having feelings for him—to get in the way, and she'd used her magic to save him. And it hadn't been some tiny flicker of fire or a few snow flurries. She'd set a whole freaking stone tower on fire. She'd set off an earthquake under it. And she'd poured her magic into a glyph to teleport them across San Francisco. In short, she'd been as subtle as a stampede of warring centaurs.

She was so screwed.

"Sorry," she told Kai. "My nerves are shot right now."

Just one day left until the Magic Games. One day to figure out how to survive the Magic Council's mind games.

"You have been helping me." She reached toward him —but dropped her hand to her side before it made contact. Touching was a bad idea. "And I really appreciate it."

According to Kai, they had cracked him back when he'd been in the Games. Him. Kai Drachenburg, the world's most powerful mage. The man who turned into an enormous dragon. The man who stomped on werewolves and toppled armored military tanks. The man with more self-control than anyone she'd ever met. If his mind hadn't held up, how could she entertain even a glimmer of hope that hers would? She pushed the thoughts from her head. They would only paralyze her.

"Sera," he said, setting his hands on her shoulders.

A tingle of magic lingered on his fingertips, the soothing vibrations rippling across her skin. Whatever he was doing, she wished he would keep doing it. Forever.

See? Touching is bad.

She shifted her weight to put some distance between them. He didn't try to hold onto her; his hands just rolled off her shoulders. Sera had to admit she was disappointed —even knowing that touching was bad. Touching led to kissing. And kissing Kai cracked her self-control faster than anything the Architect of the Magic Games could throw at her.

"You spent years killing supernatural beasts, using no magic whatsoever," he told her.

"That's not true. Sometimes I cheated." She gave him a half-smile. "When no one was looking."

"Very well. Using minimal magic and only when no one was there to see it," he said. "How often did that even happen?"

"How often did I use my magic? Almost never," she admitted. The monsters she'd faced in battle were nothing next to the beasts that sat on the Magic Council—those mages, vampires, fairies, and ghosts who had labeled her kind abominations and sentenced them to extinction.

"Your magic is beautiful," Kai said.

He rubbed two of his fingers together, sampling the magic in the air. Her magic. And his. They'd become entwined, just as they always did whenever he was within ten feet of her. She could tell her hands not to touch Kai, but ever since that incident in the burning tower—no, basically ever since she'd met Kai—she'd had no luck whatsoever reining in her duplicitous magic. It had decided that it liked his magic. Like *really* liked it. Right now it was purring like a winged cat in heat.

Get a grip, she told it. So now she was talking to the voice in her head and to her magic. If that wasn't crazy, she didn't know what was.

"Would you like to take a break from training? I'm

sensing that you're…" Kai's gaze slid up her body. "…distracted."

"Keep your shirt on. I'm fine."

He looked at her, clearly perplexed. "My shirt?"

"It's an expression," she told him. And apparently one that German dragons didn't know. Or he was just being coy.

"So it has nothing to do with actual articles of clothing?" His puzzlement melted to amusement. "Or the removal thereof?" He stepped closer.

She backed up, matching him stride for stride, trying to maintain a safe minimal distance. Whatever that distance was. Jupiter might be far enough away.

"No," she croaked out. "No clothing."

His grin widened. Shit.

"Uh, I mean it has nothing to do with clothing," she spluttered. "It means stay calm."

"You're not calm," he said, gliding to a smooth stop. "You're nervous." His smile waned.

"Of course I'm nervous. A dragon is looking at me like he wants to eat me for dinner."

He frowned. "You shouldn't be nervous around me."

"Then maybe you should stop trying to make me nervous."

"I'm not…" He stopped, looking up. Like he was actually chewing that over. A few moments later, his gaze returned to her. "Am I?"

"Yes, you get a kick out of intimidating people," she said, then, realizing she was being unfair, added, "Maybe it's so engrained that you don't realize you're doing it."

The dark glint in his eyes told her she'd said the wrong thing. Usually, she didn't trip over her tongue like this. It was those damn Games. The stress of them was throwing her off her game—and they hadn't even started. What would she do when she entered the fighting pit? When the Magic Council threw every weapon in their mind-frying arsenal at her? Her pitiful twenty-four years was nothing compared to their centuries of research and experience. They'd been breaking mages for *centuries*.

"I'm sorry," she told Kai. "I shouldn't have said that."

He looked at her, his expression guarded. "It was never my intention to intimidate you."

"What was your intention?" she asked.

Smooth. Real smooth, the voice taunted.

Shut up, she told it. But it was right. She was mangling everything.

"I think I've made my intentions clear, Sera," Kai said.

Heat flooded her as she remembered the kisses they'd shared. They had made out on his desk, and they'd have done a whole lot more than that if his secretary hadn't walked in on them. Sera pushed thoughts of Kai's hands sliding down her body—of his magic caressing hers—out of her head. She turned away from him. It was hard not thinking about those things when he was right in front of her.

"Wait," he said, taking her hand.

She stopped, but she didn't turn around. She didn't trust herself. Just the feel of his hand against hers was scrambling her thoughts enough already as it was.

"You're tense," he said and let go of her hand.

She cleared her throat. "We should keep training."

He lifted his hand to her face, brushing away a few strands that had come loose from her ponytail. His fingers lingered on her cheek, feather-soft, teasing.

"Kai."

He stepped back, his face serious once more. "You're

right. The Magic Games start tomorrow. It's time I gave you a real challenge."

"A *real* challenge? Then what would you call the grueling fights these past three weeks?" she demanded.

"Merely a warmup."

Magic rumbled in his chest, deep and primal. The air grew heavy with the scent of burning wood. It flooded her nose and singed her tongue. Uh-oh.

Kai exploded in a burst of magic and fire. Before Sera could blink, a dragon stood in his place. Way over twenty feet tall, he was as black as a starless night, but when the light caught his body at just the right angle, his scales and wings shone with an inky blue-green sheen. Just like in his human form, his eyes were electric blue. He was beautiful.

Beautiful and deadly, she reminded herself. The last time she'd seen him shift into a dragon, he'd crushed a werewolf into a bloody mass. She took an instinctual step back.

What few people had ventured out to the shore at this early hour clearly didn't share her sense of self-preservation. Instead of fleeing for their lives, they stopped and stared. A bunch of them pulled out their phones and began to shoot videos of the big, bad dragon, framed against the Manhattan background. Kai dipped his chin to them, puffing smoke out of his nostrils. One of the women swooned.

Sera rolled her eyes, then stared up at the dragon. "You're not playing fair. No dragons allowed in this fight."

She'd never seen a dragon shrug, but Kai made a solid effort. His thick, muscled shoulders rolled back, magic sparking up as his scales scraped together. He smirked down at her, his smug confidence as clear as day—even on that dragon face. Well, of course he was confident. He could wipe the floor—err, the grass—with her in his usual form. As a dragon, he'd stomp her into oblivion.

Kai's dragon mouth opened wide, and fire spilled out like a flaming waterfall. Sera darted away, the fire licking at her heels. She kept running until she made it to the park bench. A dragon claw slashed toward her. She ducked and reached under the bench, grabbing her sword off the ground. Turning as she rose, she met the dragon's second slash mid-swipe. Her blade hit his hard scales in a flash of magic, the impact of the collision throwing her off her feet. Her back hit the ground, nearly knocking the wind out of her. Above her, the dragon snorted.

"I'm glad you're enjoying yourself," she growled, peeling her sore body off the ground.

His eyes narrowed.

"I know, I know. I have to use magic, not brute force," she said, tossing the sword aside. It was enchanted with magic—more than enough to deal with most monsters. But apparently not to break through Kai's magical defenses.

She reached for her magic, and this time it responded right away. A tornado burst out of the ground beneath the dragon, catapulting him onto the nearby gravelly shore. He jumped up and stalked back toward the grassy field, his enormous clawed feet sliding over the shifting rocks. She had to find a way to keep him on the shore, where the uneven ground would slow him down. And she had to do it soon.

She summoned another tornado—and was surprised by how quickly it came. The swirling cyclone blasted toward Kai and hit him hard in the chest. He grunted but held his ground. This time, Sera didn't hesitate. She summoned tornado after tornado, firing them in rapid succession at the dragon. They smashed against his body, doing no damage. But that wasn't the point. Her attacks were driving him back, sliding him closer to the water.

She kept up the machine gun pace of tornado bullets. Sweat dripped down her neck and splashed her top, but she didn't slow. And she didn't stop. She reached for more magic. Different magic.

The gentle, silky rhythm of the lapping river hummed louder. Waves rippled across the surface, growing higher and higher. And higher. They swooshed and crashed and rocked. As the final tornado blasted against Kai's chest, pushing his back foot into the river, a solid wall of water smashed into him from behind. The wave rolled over his body. An enraged growl gurgled through the salt water. Then, as the water slid down his body, retreating back into the river, he glared back at Sera.

"Well, you did tell me to use magic," she said.

She gave him that same slow, relaxed shrug he'd given her earlier. Truth be told, she wasn't relaxed at all—not with the strain of managing that much magic—but she wasn't about to tell him that.

The magic was popping across her skin, so she didn't have to reach far for it this time. She summoned earth, and the wet sand beneath Kai's feet collapsed. Before he could free himself from the deep pit, she drew the water forward, flooding it. The dragon thrashed and splashed—and flung himself out of the hole. He glared across the shore at Sera. There was no humor in those eyes now.

Wind slammed against her back, tossing her onto the beach. As she fell, a ring of rocky fangs split out of the sand all around her, swallowing her. She stared at the rocks until they froze solid—then crumbled to sandy ash.

While she'd been busy with that rocky prison cell, Kai had stomped over to her. He towered high above, and right now he was definitely trying to look intimidating. She glared right on back, and a small cloud formed over his back, sprinkling tiny snowflakes down on him. He sneezed.

Sera pulled a tissue out of her pocket and offered it to him.

He snorted at the offering, and fire bathed the thin paper, crumbling it to ash. He opened his mouth wide, giving her front row seats to the furnace burning inside of him. The fire was spreading up his throat, pouring into his mouth.

Sera waved her hand over her head, drawing an ice umbrella. It began to melt immediately, but it bought her enough time to make a run for it. As she sprinted away, the umbrella shattered, shooting tiny ice particles all across the shore. Sera scrambled for the grass. She needed to get off this slippery beach.

Something yanked on her foot, tripping her. Her legs hit the gravel, but she managed to throw out her arms just in time to avoid a face full of rocks. She glanced back at her foot and found a tentacle of glowing magical energy wrapped around her ankle. A second arm split from the first, and it began to slide up Sera's body. It had a familiar masculine, spicy scent. Kai's scent.

"Let go of my leg," she growled at the dragon.

A deep laugh rumbled in his chest.

Fine. Two could play at that game. She collected her magic, channeling her agitation until it burst from her in a pulse of tangled wind and lightning magic. The tentacles dissolved, and she jumped up. Even before she landed, she was winding up a fireball. As her feet hit the sand, she hurled it at him.

Except Kai wasn't the one standing in front of her anymore. There was someone between them. Her brother Riley. The fire roared toward him like a firestorm, its magic potent and deadly.

Before she could lift her hands, the fireball froze. It hung in the air for a moment, then smashed against the ground, revealing Kai. Human Kai.

"Are you all right?" he asked Riley.

Riley nodded, his smile shaky. His breaths were deep and heavy. Sera set her hand on his shoulder.

"You're not hurt?" she asked him.

"No."

Sera drew in a deep breath, relief spreading through her. "Good." She dropped her hand from his shoulder. "Have you completely lost your mind?!"

He swallowed hard.

"You could have been hit, Riley," she said, her crashing adrenaline making her tired. And cranky. "What the hell possessed you to jump into the middle of a mage duel?"

"Sera," Kai said, touching her arm.

She spun around to glare at him. "What?"

"He was watching us from that bench over there and got sucked in by one of the cyclones you were tossing out," Kai told her.

For the first time, Sera noticed her brother's honey-colored hair was messy. And his clothes were ruffled. As though he'd walked through a wind tunnel. The fight died in her, and her shoulders slouched over.

"Oh, Riley. I'm so sorry." Guilt flooded her body—and dread of what could have happened. "I need to get a better handle on my magic."

15

"I'm ok," he said with a smile. "And what you really need right now is a break." He handed her a bag from Spells & Sandwiches. "How about a proper New York lunch?"

CHAPTER TWO
Dragons and Assassins

SERA'S CHICKEN SANDWICH was pretty good. Not pizza-good, but it wouldn't be fair to hold that against it. Riley and Kai sat across the table from her, eating their own sandwiches. Kai's was so tall that it was a wonder he could fit it into his mouth without shifting into a dragon. Sera propped her elbows on the rickety tabletop and leaned in for a closer look. The scents of beef and red onions wafted up from his gigantic ciabatta roll.

"Hungry?" she asked.

"Fighting you requires a great deal of energy, Sera."

She grinned at him. "Especially when you're losing."

His sandwich paused before his mouth. "I was not losing. I was in complete control of the situation."

"Yeah, right." She snorted. "You looked really in control flailing about in that hole in the sand."

"You did a good job linking those spells together. I knew you could do it if you put your mind to it," he told her. His eyes hardened. "But you are mistaken if you believe you had me bested."

"If we'd finished our fight, I would have won."

17

A smooth smile slid over his mouth. "You just keep telling yourself that, sweetheart."

"I'm still trying to decide if it's disturbing to hear my friend call my sister 'sweetheart'," Riley said.

"Yes," Sera said, just as Kai said, "No."

Riley chuckled. "You two might want to work that out."

"There's nothing to work out," she lied. There were about twenty million things to work out between her and Kai, but she wasn't going to think about that now. Or maybe ever. So she changed the subject. "Are you going to be able to get us in for an early peek at the fighting pit?"

"I'm still working on it," said Kai. "The Magic Games security is being obstinate."

"Maybe you can sneeze smoke at them," Sera said.

"Or just go over their heads," Riley suggested.

"Oh, I intend to."

The look on his face was downright frightening. Sera was glad she wasn't the head of the Magic Games security.

"I will get us in before tomorrow afternoon," he said.

Tomorrow. The Games started tomorrow. Her stomach sank like a stone. She dropped her sandwich onto the crinkled bag. Suddenly, she didn't feel all that hungry.

"You'll be fine," he said. "You just need to remain calm. Luckily, I have something to distract your mind."

"A job?"

"Yes."

Kai wasn't just her coach for the Magic Games; he was also her sponsor. Most mages had a family to sponsor their entrance into the Games, but Sera wasn't from a magic dynasty—or at least not one she was willing to admit to. In cases like hers, the Magic Council took on the cost of the Games for the mage, but that help came with a heavy price. She would have to work it off later. As in, work for the Magic Council. And Sera wanted to stay as far as possible away from them.

The other option was to pay the costs herself, but she didn't have that kind of money. She was due for a pay raise at Mayhem, her mercenary guild, now that it had come out that she was a mage rather than just a human. The monster-hunting guilds paid you based on your magic rating, which was pretty elitist, but no one had challenged the system yet. Human mercenaries crazy enough to hunt monsters tended to be too desperate for cash to be choosy.

Sera and Alex had been two of those desperate mercenaries four years ago when they'd come to San Francisco with Riley. Their genius brother had gotten into the prestigious program at San Francisco University of Magical Arts and Sciences, but tuition wasn't cheap. They'd had to kill a lot of monsters to keep him in college. But overtime was better than death, which was what would happen if anyone found out Sera and Alex were Dragon Born. So they'd taken the crap pay, hiding their magic just like their father had always told them to do.

Sera's new salary would kick in after the Magic Games. Simmons, the head of Mayhem, was a stickler for protocol—and a complete cheapskate. He wasn't going to pay her a penny more until her results came back. Sera only hoped that those results wouldn't be her death sentence. She had to stay focused, no matter what the Game Architect threw at her. And above all, she needed to remain calm. Kai was more right about that than he knew. She couldn't afford for them to crack her mind. Or her secrets.

So since she couldn't pay her entrance costs herself, and she didn't want to be in debt to the Magic Council, that left only the private sponsor option. When Kai had made the offer, she'd taken it, knowing it was the best she was going to get. His condition was that she do a few jobs for him. Since all her jobs had to go through Mayhem, he and Simmons had hammered out a deal behind closed doors. Kai must have offered him a lot of money because Simmons had looked really happy after that meeting. He'd even whistled down Mayhem's main corridor. And Simmons *never* did anything as whimsical as whistling. Especially not anywhere that anyone would catch him at it.

"What is the job?" Sera asked Kai.

"I've received a tip that a group of vampires is planning something at the Magic Games," he replied.

"Something bad, I take it?"

"It didn't sound like they wanted to throw us all a party." Looking up thoughtfully, he rubbed his chin, which was sporting a two-day stubble. Usually, he was so well-groomed. "Have you heard about the Blood Orb being stolen?"

"Yes, Alex told me about it. She said a group of supernatural haters is trying to use the Orb to control the vampires."

"They aren't just trying. They've succeeded," he said. "Over the past few weeks, there's been an increase in attacks perpetrated by vampires. After each attack, the vampires claimed they were being controlled by magic."

"And you think this hate group is planning to unleash vampires on the Magic Games?"

"I've heard rumors to that effect, yes."

"Ok." She swung her legs around the chair and stood. "I wanted to give Alex a call anyway. I'll ask her if she knows anything more about the Blood Orb or the vampires." Sera started to walk away from the table.

"Hey, where are you going?" Riley asked her.

She looked over her shoulder. "I need some privacy. I have to talk to Alex about…something personal."

Riley turned his head toward Kai. "Do you think that's code for girl issues?"

Kai shrugged.

"Do you want me to give her a message from you?" Sera asked Riley.

"Tell her I liked her latest photos from Madam Meringue's chocolate factory," he said with a grin.

Sera nodded and continued walking in the direction of the Brooklyn Bridge. When she felt she'd gone far enough, she stopped and pulled out her phone. She didn't want Kai to overhear what she had to say to Alex.

"Uh, hi, Sera," her sister answered after a few rings. A bed creaked, probably as Alex sat down on it. "How are you?"

"I…well, I'm managing."

"The Magic Games are tomorrow, right?"

"Yes."

"Good luck," Alex said.

"Thanks."

Neither of them mentioned that Alex was an unregistered mage too. Maybe the Magic Council hadn't figured it out yet, or maybe Alex's super-important client was protecting her. In any case, Sera wouldn't have wished the Games on her worst enemy—and certainly not on her own sister.

"Alex," Sera began. "I wanted to talk to you about the

Blood Orb."

"The Blood—" Alex paused. "Just a minute." Something thumped in the background. It sounded like a shoe hitting the wall. "Logan, get your paws away from my underwear drawer!" she shouted away from the phone, then spoke into it again. "Sorry about that, Sera."

"Am I interrupting something?"

"No." A second shoe hit something—no, make that someone. A man grunted. "That's just the assassin in my room."

"An assassin? You might want to hit him with something harder than a shoe. Like a knife," Sera suggested.

"Na, then he'd just bleed out all over my floor."

"That would be a huge mess to clean up."

"Exactly," Alex agreed. "So, the Blood Orb, you said?"

"Yes. Apparently, someone looking to stir up trouble is sending a bunch of vampires to the Games."

"What kind of trouble?"

"We don't know," said Sera. "But we think it might be the same people behind all those recent vampire attacks. The ones controlling the vampires with the Blood Orb."

"The Convictionites," Alex said, her voice devoid of humor. "They're called the Convictionites."

"Do you know of any way to break the Blood Orb's control over the vampires?"

"We're working on it, but no, not yet. At least not on a wider scale. A strong Magic Breaker could probably do it on individual vampires. Or maybe a whole group. But you'd have to get close to them."

"How close?" Sera asked.

"Grappling distance."

Awesome.

"Sera, if you're fighting these people, please be careful. Do not underestimate them. They have very powerful magic at their disposal."

"I thought they hated magic."

Alex sighed. "Yeah, well people don't always make sense. As far as I know, they don't have magic themselves, but they do use magical objects and weapons. Your best bet in a fight is to disarm them."

"Thanks for the tip."

"They're devious," Alex added. "They will stay out of sight, keeping to the shadows."

"I'll have my dragon step on them."

"Your…dragon?" Alex's voice trailed off. "Ah, you mean your new boyfriend."

"He's not my boyfriend. Why does everyone keep saying that?"

Chuckles buzzed through the phone.

"He's just my coach for the Magic Games."

"Sure thing, Sera." Alex didn't sound convinced. "Sera…" Her voice grew serious. "Do you ever…well, have this voice…in your head?"

"Yeah." Apparently, Sera wasn't the only one hearing voices. That was oddly comforting.

"You should listen to that voice," Alex told her.

"Listen to the voice in my head?"

"Yes." Alex paused. "I have a lot I want to tell you, Sera, but not over the phone. It's so impersonal."

Translation: someone could be listening, so it wasn't safe for Alex to say more.

"We have to get together soon," Sera agreed. "How long will you be in Zurich?"

"At least until this mess with the Blood Orb is sorted. And then there are all these hybrids springing up. Things are busy here."

"Busy with that assassin?"

"Logan? He's my partner. Work partner," she tacked on quickly.

"I don't remember any of your other work partners ever having access to your underwear drawer," Sera teased her.

"He doesn't have access. He only wishes he did."

Something in Alex's tone made Sera think her sister wished it too, so she decided more teasing was in order.

"Are assassins good kissers?"

"That one is," Alex said in a whisper. Maybe she didn't want him to hear.

Sera chuckled.

"And are mage shifters good kissers?" Alex asked her.

Sera choked on her own chuckles. "Um, what?"

It was Alex's turn to laugh. "Oh, come on, Sera. I know you've been running around with Kai Drachenburg."

"You've been talking to Riley."

"Yep," Alex said brightly.

"By the way, Riley says he likes the pictures you sent him of Madam Meringue's chocolate factory," Sera told her.

"The ones I sent him last week? We went on a tour of the inside."

"You went on a tour of a chocolate factory...with an assassin?" Something about that was just too funny.

"Yes. Yes, I did," Alex said. "But we were talking about your new man."

"He's not my man."

"Then what is he?"

"Kai is...complicated."

Alex laughed. "Aren't they all? Though I do hear he was on the cover of Mages Illustrated."

"And you've been talking to Naomi too."

"She e-mailed me. Wrote that I should encourage you to 'let loose every now and again'."

"Actually, I wanted to talk to you about that," Sera said.

"Oh?"

"Don't you think 'letting loose' with someone like Kai would be…irresponsible?"

"I'm sure you know how to take the proper precautions."

"I'm not talking about letting someone into my pants, Alex. I'm talking about letting him into my life."

"And your heart?"

"Yes."

"It sounds like he's already there," Alex commented.

Sera tried to ignore the sharp twinge in her chest. "Yes. I've already let things go too far. And because of that, tomorrow I'll be neck-deep in trials designed to break me. And it could have turned out far worse. For others."

"Oh." Alex seemed to understand the meaning: that she could have been exposed too. "Sera, I really think you're rewriting history to torture yourself. You're going to the Magic Games because you used magic to save San Francisco, not because you played footsie with the dragon. You can't stop living life because you're afraid of what will happen if you let yourself be happy. I think we've both been doing that for far too long. Besides, I'm not going to let you hog all of the blame. I've been a bit irresponsible myself."

"By playing footsie with the assassin?"

"Something like that," said Alex. "And you know what? It was so worth it."

"Hmm."

"Do you like him?" Alex asked.

"Kai? Yes, I really do."

"Then go for it," Alex said. "Just make sure you make him work for access to your underwear drawer."

Sera laughed. "Sure thing."

"Ok, there's an assassin standing over me, tapping his egregiously overpriced watch. We have to go."

"Hot date?"

"I wouldn't call street-side warfare with a motorcycle gang of mage delinquents a hot date, but the night is still young. Maybe my assassin will woo me with chocolate later. Talk to you soon, Sera. Kick some serious butt in the Magic Games."

CHAPTER THREE
Leather & Denim, Blood & Gore

AFTER ENDING THE call, Sera walked back to the table. Kai was still sitting there, but Riley had moved out to the middle of the field. He tossed something up into the air, then hurried back a few steps. Magic exploded overhead, sizzling and sparkling like fireworks. Green and blue and black, the magical lights coalesced into the shape of a dragon that looked an awful lot like Kai. The fiery dragon shot past Riley, looped a few times in the air, then dove for the table.

Kai's cool blue eyes watched its descent. He didn't stand—or fidget—even as it hit the tabletop in an explosion of magic and light that rumbled the wooden planks. The aroma of lilacs and redwoods saturated the air, tingling Sera's tongue.

Kai looked at Riley. "The lilac was a nice touch," he told him calmly, as though a magic bomb hadn't just exploded in his face. "It covers the stench of sulfur."

"Actually, I got rid of the sulfur by switching fire and lightning ingredients for ice and earth. The natural scents are from the earth. I thought it made the magic more palatable."

Kai brushed his finger across the tabletop, then licked the tip, tasting the magical residue. His eyebrows lifted. "Good. You're hired. I need someone with your sense in my labs. Last week, they tried to sell me on a new line of magic-retardant suits." He crinkled up his nose. "They smelled like burning plastic."

"No," Sera said.

Kai looked at her. "Yes, they actually did. I couldn't believe it either."

"No, I meant that you can't hire Riley. He has to finish school."

"My courses are over," Riley said. "I graduate in just a few weeks. All I have to do is walk across the stage, give my magic presentation, then claim my diploma."

"At which point, you and Kai can discuss lilac and sulfur all you want." She gave Kai a hard look. "But not before then."

Riley frowned. "You really need to chill, Sera. I won't drop out of school a few weeks before the finish line. I'm not stupid."

"Of course you're not," she told him. "You're really smart. And since you're really smart, you realize how much that diploma will be worth. It's something no one will be able to take away from you. Unlike a job."

She made a conscious effort not to look at Kai as she spoke. She couldn't, however, miss the smoky sizzle electrifying the air—that of his magic flaring up at her last statement. Well, he could huff and puff all he wanted, but he knew she was right. He'd certainly pay Riley a lot of money to come work for him, but without his Magical Sciences degree, Riley would have trouble getting any other job. What if something came between their friendship, and they started hating each other? Would Kai fire him? Or would Riley just quit? Sera had a pretty good idea what—or more like who—could come between them. She could never, ever let Kai find out that she was Dragon Born. It wouldn't just end her life; it would ruin Riley's.

Suddenly, she felt really tired. "I'm beat," she told them, stuffing what was left of her sandwich into the bag. "I'm meeting Naomi in a couple of hours. I need to get back to the hotel and shower first."

Kai rose smoothly to his feet. "I'll drive you."

"Thank you."

Kai walked down the path, shifting gravel crunching beneath his shoes. Sera and Riley followed him out of the park. Only one car was parked on the road—actually, on the sidewalk. Kai had a history of delinquent parking.

A black rental SUV, a perfect replica of his own car, blinked in greeting as they approached. It looked like the sort of car the FBI would drive—or the type the military would use. Sera often teased Kai by referring to his beloved car as 'the tank', but she wasn't in the mood for teasing now. A morning of elemental warfare had left her drained, and worrying about the Magic Games looming on the horizon wasn't helping either.

She couldn't help but think about what Alex had said. Her sister was right. She liked Kai. But how could she be with him while lying to his face about who she was? The safe thing—the responsible thing—to do would be to stay away from him. If she could even do that.

Riley made up her mind for her. He cut in front of her, hopping into the back seat of the car. Then, giving her a wink, he shut the door behind him. Sera sighed and climbed up into the front seat. As Kai slid into the driver's seat, his devastating eyes meeting hers, she quickly looked away to focus on her seatbelt. Then she turned forward and stared straight through the windshield. By then, Kai had started the car and was pulling away from the sidewalk.

They passed the long drive in silence. Well, at least Sera did. A couple minutes after they hopped into the car, Riley and Kai started talking about the shoreside run they'd be taking later. Sera leaned against the window and closed her eyes.

Before she knew it, the slam of the car door rattled her awake. They were in the hotel's underground garage. Riley passed by her window, his sneakers squeaking across the garage. Sera released her seatbelt and was reaching for the door when Kai caught her hand.

"Wait," he said.

She turned and gave him a wary look, but he didn't try anything else. He'd even reeled in his magic, coiling it tightly inside of him. Sera could still feel it—there was no hiding that much raw power—but it wasn't caressing her magic like it sometimes did, or teasing her with the delectable spicy taste of dragon.

"Yes?" she croaked, then cleared her throat.

"I wanted to talk to you about later today," he said, his face unreadable. His magic was unreadable too.

"I'm meeting Naomi in a few hours, but we can practice this afternoon."

"I have work to attend to in the afternoon."

"Oh," she said, trying not to sound disappointed.

Of course he had work to do. His whole life wasn't centered around helping her with the Magic Games. He was managing larger chunks of his family's company, not sitting on a yacht all day sipping mojitos and listening to banjo music.

"But I need you to meet me tonight at nine," he continued, then paused, as though he wanted to gauge her response to his next words. "At Trove."

She suppressed the frown crinkling up her lips. Trove was New York City's equivalent of Liquid, San Francisco's high-end mage club. Sera had never been to either—if she went within five feet of the door, the bouncer would turn up his nose at her and shoo her away like a stray dog—but she knew the sort of people who did go to those places. Every single one of them was a member of an elite magic dynasty. People like Kai. Not like her.

"A job?" she asked, her stomach doing a bellyflop. Usually, she just ignored snooty people who looked down on her, but it was awfully hard to ignore a whole club full of people looking down on her.

"Yes, an important job," he said.

Over the last three weeks, in addition to training, she'd done more than a few jobs for him. Mostly taking care of monsters annoying one magical dynasty or another. It turned out Kai was a master strategist; he'd collected more favors in three weeks than most people could in a lifetime. Sera tried not to feel like a pawn in his game. It was training. Through it all, he'd fought alongside her, explaining how to use magic—not brute force—to take out their foes.

"What is it this time?" she asked. "Centaurs? Harpies? Jumbo caterpillars?"

She hadn't heard of any monsters plaguing Trove lately, but she hadn't known about any of the other attacks either. The elite magic dynasties had centuries of practice hiding their problems from the general public.

"It's a surprise," Kai told her.

She cringed. The last time he'd threatened a surprise, she'd found herself caught in the crossfire of a mage duel between two telekinetics. He seemed to think that throwing her into dangerous, unknown situations was good practice. Kai was firmly in the camp of 'what doesn't kill you, only makes you stronger' folks. He was probably right. Not that she'd ever admit it to him.

"I'll bring my sword," she told him, doing her best to put on a cheerful smile.

"No sword."

Drat. "Knives?" she asked.

He shook his head. "Weapons are not permitted at Trove."

This was just getting better and better. "Then how am I supposed to fight this unknown evil?"

"Bring your magic," he said. "This will be good practice, not having your weapons as backup."

Except Sera felt naked without her weapons. Sure, she'd come a long way with Kai's help, but she still wasn't in complete control of her magic. This morning she'd had a good day. Other times, she hadn't been so lucky. Her magic was unwieldy and temperamental.

Kind of like your hormones, said the voice in her head.

She didn't tell it to shut up. Not this time. Alex had told her she should listen to the voice in her head. Sera nearly laughed aloud. That there was crazy talk.

"Sera."

She looked at Kai. Apparently, he'd said something, and she hadn't heard…because she was listening to the voice in her head.

"Yes?" she asked.

"I was explaining the dress code at Trove. This is very important, so please pay attention. They won't allow you inside if you don't follow it to the letter."

"They won't let me in either way," she grumbled.

"I've put you on the list," he said. "Now, the dress code. No torn or dirty clothes." His gaze slid down to her thigh, where a sliver of skin peeked through the tear in her leggings.

She set her hand over the tear. "Hey, they weren't torn when I put them on this morning. Fighting you is hazardous to the health of my clothing."

"No military wear."

"I don't own anything of the sort."

"You have a pair of combat boots," he pointed out.

"I only wore those boots once, and that was to the pier. At midnight." She shivered. "Who starts a fight at that hour anyway? It's indecent." She shivered again. "And cold."

"No monster gore or blood."

"So I take it vampires aren't allowed at Trove?"

"No leather," he said.

"I guess I'll just cancel that order of leather lingerie then."

One of his dark brows twitched. "No jeans."

She gave his jeans a pointed look.

"Yes, even for me," he said.

"I've never seen you in anything but jeans and a dark t-shirt. I've decided that you have two hundred copies of the same exact outfit in your closet."

"I do own other clothing."

"Like suits?" she asked.

"Yes."

Sera snickered.

"Are you ready to take this seriously?" he asked.

"It's just that you said you found suits to be so stiff

and uncomfortable and…" She stopped at the chilling look he was giving her. "Uh, yeah, I'm ready."

"Do try to wear something nice to Trove, Sera. And keep your smart comments to yourself. Not everyone finds them as endearing as I do. I'd hate to have to break up a fight between you and the bouncer."

"I bet I could take him," she muttered.

"Of course you could," he said with strained patience. "But the owner of Trove is a business partner of mine. Isaac has a sizable ego, one that would suffer a severe blow if his big, scary bouncer were beaten up by a woman. Don't embarrass him. That would put a strain on my partnership with him."

"I'll try to behave myself," she said.

"Start by following the dress code."

"Yes, fine. I'll follow the silly dress code. How hard can it be to find something in my closet that isn't denim, dirty, leather, torn, bloody, full of monster gore, or designed for military warfare?"

His blue eyes pulsed once. "Do you have time to go shopping before tonight?"

She punched him in the arm. "Not funny." She shook out her hand.

"Are you all right?" he asked, watching her curiously.

She'd hit him, and he was wondering if she was all right? Punching Kai was like hitting a boulder: it hurt her more than it hurt him.

"Fine," she said. "I will find something to wear. Even though anything that will get me through the door of Trove is probably impossible to fight in."

"You have finesse, Sera. I have every confidence in your ability to use magic while maintaining the club's dress code. And I'll help you," Kai added, brushing aside a loose strand of hair from her face. He tucked it behind her ear, but allowed his hand to linger on her cheek. His finger traced her jawline slowly.

Heat flushed her face, spreading from his hand, sliding with liquid ease down her neck, cresting her breasts... Sera fumbled with the door handle. The door opened, and she fell out of his car. She landed—ungracefully, but at least on her feet.

"See you tonight," she said, not meeting his eyes as she swung the door shut.

She hurried across the garage. She could hear him step out of the car, but she didn't stop. She didn't even slow down until she was walking down the hallway to her suite. Kai's suite was on an entirely different floor.

Riley stood in the open doorway, watching her come down the hall. "What's wrong?" he asked, stepping aside as she reached the door.

She hurried inside and shut the door after them. And only then did she dare to breath. "Nothing. Just Kai's next job for me." She slid out of her shoes, her toes screaming in relief. She'd been on her feet since before dawn—well, except when she was being hurled across fields. "This exclusive work sure is annoying sometimes. Being at the client's beck and call."

Riley grinned. "And keeping your smart mouth in check?"

"Yeah."

"Kai's not so bad." He set down his backpack. "Not like that purple poodle lady."

Sera snorted. "True."

Kai was no purple poodle lady—that was for sure—but that didn't mean he wasn't big trouble. Maybe even bigger trouble than the Magic Games.

CHAPTER FOUR
Army of Clean

SERA TOOK A long, hot shower, scrubbing her dirt-freckled skin with copious helpings of the hotel's flowery body wash. It came in teeny-tiny pretentious bottles, so it must be the good stuff. Sera drained four bottles, and she didn't even feel bad about it. She'd earned it. That morning, she'd woken up at an unholy hour, and the extended ass-kicking session by the dragon that had followed hadn't helped matters.

She stepped out of the shower with a stretch and a yawn, smiling as she oozed her toes into the plush bath towel. Two chocolate peanut butter granola bars and a tall glass of cold milk later, she grabbed her pink scooter Lily and kicked off toward Mayhem.

About two years ago, Mayhem had opened a New York branch. Monster infestation was a global phenomenon, and Simmons, the head of Mayhem, wasn't one to ignore the call for profit.

Mayhem's NYC office was located inside the posh 'Magic & 8th Avenue' building, the city's goto place for all shops and services of the supernatural persuasion. Sera walked through the main entrance, right into the middle of a magical shopping paradise. There were shops for magic pets, magic potions, magic artifacts, magic books… It was all very boutique, and most of the magic they were selling there was actually legitimate.

She navigated an obstacle course of frenzied shoppers, heavy bags, and miniature purse poodles that smelled of mint perfume and self-entitlement. One of them—a pink dog with a gem-studded collar—turned its nose up at Sera as she escaped into the elevator. Apparently, even the dogs here looked down on her. She stuck her tongue out at Pinky. In response, it began to yap rapidly, like it was telling her off for her impudence. Its owner, a fairy with a flower crown, turned to see what all the fuss was about, but Sera had already mashed the button to the twelfth floor. The elevator doors slid shut, the sound as soft as whispered silk.

Alone at last, Sera checked her workout suit for any tears that might have gotten the pink poodle's tail in a knot. Ha! She didn't find any. There was, however, a bloodstain left over from the fight with the dark ponies last week. Her blood, not theirs. Those My Little Pony lookalikes hit hard. Maybe Kai was right. Maybe she should go shopping before tonight.

The elevator doors spread open, and she stepped into Mayhem. Here, the floors were marble, the walls frosted glass, and the high ceiling of painted angels as grandiose as an opera hall. Grace, the receptionist, sat primly behind a glass desk. Dressed in silk and cashmere, she looked like the twin of Fiona, the San Francisco office's receptionist. The perfect lady, her ankles were tucked neatly together.

The sweet, seductive aroma of roses filled the air,

mixed in with a little caramelized magic. It was the perfect atmosphere to woo the magical elite. They didn't know the fragrance was also a weapon. On its lowest setting, the mist was merely soothing; on its highest, it could knock out a first tier mage. The same could be said for Grace. The dainty receptionist was hiding a stash of knives and an automatic rifle in the cabinet beside her desk. She had a few grenades tucked away inside the secret bottom compartment of a nearby potted palm tree too. That woman was as scary as any of Mayhem's mercenaries.

"Grace," Sera greeted her.

"Ms. Dering." She returned the nod. "You and Ms. Garland have Gym 4 reserved from one to three o'clock today."

"Yep."

"Please allow me to draw your attention to the gym rules. Due to high demand, you may use the gym only during your reserved hours."

Sera didn't point out that it was Sunday—and therefore over half of the mercenaries weren't working at all. When she and Naomi had put in their reservation yesterday, all the gyms had still been available. She bet they still were.

But Grace continued to rattle off the gym rules anyway. "Before you leave, all pieces of equipment must be returned to their designated storage positions."

"Sure thing. We always clean up after ourselves."

One of Grace's blonde eyebrows arched upward. "The Mayhem Disposal Team would beg to differ. I've read your file, Ms. Dering."

Sera shrugged. "Monsters are different. I don't fight them in the gym."

Grace looked like she wanted to sigh, but she continued with the rules instead. "Please refrain from severely injuring other employees of Mayhem while training. Injuries increase the guild's accident insurance premiums."

"Does that mean she can't toss me up in the air?" Naomi asked, wrapping her arm around Sera's shoulder as she joined her at the reception desk.

"I guess that depends on my aim," Sera said.

"I'd like to practice my flying today," her half-fairy friend replied with a wink.

They'd picked Gym 4 because of the rings and ropes dangling from the ceiling. They were useful for throwing maneuvers. Naomi couldn't fly as high as a full-blooded fairy. Sometimes, Sera had to give her a boost.

"Please pull out the mats if you plan on throwing each other across the gym," Grace told them. She looked at Sera. "They are also fire-retardant."

Sera frowned at her. "I'm not going to set the gym on fire."

Grace folded her hands together, her expression guarded. Even wary. Apparently, word had gotten out about the tower Sera had set on fire when her magic had gone out of control. But how did anyone know about that? Finn, the madman behind the magic cult she and Kai had thwarted, was sitting in a cell inside some secret prison, and his minions hadn't been heard from since they'd fled the scene. They were too busy hiding to spread rumors.

"Really, I won't," Sera assured her. What else could she say?

Grace's shoulders relaxed, if only slightly. "I hope so. Because a fire would increase the guild's fire insurance premiums."

Insurance premiums again? It was no wonder a tight purse like Simmons had hired her.

"Come on, Sera," Naomi said.

Her arm still wrapped around Sera, she nudged her toward the shaded glass doors that led into the underbelly of Mayhem. The doors slid open, revealing a man in neck-to-toe leather. He had enough knives and guns on him to send a metal detector into epileptic shock. The other mercenaries called him Raze, which basically summed him up. There was a rough look about him, like he chewed bullets for breakfast. There wasn't, however, a single speck of magic in him. He was one hundred percent human. He'd worked for Mayhem for over twenty years, outliving even most of his supernatural colleagues. And he was proud of it.

Two years ago, Simmons had sent Raze to New York to build up Mayhem's presence here. Before that, Sera had worked with him a few times. He'd always liked her because she was human too. At least she'd pretended to be. The hard look on his face told her Raze now knew she was really a mage. And he didn't like it. He nodded at Naomi, but only glared at her, his cold eyes following her like a laser sight. Sighing, Sera turned back toward Naomi, and they entered the real and rugged Mayhem beyond the pretty front.

"Raze looks like he's swallowed a razor," Naomi said as they walked down the ugly corridor.

The red paint glossed over the floor only partially hid the rippled, raw concrete, and lamps that resembled upside-down flying saucers dangled from the pockmarked ceiling. It was pretty much identical to the San Francisco office. Simmons was nothing if not consistent.

"I lied to him. To everyone." The words gurgled in Sera's throat, threatening to choke her. She couldn't even meet Naomi's eyes; she'd lied to her too. "I'm sorry."

Naomi's hand closed around her arm, giving it a gentle squeeze. "Do you want to talk about it? I mean, you don't have to. But if you want someone to talk to, I'm here."

"I…"

She dared a quick glance at Naomi, surprised to find no anger on her face. She should have been furious. Like Raze was. Well, at least Naomi didn't know that Sera was Dragon Born.

Legend said that the Dragon Born had once been the most powerful mages in the world, a consequence of their unique birth. They were twin souls—in this case, Sera and Alex—born into one body and later separated by magic. Just like the dragons were born. For centuries, the Dragon Born had lived as part of the mage community, accepted and even respected.

But all that had changed. Sera wished she knew why the rest of the supernatural world had turned against her kind. Ever since that happened, the Dragon Born had been branded as abominations. The sentence of being born was death. If the Magic Council ever found out what Sera was, they would tear through her life to get at her. Everyone she cared about was at risk, including her friends. So, no, she couldn't let the Council find out, even if it meant lying to her friends.

"When I was sixteen, I had a bad experience with magic," she told Naomi. It was the understatement of the century, but half-truths were all that she dared tell. "A powerful mage killed my father." The assassin who had discovered her and Alex's secret and had come to deliver punishment. "We weren't able to stop the mage. When our dad died, we...snapped. We lost control of our magic, and it killed the mage. Painfully. We boiled his blood from within. We froze off his fingers and drowned his lungs. We peeled the skin from his body..."

Sera looked into Naomi's horrified face. The weight of the memory crushed her head and crunched at her heart. "After it was all over—after the magic high had worn off —we looked at the mage's...remains. And we realized what we had done. We swore off that dark part of ourselves. We didn't use magic anymore. We just wanted to get as far as possible from that world. To not be monsters. And so we became human and took up killing monsters."

Naomi watched her in silence for a few moments, her usual mischievous expression subdued. Finally, she said, "I think I understand. In your place, I might have done the same. You don't have to explain yourself to me, Sera. I'm not upset. I'm still your friend. I'm sorry you had to go through that. And now the Magic Council is forcing you into the Games. It's a wonder you've escaped their notice this long."

"I'm good at hiding my magic," Sera said. She'd been doing it since she was old enough to understand what would happen if she didn't.

"That I can believe. I never had a clue you're a mage."

Neither had anyone else. Well, not anyone except that assassin and then later Kai. Every mage was tested in the Magic Games at the age of sixteen. Sera had escaped that fate the first time by burying her magic so deep down that even the Council's best magic Sniffers couldn't find it. As her unease flopped and sank beneath the despair in her stomach, she wondered if she should have just let Finn and his psychopaths overthrow the Magic Council. Why had she helped the people who wouldn't hesitate to condemn her to death?

"I just wish things would get back to normal," Sera lamented. "Even though I know nothing will ever be the same again."

"Some things will always be the same," Naomi said, pointing down the hall.

Cutler was there, headed straight for them like a man on a mission. Sera didn't know what he was doing here, all the way across the country. And she certainly didn't have time for whatever was responsible for the huge grin plastered across his face. As his eyes met hers, the grin widened. He was smiling so hard, it looked like his jaw would break. Sera considered ducking into the locker room to escape him, but the only one in sight was the men's room. That wouldn't stop Cutler from following her. In fact, even running into the women's locker room wouldn't stop him.

"Sera," he said, his voice as smooth as melted chocolate.

Magic hung in the air, crackling against Sera's skin. Cutler's magic was forced, rough, acidic—like a squirt of lemon in the eye. He thumped it against her with unabashed fervor.

"You feel that, don't you?" he said, delight dancing in his eyes.

Sera folded her arms across her chest and glared back at him. Cutler was a first tier telekinetic—in addition to being a first tier pain in the ass.

"You've been holding out on me, Sera." He leaned his arm against the wall in a completely unsubtle attempt to flex his muscles. "I know about that magic you did in

Alcatraz."

Cutler came from one of San Francisco's important magic dynasties, its members characterized by an overabundance of magic and money. If his behavior were any indication, they were also characterized by a shortage of sense. No one at Mayhem wanted to work with Cutler because if his recklessness got him hurt—which it inevitably did—his mommy showed up on his partner's doorstep with steam coming out of her ears. Literally.

"I want to see this magic of yours," he said with a lazy wink.

"No."

"No?" He looked amused, as though rejection were a foreign word he didn't understand. "Oh, come on. Just give me a little taste of your magic." He leaned forward, a wicked grin on his lips. "I promise not to tell anyone."

"Even your mommy?" Naomi muttered under her breath.

Sera snorted.

"Playing hard to get, are you? Is that your game?" Cutler asked as the overhead lamps shuddered and shook.

"The only one playing games here is you," Sera told him and pointed at the ceiling.

The lamps stopped shaking. Their cables went as limp as wet spaghetti. Before Sera could breathe a sigh of relief —she was *not* in the mood to fight Cutler—two doors blasted open behind him, expelling a tangled mass of brooms and buckets and mops. The cleaning supplies hopped up immediately and marched into picture-perfect lines, standing behind their master like an army of ill intentions. It was as though Sera had stumbled into a children's cartoon. If it hadn't been for the determined look on Cutler's face, she might have even laughed.

The broom and mop soldiers charged forward, tin humming as the buckets swung above them like battle hammers being wound up for a mighty release. The buckets shot toward Sera and Naomi in a tidal wave of magic and metal. Naomi pushed out her hands, blasting them with Fairy Dust.

"Uh, Sera," she said when the buckets cut right through the cloud of pink and silver sparkles.

"On it," replied Sera, throwing herself against Naomi to push them both into the men's locker room.

Zan, one of Mayhem's veteran mages, gave them a curious look as they tripped over a bench, but he was the least of Sera's worries right now. She hurried back to the door and peered out just as the buckets bounced past on their way back to the broom and mop soldiers. Metal echoed hollowly down the hall, bouncing off the bare concrete walls. The whole area stank of souring citric acid and wilted flowers, the after-stench of Cutler's telekinetic spells.

"Ready to be reasonable, Sera?" he called down the corridor to her.

There was no point talking to him. He didn't even realize how insane he was. Sera reached down, sliding two knives out of the straps buckled to her thighs. Before he could send the Army of Clean at her again, she launched the knives. They met their marks, sinking through the wooden handles of a mop and a broom.

"Cute," Cutler chuckled. "But these aren't monsters. And they can't be stopped by knives."

The brooms and mops marched forward, Sera's two victims leading the way. Had they been monsters, those knives would have gone right into their eyes. Unfortunately, as Cutler had so cheerfully reminded her, his soldiers weren't even alive. Sera ducked back into the locker room, scanning the area for something she could throw at them. Anything.

The only thing that might slow them down was a locker, and she wasn't strong enough to rip one of them off the wall and hurl it at the mops and brooms. Well, she could try tossing Zan at them, but she didn't think the seasoned mage would find that funny. Sera wished he weren't even here. With him as a witness to this ridiculous fight, she really *had* to defeat Cutler's Army of Clean—or risk becoming the laughing stock of the guild.

"Fine," she muttered under her breath, then stepped into the corridor. If it was a fight he wanted, she'd give it to him.

The buckets were already winding up for another toss. Sera didn't wait. She reached for her magic, deep and dark. A gust of wind rushed past her, kissing her cheeks on its way toward the buckets. It smacked into them so hard that it knocked every single one of them off its twirling axis. Spinning out of control, they shot in every direction. The veins in Cutler's face bulged from the strain of trying to steady the wayward flights of two dozen tin buckets.

Fire poured down on the brooms and mops, bathing them in flames. Cutler spun toward them, the buckets forgotten. Wide-eyed and for once speechless, he gaped as the burning mops and brooms dissolved to ash.

The siren's call of the fire magic sang out to Sera. It burned through her veins and bathed her skin in pure rapture. She wanted to make it blaze higher and hotter, to allow its magic to consume the world as it had her.

Whoa, there. Let's rein in the crazy, shall we? The world doesn't want to be consumed by fire, said the voice it her head.

As soon as it spoke to her, she knew it was right. She lowered her hands, and the flames died out. Her whirlwind fizzled out too, and the buckets that had been caught inside dropped to the floor. Sera's plunging magic almost made her drop too. She wiped the sweat from her forehead and scanned the battlefield. Thankfully, the only casualties were a few brooms and mops.

"You're a freaking psychopath," Cutler said, his eyes still wide in shock. He didn't even notice that the tips of his hair were on fire.

"Your hair," she coughed out. It felt like a car engine had exploded in her lungs.

Cutler patted down the tiny flames. "Psychopath," he repeated.

"Pretty much," Sera said.

As he met her eyes, his grin returned and manic delight spread across his face. "You're even hotter as a mage than you were as a human."

And Cutler was even crazier than she'd thought.

"Go out with me. Tonight."

Sera sidestepped his grasping hand. "I'm busy tonight."

"What could be more important than going out with me?"

Uh, anything? "Work," she said instead, hoping that would avoid another battle with brooms and mops. Assuming she hadn't just burned Mayhem's entire stash of them to ash.

"You're on leave." His eyebrows scrunched together in suspicion.

"Not exactly. I have to pay back my Magic Games fees somehow. Not all of us were born with a magic money tree in our front yard."

"Drachenburg," Cutler said, frowning. "You're working for Drachenburg. I saw him leaving Simmons's office last month. What are you working on with the dragon?"

Ha. So she wasn't the only one who called him the dragon.

"Hunting monsters mostly, just like I always do," she said.

"Except with magic."

She shrugged. "Kai is helping me."

"Sera, that man is out of his mind. He ate my three-headed guard dog."

"He ate your what?" Naomi asked, walking up beside Sera.

"My three-headed guard dog."

"He did that as a mage?" Sera asked.

"No, as a dragon." He frowned. "But that's beside the point. He's the same person, whether mage or dragon."

"Was the three-headed dog in question terrorizing innocent people by chance?"

"He was only *playing*," Cutler pouted. From the look on his face, he'd had this conversation before. Probably with Kai. "You need to stay away from Drachenburg. He's not good people."

She arched her brows. "And you are?"

"Of course, darling." He gave her a dazzling smile, the kind you could bounce marbles off of. "I'll protect you from him."

"Are you so sure? You couldn't even protect your dog from him."

The arm he'd tried to wrap around her dropped to his side. "Blow him off," he said, regaining his composure.

He tried to sizzle her with another smile. "Come with me tonight. You'll have more fun hanging out with me than sloshing through monster guts with him."

"Sorry." She shrugged his arm away. "Busy."

"Tomorrow?" Cutler asked. He just didn't get it.

"I'm busy every night," she said, then grabbed Naomi's hand and hurried toward the women's locker room.

CHAPTER FIVE
Mages Illustrated

"DO YOU THINK he'll follow us in here?"

Sera looked away from her open locker, meeting Naomi's amethyst eyes. "No. As we walked away, Zan went to go talk to him. I heard something about 'insurance premiums'."

"Grace must have called Zan during the fight."

"Likely," Sera agreed, then tossed her shoes into the locker.

"So, what's the plan?" She hitched her thumb over her shoulder, indicating the door that led to the gym. "You mentioned you wanted my help with something in there."

"Yes. I need to practice for the Magic Games."

Naomi's rosy cheeks paled. "I'm not sure I can help you with that. I was never in the Games. It's only for full-blooded mages. Thank goodness," she added under her breath.

"Actually, I need your help because you're not a full-blooded mage."

Naomi's indigo brows lifted. "Oh?"

"Kai says I need to prepare for all types of magic.

Who knows what they'll throw at me in the Games," Sera said. "I want you to try to blast me with Fairy Dust. And any other tricks you might have."

"Well, I do have a lot of tricks." Naomi winked a pale blue eye, and when it opened again, it was chocolate-brown. "Just remember that my Fairy Dust isn't as powerful as a full fairy's."

"You're also half mage. That hybrid magic is special and strong, and I need to figure out how to fight it too."

Naomi set her hand on Sera's shoulder. "You're really worried about this, aren't you?"

"Yes." Sera stared into the dark depths of her temporary locker; it was about as welcoming as a black hole. Maybe she should put pictures up. With pink flowered borders.

"I will do whatever I can to help," Naomi said seriously—then, more playfully, added, "Though I have a sinking suspicion this girl power training session has as much to do with training as it does with avoiding someone."

"Like who?" Sera asked warily, turning around to face her. She wasn't surprised to see the wide grin on Naomi's face.

"Kai Drachenburg."

"That's ridiculous. Kai is helping me train for the Games. It would be stupid to avoid him."

"Indeed."

"So I'm not," Sera added. "...uh, avoiding him."

The look on Naomi's face told Sera her friend didn't buy it for a second.

Sera tried again. "He's working right now. I couldn't have trained with him if I wanted to. Which I don't," she tacked on quickly.

"Because you're avoiding him."

"Yes. Wait, no." Sera frowned at her. "You're trying to trick me."

"Am I?" Naomi asked, her face the epitome of innocence. Her magic, on the other hand, was as wicked as they came. It bubbled with delighted hiccups and smelled strongly of bubblegum.

"I'm not avoiding him. Not that I mind a respite from his attacks," Sera admitted. "Kai is a tough coach. He hits hard. Like wrecking-ball-demolishing-a-building hard."

"That's to be expected of a first tier mage who shifts into a dragon. But that's not why you're hiding from him, Sera."

"I don't know what you mean."

Naomi flashed her pretty white teeth at her; they sparkled like polished marble. "You *like* him." She nudged Sera. "Admit it."

"I do not 'like' the dragon," Sera replied, trying to keep her face perfectly neutral.

"So that's why you kissed him? Because you don't like him?"

"He kissed me."

Naomi's grin widened. "And you liked it."

"He's a good kisser." Sera tried for a nonchalant shrug, but it came out stiff. After three weeks of torturous training, her body was screaming for a massage.

"I know all about what happened. All about how you saved Kai." Naomi began to pace around the locker room in hyper, prancing steps. "You two shared an amazing adventure. Adventures like that bring people closer together. You like him. And he likes you. Otherwise, he wouldn't be training you so hard."

"I'll try to remember that the next time he blasts me onto my back."

Naomi snickered.

"Seriously?" Sera asked her. "You're going to turn that into something dirty?"

"Sorry." Naomi's hand disappeared into her locker, then she pulled out a magazine. "Do you know what this is?"

"Mages Illustrated," Sera read the magazine title off the cover.

"Not just any Mages Illustrated," Naomi said. "This is the Mages Illustrated with Kai on the cover. Topless."

Sera took a closer look at the man flexing his muscles on the cover and nearly snorted. That was Kai all right. And he looked like he really needed to kill something. Like the photographer. Or the person who had made off with his shirt.

"That's the dragon all right," Sera said.

"He's one gorgeous man." Naomi slid her finger down the magazine cover, tracing Kai's contours.

"Shall I leave you alone with him?"

"No." Naomi took one final, longing look at the magazine, then pushed it into Sera's hands. "Does he often go around with his shirt off?"

"Uh, no." She rolled her eyes for effect.

"Oh, come on." Naomi wrapped her arm around Sera, drawing her in closer. "It's just us girls here. You can tell me how you feel about Kai."

"He's arrogant and controlling. And his car looks like a tank," she added.

"Is that a bad thing?"

"It's a…thing," Sera finished eloquently.

"His magic is off the charts."

"That's probably what's responsible for those arrogant and controlling qualities I mentioned. Kai is an alpha male. With a capital A."

"You say that like it's a four-letter word."

"Yep."

Naomi snickered. "So, he's arrogant, controlling, and alpha. And?"

"And he's a good kisser. That might make up for two of the three. But not all three."

Naomi's merriment melted and she said seriously, "You're so in over your head, girl."

"I know." Sera sighed. "But I have more important things to worry about right now. I have to train for the Magic Games, then survive those Games. And all the while in between training and not having my mind cracked open like an egg, I need to figure out what some naughty vampires are up to at the Games. But at this very moment, I need your help, Naomi." She handed the magazine back to her.

Naomi shook her head. "Keep it," she said with a smile. "You never know when you might need it."

Sera didn't think that was likely. She couldn't do anything remotely useful with a magazine. Sure, maybe she could roll it up and smack people with it, but she had fists that could do that just as well. And when those failed, she had her knives.

But Naomi didn't look like she was going to take no for an answer, so Sera tucked the magazine into her locker and shut it. She didn't have time to argue—not when her life depended on training for the Magic Games.

CHAPTER SIX
Centaur Storm

"HOW ABOUT THIS one?" Naomi asked, holding up a hanger.

Sera cringed at the tiny whisper of a black dress hanging from it. "Are you sure you didn't pick up a swimsuit by mistake?"

"This is the twenty-third outfit you've shot down." Naomi expelled a heavy sigh and put the hanger back on the rack. "You need to stop being so picky."

"Trove is the picky one," Sera mumbled, skimming through another rack.

They'd been shopping for nearly half an hour, which was half an hour too long. Every floor of Macy's was flooded with Sunday shoppers. Rushing, aggressive, shoving Sunday shoppers. Sera would have preferred monsters. You were at least allowed to poke monsters with your sword when they acted rude.

One of the floors dedicated to the Rich Witch brand. That's where Naomi had dragged her. She'd described the brand as 'trashy chic'. Looking around at the offerings on the rack, Sera had to agree.

"How is Trove being picky by expecting their clientele to wear clean clothes that aren't torn?" Naomi asked.

"I can't even make it two hours without having to fight off a monster or mage or some other supernatural crazy. Clothes get torn. And dirty. I can't go shopping for new clothes every two hours."

"You're making this entirely too complicated," Naomi said.

Sera shrugged. She hadn't wanted to go shopping. Naomi, being of the same mind as Kai, had talked her into it. Right now, Sera was missing out on dissecting more vampiric tapeworms with Mayhem's disposal department. Yes, that was every bit as disgusting as it sounded, which is why it hadn't taken much convincing from Naomi.

"My life has recently taken a complicated tur—"

A shrill shriek split through the room. Before Sera could turn to see what it was all about, a chorus of screams echoed the first, followed by a stampede of fleeing footsteps. Towering high over the panicking crowds, their heads nearly bumping the chandeliers, a horde of centaurs stomped across the store. Their eyes, gleaming with hate, glared at a second centaur horde galloping down the wooden escalator. Armor covered the centaurs' chests, arms, and backs, clinking like a bundle of tin cans as the two factions clashed.

"See what I mean?" Sera said to Naomi over the clamor of hooves and clang of steel.

"You always seem to be in just the right place at the right time for trouble," her friend agreed.

They watched the battle that had taken over the store. Centaurs leapt and galloped and hollered. The shoppers were hollering too. They ran in erratic, panicked zigzags, squealing at the top of their lungs. Speckled here and there between the chaos, a few calmer shoppers had hunkered down behind overturned clothing racks and were shooting videos of the fight.

"Do you think we should do something?" Naomi asked as a centaur galloped after a fleeing group of humans. "All the screaming is riling them up."

"Centaurs are always riled up," Sera said, drawing two knives. "Drama queens."

She picked out the two leaders in the crowd, who were entangled in a hoof-to-hoof brawl. How convenient. A knife in each hand, she sprinted forward and slammed a blade into each. The centaurs reared back, but they didn't stop fighting each other—not even to kick her away.

"Hit them harder?" Naomi suggested, stepping up beside her.

"I didn't bring my sword." She hadn't expected to need it while shopping. Wishful thinking. She *always* needed her sword. "But I can try something else."

Focusing on the knives inside the two centaurs, she drew on fire. She poured the magic down the blades, searing flesh and burning blood. Through the crackling snap of her magic, something was humming. The raw song tickled her ears and buzzed down the back of her neck. A hand tore Sera out of the trance. She looked back into Naomi's horrified eyes.

"Sera." She pointed.

The two centaur leaders were rolling on the floor, screaming out in agony. All the others had stopped fighting. They were hardly moving. They watched their leaders, the same horrified look that was in Naomi's eyes was in theirs too. Sera severed her magic, pushing it back down where it belonged. The centaurs' screams died, and a moment later they stood.

"You are a powerful warrior," one of them said to Sera, respect in his eyes. He glanced back at the knife sticking out of his flank. "What kind of enchantment is on that weapon?"

Sera gave the knife a rough tug, and it tore out of him. Coddling a centaur was a surefire way to send him into a rage. They believed in strength and bravery, not hugs and kisses.

"A warrior doesn't share her secrets," she said and yanked the knife out of the second centaur.

"Indeed," the first said, laughing.

Sera sheathed her knives. "What are your names?"

"Apollo," said the first.

"Thor."

Wow. Someone had delusions of grandeur. Sera turned to the second centaur.

"You only have a sword," she pointed out.

Thor gave her a perplexed look. Or maybe that was annoyed.

"Thor is supposed to have a hammer," she said.

Apollo let out a snort worthy of a stallion.

Thor's grip tightened on his sword. "My other weapon is a war hammer."

"That would make a great bumper sticker," Sera said, glancing at his flanks.

Beside her, Naomi slapped her hand against her forehead.

Sera frowned at her. "You did not just facepalm my joke."

"That was supposed to be a joke?" Naomi asked with a sassy smirk.

Sera sighed. "Never mind." She looked at Apollo and Thor again. "You two will need to take your lovers' spat elsewhere. This establishment is under my protection."

"Since when?" Thor asked, a challenge in his eyes.

"Since now," she told him. "So if you two don't want to end up squealing like pigs on the floor again, move on out."

Apollo grinned at Thor. "I like her. She's spunky."

Thor's frown deepened. "You can't take all of us at once," he told Sera.

"You're welcome to find out," she replied. "But I have more than just knives at my disposal."

Thor glared at her, like he really was going to test her. Even at their calmest, centaurs' magic was heavy and musky, which wasn't all that surprising considering that they were essentially part horse. Right now, Thor's magic wasn't just heavy and musky. It was as thick as butter—but not nearly as tasty. He stared down at her, his eyes dark and cold, his magic a storm of thunder and fire.

Then, just as his anger was reaching the boiling point, it deflated. He turned and walked away. Apollo gave her a brusque nod, then he headed for a different exit. The other centaurs streamed into two neat groups and followed their leaders.

"Well, that went surprisingly well," Naomi said, looking across the battlefield of overturned racks and scattered clothing.

With the centaurs gone, the scared shoppers were starting to venture out of their hiding places. A few of the braver ones were already showing one another their videos of the fight. New shoppers were filtering into the store from outside, and a bedraggled woman with a 'manager' bar pinned to her blue blouse was giving the mountains of mess a weary look.

The respite didn't even last a minute. Before Naomi could show Sera another dress, a horde of vampires flooded the store, their eyes gleaming crimson.

CHAPTER SEVEN
Vampire Apocalypse

THE SHOPPERS SCREAMED and scattered like the vampire apocalypse was upon them. They stumbled over snapped coat hangers and rumpled clothing. Of course the vampires took chase. The only thing that got a vampire riled up as much as blood was fear. And the Sunday shoppers were giving these vampires a real tasty appetizer.

"Stop!" Sera shouted over the shrieks and the thumps of stampeding feet. "Your hysterics are only making the vampires' bloodlust worse. Hey, stop! Listen!"

Unsurprisingly, they didn't stop, and they didn't listen. They were too busy panicking. Or shooting videos. Again. Sera glared at the group of teenage boys following the vampires around, their phones recording the mayhem. Those kids had a death wish. Their silly hats weren't the only thing they'd put on backwards today.

A fist swung toward Sera's head. She ducked and spun, giving the vampire a solid shove as she turned. He threw out his hands to catch his fall, but Naomi hit him with a blast of Fairy Dust. His body went limp, and he smacked hard against the floor.

Three more vampires charged forward, drool dangling from their fangs. As Sera dashed past the first, she landed a knife in his back. She launched another knife over his falling body, at a vampire chasing a little girl across a tabletop of scarves. The blade sank into his forehead, and he crashed down onto an umbrella display. Sera drew two more knives and downed the vampires creeping up on Naomi.

"Hey, are you going to leave any for me?" her friend protested.

Sera shrugged. There were plenty more vampires in the store, twelve by Sera's count. No, make that sixteen. Four vampires had just stalked out from the shadows, slinking up behind a group of mages shooting lightning bolts and high-heeled shoes at any and every monster in sight. For a bunch of men in sleek, custom-cut business suits, those mages sure were efficient monster slayers.

As for the vampires stalking them…well, their behavior was downright odd. All the other vampires in the store were sporting gleaming blood-red eyes and some serious fang. These four had neither red eyes nor big, pointy teeth. Their magic didn't smell like rotting meat either. It didn't smell like anything. Odorless magic? Sera had never come across anything like it before. The pale sheen on their skin, though, was undeniable. Those were vampires.

There was a sense of purpose to the four vampires' movements. Vampires caught in the throes of bloodlust didn't stalk with purpose; they pounced and bit and tore.

"They're not together," Sera said as she slammed a vampire face-first into a glass display case. It shattered on impact.

"Who?" Naomi asked.

"All these vampires." Sera indicated the blood-thirsty bunch. "And those four over there. The ones going after those mages."

By now, the mages had noticed the sneaking vampires. One of them shot an enormous fireball at those vampires, but the magic just bounced off their bodies.

"Well, that's new." Naomi pushed her hands forward, giving the two vampires she was fighting a face full of Fairy Dust. On their way to dreamland, they tripped over each other and fell to the floor in a tangled mess.

"Nice."

Naomi grinned. "Thanks." Her eyes shifted to the business suit mages. "Should we help them?"

There were now two mages shooting fire at the stalking vampires, but whatever they were doing wasn't working. The vampires continued stalking forward, the mages' magic simply bouncing off of their armor. Fear was slowly whittling away at the arrogance on the mages' faces.

"Yeah, we probably should. Just a sec," Sera said.

She threw an umbrella at one of the raging vampires tearing through the store. It clunked hard against his head. But rather than going to sleep like a good little monster, he turned his crimson eyes on Sera and roared, splattering the nearby teenage boys with monster drool. The boys shouted out in disgust and scrambled off the battlefield. The drool succeeded where common sense had failed. Monster video-making hour was finally over.

Sera launched a knife at Mr. Spittle, and this time he did go down. "Ok, ready. Path is clear."

She ran toward the mages. They had abandoned their cool-faced extermination of the raging vampires. All five in front were now shooting magic at the armored vampires. Their faces weren't calm anymore either. Panic speckled the heavy cloud of first tier magic brewing around them. Their unease grew with every spell that bounced off the vampires.

"We need to get the vampires out of that armor," Sera said.

"How do you suggest we do that?" Naomi asked.

"I'll think of something. Can you handle the bloodlust crowd in the meantime?"

Naomi's eyes scanned the area. There were still a few vampires left. They were chasing the human shoppers from one end of the store to the other. They hadn't hurt anyone yet. It was as though they were only meant as a distraction.

"Sure. Go get 'em, Sera."

Sera darted around the closest vampire. Drawing a knife, she grabbed him from behind and sliced her blade at the bonds holding the armored breastplate to his body. He spun around, swinging his arms at her, but she ducked, splitting the armor's remaining bonds as she dropped. The breastplate peeled off of him. She smashed it into the vampire's knees. As he collapsed, she clobbered him over the head, finishing the job.

Well, kind of. There were still three more vampires. They were almost upon the mages, who continued to shoot magic fireworks like it was New Year's Eve. Sera ran toward the next two vampires, slashing out with her knives as she passed between them. Unfortunately, that also put her directly in the line of the mages' fire. As the vampires' armor tipped to the side, she dove under the firestorm and rolled.

"Your magic isn't working," Sera told the mages,

hopping to her feet beside them. "I've cut an opening in the armor of those two." She pointed at the vampires with the lopsided breastplates. "Aim your spells for their sides. I'm going to take care of the next one's armor."

One of the mages, a silver-headed stately sort of man whose last haircut had probably cost more than everything Sera was currently wearing, poked his head out of hiding. He turned his cold dark eyes on her. "You dare to give my bodyguards commands? Do you have any idea who you're talking to?" He was pretty opinionated for someone who was letting the other five mages fight for him.

"Look, mister. I don't care if you're the president. Those vampires are out for blood—your blood—and your way isn't working. You can either do as I say and live, or you can stick your nose in the air and die. Your choice."

Mr. Silverhead's nostrils flared. "Of all the impudent, ill-mannered—"

"She took out one of them," another mage said, pointing at the vampire on the floor.

Mr. Silverhead looked at Sera. She shrugged and smiled at him, which was apparently not the response he was looking for. His magic buzzed with anger.

"Fine. If you're not going to do as I said, then just try not to shoot me," she said. She certainly didn't have time to babysit prissy mages.

"We should listen to her," one of the bodyguards said to the others. "She looks like she slaughters monsters all the time."

Sera wasn't sure whether the bodyguard intended that as a compliment or an insult. In either case, it was true.

"Fine," Mr. Silverhead growled. He turned toward the other mages. "Aim for the gaps she made in the vampires' armor."

As a fresh round of magic singed the air, Sera ran for the last vampire. Like the others, he had that same invisible, odorless magic around him. No, not exactly invisible or odorless. It was a kind of white noise, a background magic that masked all ambient magic. Odd as it was, it didn't make him stronger than any other vampire. If anything, he was slower, like his movements were delayed by half a second. Sera slashed the bonds on his armor and caught the breastplate as it fell. She smashed him in the head with it, but he didn't go down. Maybe he was stronger after all.

He swung his gigantic fist at her. Sera lifted the breastplate to block his punch. He kept swinging, again and again. And again. Sera's armor shield dinged like a clock tower sounding out the hour. Blood dripped down the armor, speckling the white floor with crimson drops. Still the vampire didn't stop.

Sera stole a glance back at the mages. They'd taken down the other vampires and were now watching her fight with this one. More than one of them looked completely horrified. Just not Mr. Silverhead. Apparently, it took more than a bloody-fisted vampire with a look of cold, calculated murder in his eyes to rustle up that mage.

A streak of lightning zapped past Sera, nearly sizzling her hair. It missed the vampire completely. She shot an irked look at the mages.

"Watch where you're shooting," she growled at them.

She shoved the breastplate at the vampire, then hopped back to put some distance between them. The second lightning bolt hit him square in the chest. The vampire convulsed for a few seconds, his eyes rolling back, then he went down.

Mr. Silverhead walked up beside Sera and gave the unconscious vampire a cold sneer. "I need you to hand over that armor," he told Sera, holding out his hand.

"I don't think it's your color."

Shockingly, he didn't laugh. "The armor. Now."

"You have three sets of armor over there." She pointed at his bodyguards, who were looting the other three vampires. "This set is mine."

"You seem to be confused as to our respective positions here," he said, drawing his magic around himself like a regal cloak. "I command. You obey. I have jurisdiction. And you have the honor of serving the Magic Council."

The sarcastic quip sizzled out on her tongue. The Magic Council. She couldn't afford to incur their wrath. She'd already attracted far too much of their attention.

"Good. You're more agreeable when you don't talk," he said. "Now hand over that armor."

"Fine." She shoved the breastplate into him, then walked away.

"Are you all right?" Naomi asked her as they headed toward the exit.

"Yeah, fine."

"You looked like you wanted to punch that mage."

"Yep."

"But you didn't."

"He hid behind his Magic Council shield," Sera told her.

Naomi glanced back at the group of mages. "He's on the Magic Council?"

"Yes," Sera grumbled.

"You look like you're regretting saving them."

"Yes."

The manager in the blue blouse stepped in front of them. Her neat bun had come undone, and her pantyhose were torn. She looked like she'd just survived a night of hell. Maybe the centaurs and the vampires had been too much for her.

"You don't usually get monster attacks here, do you?" Naomi asked, her smile sympathetic.

The woman brushed down her expensive skirt and made a solid attempt at standing tall. Her messy clothes and broken heels somewhat diminished the effect.

"This is not a fighting pit," she said stiffly, sweeping her hand across the trashed store. "Who is going to pay for all this?"

Sera pointed at the mages. "Talk to those guys. They have jurisdiction."

The manager hustled off to the mages. She actually looked relieved. Sera hoped Mr. Silverhead wasn't nasty to the poor woman. She wanted to hear how they were going to fix her store, not eloquent speeches about 'serving the Magic Council'.

"First centaurs, then vampires," Naomi said as they stepped outside. "What do you think this was all about? And why do monsters always attack wherever you are?"

Kai had told Sera magic was a monster-attracting beacon, but she wasn't going to take the blame for this one.

"The vampires were after those mages. No, that one mage. Mr. Jurisdiction," she said. "We were just in the wrong place at the right time."

"Or the right time to save their asses."

"Yes."

"And the centaurs?"

Sera shrugged. "Bad luck. I don't think they have

anything to do with the vampires."

"Those vampires were acting weird," Naomi said. "Well, the four armored ones, anyway. The others were just common vampires caught up in bloodlust."

"They were the distraction so the other four could take out Silverhead. No, not just the distraction. The cover. Someone was controlling the vampires. I bet you a tub of double chocolate ice cream that they wanted to make that mage's death look like a random casualty."

"I'm not taking that bet," Naomi said. "This whole thing is as fishy as a Wizard House Pizza Seafood Special. It's too bad the mages wouldn't let you take a piece of that magic-proof armor. It might be able to lead us to whoever is behind this."

Sera pulled a knob out of her pocket. "I might have swiped a piece of armor."

Naomi's eyebrow twitched. "You stole it from right under Mr. Snooty's nose?"

"Sure. And if he hadn't been so busy waxing poetic on the joys of serving the Magic Council, he would have noticed too." Sera rolled the knob between her fingers. With the magic-nullifying effect of the armor broken, it smelled an awful lot like burning plastic. "I need to get this to Kai."

"Why?"

"Because I think the armor is from Drachenburg Industries."

CHAPTER EIGHT
Trove

SERA GAVE HER closet a wary look. The shopping trip had been a bust, which left her back at square one. Sure, she'd insisted to Kai that she had plenty of clothes that wouldn't get her turned away from Trove, but she'd also been totally lying. She actually was having trouble finding something that wasn't denim, dirty, leather, torn, bloody, full of monster gore, or designed for military warfare. What did the magical elite have against denim anyway? Even Kai wore jeans, and he was practically perched at the top of their silly hierarchy.

"Maybe I'll just wear my running suit," she muttered as she pushed all her jeans to one side of the closet.

Her stomach growled in response. Lunch with Riley and Kai felt like weeks ago. Probably because in the last few hours, she'd fought through centaurs, vampires, and Cutler. And she'd had to put up with a mage from the Magic Council. Stupid Mr. Snooty Pants. She'd rather have fought more monsters.

After the ill-fated shopping trip, she'd gone back to the hotel for a nap. She probably should have gone to Kai right away and shown him the armor piece, but she was too tired to deal with him right now.

Her stomach rumbled again. Apparently, the sandwich she'd snarfed down after showering hadn't been enough to satisfy it. Well, it would just have to wait its turn.

Sera wished Alex were here to help her pick out something to wear—or at least mock Trove's snooty clientele with her. She would have settled for Riley, except her brother was off exploring the city tonight. Maybe he'd meet a nice girl, one with zero drama. And with no monsters in her closet.

Sera sighed and returned her attention to her own closet's paltry offerings. Right now, she would have killed for a monster or two in her closet. Anything to get her out of this latest assignment. Trove. Bah. A midnight fight at the pier was suddenly looking really appealing.

Sera's phone dinged, telling her she had five minutes to get her butt in gear and leave the hotel. She grabbed a skin-tight red shirt and a pair of even tighter black pants, a little outfit Naomi had picked out for her from the hotel store. Sera had been avoiding the outfit because she knew it would make her look like a streetwalker, but it was the only thing she had that might satisfy Trove's stupid dress code. Staring into her closet for the next five minutes wouldn't change that.

She grabbed a pair of black dress shoes—yet another gift from Naomi. The heels were way too high, but Sera couldn't very well wear flats with an outfit that was essentially a bodysuit. *That* would have been ridiculous. So she slipped on her streetwalker shoes to go with her streetwalker costume. If a monster attacked her tonight, she'd just skewer it with her dagger heels.

She dropped her phone into her purse, which was just big enough to fit a small stash of throwing knives inside. Kai wouldn't be happy, but what he didn't know wouldn't hurt him. She was not running into a fight with magic as her only weapon.

As she fished her wallet out of the sports bag dangling from her chair, she noticed Naomi's magazine poking out of the top. She was already late, but she couldn't resist taking a quick peek. Kai stood with his hands cupped behind his head, giving the reader front row seats to his sculptured torso.

"So what if he's hot," Sera muttered. "And has raw power gushing out of his pores."

She could almost feel his magic pounding against the page, trying to break free. The memory of his magic flooded her, pulsing through her veins.

"Ridiculous," she said, forcing out a laugh. She tossed the magazine aside. "He's one of them. He's on the Magic Council."

Her phone dinged again. If she didn't leave now, she'd really be late. She grabbed her purse and hurried toward the door.

Shockingly, the bouncer at Trove let Sera in. And he wasn't even rude about it. Kai must have talked to him. She hoped bribes or threats hadn't been necessary to ensure the bouncer's good behavior, but she wasn't holding her breath on that one.

She wove her way through the crowd of overprivileged young mages, concentrating really hard on not tripping over any of them. She'd already stumbled once tonight on the hotel's steps, much to the amusement of the other guests. She had no intention of repeating the experience here. As soon as the fight started, she was tossing off those stupid shoes. She should never have let Naomi buy them for her in the first place. A new knife would have been more useful—and less dangerous.

A forest of crystal branches dangled from the ceiling, sparkling in the purple-blue light. Mages danced to the heavy beat, their bodies thrashing and buzzing in time to the music. A number of couples were making out on the dance floor. One couple was doing a bit more than making out, but no one seemed to notice. They were all too drunk—drunk on magic and on those glowing drinks the bar was serving. So much for this being a classy establishment.

Oblivious as they seemed, a few of the mages did notice Sera as she passed by the dance floor. They stared out at her, their eyes alight with magic. She didn't know if it was disdain or interest she saw in those eyes. Maybe it was just plain drunkenness. But whatever their thoughts were, the effect was the same: those staring eyes gave her goosebumps.

"What the hell am I even doing here?" Sera muttered to herself. She didn't belong at Trove.

She bypassed the horde of dancing mages and headed for the bar. The magic wafting off those glowing drinks electrified the air, crackling against her skin. Maybe she wouldn't feel so out of place after she'd had a glowy cocktail. She didn't usually drink—and especially not while on the job—but if she didn't settle her nerves, she wouldn't be fighting anyone.

The bartender must have sensed her dire need to relax because before she even sat down at the bar, he had her drink ready.

"You're with Kai Drachenburg," he said, setting down a cocktail that glowed pink. A wisp of pale purple smoke floated along the glass's rim.

"How did you know?"

"He called ahead to tell me he was meeting someone here. Said to watch for a pretty brunette who looked like she'd been forced into the club at gunpoint."

"I do *not* look like that," she protested, taking a sip of her drink. Magic fizzled across her tongue, tickling her tastebuds with ice and fire.

"Sure you do." He gave her an easy smile. "How's your drink?"

"Fantastic."

"Good. Kai thought you might appreciate one of my elemental cocktails."

Sera took another sip. This time, lightning sizzled against her tongue. "You seem to know him well. Are you two friends?"

"That man saved my life." The bartender's magic changed, his humor vanishing. It was displaced by a far more potent emotion: loyalty.

"Tell me about it?"

The humor returned to his eyes. "Next time you come here, maybe I will." Then he gave her a wink and glided over to the group of male mages who had just sauntered up to the bar.

Sera took a few more sips from her drink, relishing in the elemental sensations, each time a different combination. She'd just started to relax when she saw something that threw her agitation back into overdrive. Cutler.

He was on the dance floor, gyrating with a woman

wearing a minidress that made Sera's outfit look like full-body armor. Cutler seemed to be enjoying her...um, company—so he obviously wasn't too torn up about Sera turning him down this morning. Just in case, she turned away from him. He didn't need to know she was here.

She was too late.

As the song ended, Cutler looked toward the bar. His eyes met hers with devilish delight, and she knew she was in trouble. He leaned down to whisper something to his date, then strode over to Sera, his smile widening with every step. By the time he was standing in front of her, his grin had gone supernova.

"Sera." He dipped his chin to her as he sat down on the stool beside hers. He ordered a drink. As soon as it arrived, he spun his stool to face her. "I thought you were busy working tonight."

"I am working."

"Not dressed like that, you aren't, honey." His eyes panned up her body, lingering on her chest.

She flicked him in the chin.

"Ow!" he growled, nearly tumbling off his stool.

She shrugged. "It's not nice to stare."

He resettled his balance, his grin returning. "Now do it again, this time with magic."

"You want me to flick you with my magic?" she asked in disbelief.

"Yes, as hard as you can, baby," he said, stroking his finger along the lip of his glass. From the way he was still gawking at her chest, he was obviously thinking about touching other things.

Sera looked down at her glass, which was only half-empty. She should have downed the whole damn thing the second she'd seen him.

"What do you say, gorgeous?" Cutler winked. "Care to have some fun?"

"What do I say? That I'm too busy for this nonsense. I have work to do."

He took a long drink, and when his eyes met hers again, they were glowing. "What kind of work? Checking the drinks for poison?"

She glared at him.

He didn't take the hint. "You know what I think, Sera?" Smiling lazily, he wrapped his arm around her. "I think you didn't come here to work. I think you came here because you're pining for me."

"Pining? For you?" she said, nearly choking on the words.

He gave her a knowing nod. "Yes."

She shrugged off his arm. "You're delusional. You followed me to New York."

"Of course I did. I want to see you in the Magic Games. And don't pretend you're not glad I came." Cutler leaned in. "I know a woman in need when I see her, and you're it. How long has it been since you've had sex?"

Magic and alcohol shot out of her mouth. She coughed. "Excuse me?"

"That long, is it?" Cutler nodded. "I thought so." He stood, grabbing her hand. "But don't worry. I'm here to help. Follow me. I know a quiet spot in the back."

"Remove your hand before I do," she growled through clenched teeth. Her magic was bubbling beneath her skin, its flames fed by her rage.

"So it's like that, is it?" he said, unconcerned. "You want to be wooed first." He smiled. "Very well. Let's dance."

Sera's magic was bursting at the seams, ready to

explode. She tried to push it down, but it refused to obey. Instead, it continued to pound at her restraint, chewing away at it one bit at a time.

"Let go," she said, the words buzzing in her throat. "I will not tell you again."

He laughed, his grip tightening around her wrist. "You're sexy when you're angry. I want to see the look in your eyes when I take you over the edge."

He was taking her over the edge all right. Her magic snapped out and punched him in the gut. Cutler doubled over, his grasp finally broken. Groaning, he straightened.

"Was that hard enough for you, *baby*?"

His eyes were swirling with pain. And excitement. "Sera," he began, making her name sound like a dirty word.

Someone passed between them, cutting Cutler off. Sera looked up into Kai's eyes.

"Go," he growled at Cutler. When Cutler didn't move, he barked, "Now."

Cutler took one look at the dragon scales sliding across Kai's arm, then scurried off. When he was gone, Kai turned and sat down beside her.

"Thanks," Sera said. "I was this close to blasting him across the room." She stared down at her drink and sighed. "I still have so little control over my magic."

"You showed remarkable restraint against that punk." He lifted her drink, turning it in his hand. "Do you mind?"

"Go ahead."

He drained the glass in a single go. "My magic was close to the surface too."

"You're always in control," she said, watching the scales fade from his skin.

"Not always." He tapped his arm. "As you can see."

"I thought you were just showing off for Cutler's benefit."

"No. I was half a second from losing it. Reining in my rage was…difficult."

"I'm glad you didn't blow up the building. There are better ways to show off," she teased, giving his arm a pat.

He caught her hand as it withdrew. "Tell me." His thumb stroked her palm in slow, deep circles.

Her heart stuttered. "Tell you what?"

"I've never cared about showing off for other people."

"You don't need to. Your magic speaks for itself. It's…" She gasped as his magic slid against hers. "Kai, that's very distracting."

"What?" His eyes focused. "Oh." He snapped his magic back into himself. "I didn't even realize I was doing it. *You* are distracting."

"So this is my fault?"

"Yes." He gave her a rare smile. It was a hard smile, not sticky and slimy like Cutler's silly grin. "You made me wonder about what I could do to impress you."

"I thought you didn't show off for people."

"Not people." He took her other hand. "You."

She opened her mouth to say something surely witty —if only she could have thought of something—but he'd already dropped her hands.

A deep chuckle rumbled in his chest. "Let's get you some dinner."

"I already ate," she said, trying to ignore the beat of her pounding pulse.

"Did you?" He rested his chin on his hands and looked at her. "And what did you have?"

"A peanut butter and jelly sandwich," she told him.

He looked horrified. "That's not even food."

"How is that not food?"

"It just isn't," he said, as though that were that, no need for further discussion.

"And what do you consider food?" she asked.

He didn't even need to think about it. "A steak," he said immediately.

Sera gave her eyes a long, slow roll. A steak. Of course.

"Which is why I ordered you one," he continued. "You need your strength."

"You ordered me a steak?"

He nodded.

"At a nightclub?"

"Yes," he said.

"And you expect it will actually taste good?"

"Of course. I've had their steak before. This isn't just any club. And this isn't just any city."

Sera tore her eyes away from the groping couples on the dance floor. "I see."

"Just give it a try. If you don't like it, I'll eat it," Kai said as the bartender set a large plate down in front of her.

Her stomach betrayed her, greeting her dinner's arrival with a growl. "Ok." She poked the steak with her knife. It looked normal. And the fact that it didn't poke her back spoke in its favor. "I *am* hungry. Naomi and I trained hard this afternoon. Do you have any idea how much it hurts to be blasted with Fairy Dust thirty-eight times in a row?"

"No."

Of course he didn't. The military had shot tank ammunition at him, and he'd claimed it only tickled. It must have been nice to have super-defenses. She poked the steak again.

"Sera."

She looked up from her plate. "Yes?"

"If you don't stop torturing that steak, I'll be forced to save it from you."

She pointed her fork at him. "Says the man who steps on people."

"Only if they annoy me." A feral grin curled his lips. "Now eat."

Sera cut off a piece of the steak and set it into her mouth. As she began to chew, salt and seasoned butter melted against her tongue, splashing it with a dozen subtle flavors. The only steak she'd ever had this good was that one from Illusion. Which Kai had also gotten her. The dragon sure knew his meat.

"And?" he asked.

"It's really good. It doesn't taste at all like bar food," she replied, cutting off another piece.

"Maybe you've been going to the wrong bars," the bartender said, sliding a glass of red wine across the counter to her.

She smiled at him. "Maybe I have."

Kai took the second wine glass, frowning as he swirled it around in his hand. "Are you flirting with Connor?"

"Why? Are you jealous?" she asked, grinning as the bartender walked away.

Kai's eyes narrowed. "It's a good thing we switched to wine. That glowing cocktail went to your head. You're being silly."

"In case you haven't noticed, I'm always silly."

"On that we can agree." He sipped from his glass. "Tell me about your training session at Mayhem."

Right. Straight back to business then.

"Naomi and I spent two hours in the gym," Sera said. "She blasted me with Fairy Dust. She has some elemental spells too. They're not so bad alone, but the Dust mixed with the elemental magic hurt like hell. I thought my hands would freeze off. Or burn off. It depended on what combo she was using."

"It sounds like good training for you."

"Losing my hands?" she asked.

"Facing different varieties of magic."

"Yep. That's why I asked Naomi to train with me."

"And did you practice stringing your spells together like we talked about?" he asked.

"Uh, so… The thing is my magic wasn't cooperating so well. I might have used *some* magic or another during the fight. You know, in between repelling her with those big ropes that hang from the walls and ceiling."

"I see."

Sera hadn't believed anyone could pack so much disappointment into so few words. It…hurt. Yes, hurt. She could be mature and admit that she cared what Kai thought about her. Admit to herself anyway. Not to him. No way, no how.

"But I did kick Cutler's ass on the way to the gym," she told him. "And I only used magic. Lots of magic. With lots of stringing spells."

"Good."

He glanced across the club. A group of mages was sitting on a big sofa, Cutler and his unfortunate date included. Cutler met Kai's stare for a moment—then hastily looked away.

"I hope you're not going to pull him around back and beat him bloody," Sera said.

"I don't have to. Apparently, you already kicked his

ass."

She snorted.

"Are you going to eat that?" he asked, pointing to her steak.

"Why? Are you hungry?"

"Yes."

"If you ask really nicely, maybe I'll give you a bite."

He gave her a cool look.

"Or you can just glower at me. That works too." She cut a piece off of the steak and pointed the fork toward him. "Here you go."

"What happened after the gym?" he asked before eating the piece of meat.

"I went to go help Mayhem's Disposal Department dissect a bunch of vampiric tapeworms."

He didn't even blink—or stop chewing. "That sounds appetizing."

"It was really gross, to be perfectly honest."

"Worse than chopping up monsters?"

"Oh, much worse. When you're in a fight, you don't have much time to stop and smell the monster guts."

"Indeed." He lifted his glass to her.

She raised her glass too and took a cautious sip. The wine tasted a lot fancier than the generic stuff she bought from the grocery store. It kind of reminded her of dark cherries and chocolate. Did he know her tastes so well already? Scary.

"Then after the dissection, Naomi and I went shopping," she said.

"And bought this outfit?"

"No. Naomi got this outfit for me from the hotel store while I was napping. I was almost too embarrassed to wear it. You know, on account of it being really..."

"Provocative?"

"Slutty," she amended, biting back a blush. "But it's the only thing I have that isn't ruined or on Trove's black list. You see, not even half an hour into our shopping trip, two gangs of centaurs stormed through the mall, shaking their swords and screaming insults at one another."

"They always do that. They're just looking for attention. Ignore them, and they eventually gallop away."

"I couldn't just ignore them when there were panicking shoppers riling them up," she said. "We scared off the centaurs, but then vampires attacked."

"Your magic is very appealing to monsters. It draws them in."

She shook her head. "Not this time. The vampires weren't after me. They were after a mage. Someone from the Magic Council."

"Describe this mage."

"Rich, powerful, rude, claiming jurisdiction. Basically like someone from any of the magic dynasties."

Kai gave her a cool look.

She smirked at him. "What? You know it's true."

He remained unimpressed.

She sighed. "Ok. Fine. Male. Roughly fifty. He had silver hair, and a really bad attitude. About half a second into our conversation, I was already regretting not letting the vampires have him."

"Duncan Blackbrooke," said Kai. "What happened to the vampires?"

"There were two groups. The larger group—the bloodlust ones—ran around the store while a smaller group went after Blackbrooke. And only after Blackbrooke."

"Someone was controlling them?"

"I believe so," Sera replied. "Maybe someone with access to the Blood Orb."

"If it's really a magic-hating group behind this, they could be targeting members of the Magic Council." He pulled out his phone and began swiping away.

"Kai, you're on the Magic Council."

He didn't look up from his phone. "I can take care of myself."

"That's what Blackbrooke and his entourage of bodyguards thought."

"I am *not* Duncan Blackbrooke."

"There's something else." Sera reached into her purse. "The vampires were wearing magic-resistant armor. I managed to swipe a piece before being shooed away."

Kai looked up as she set the knob on the counter. Blue light flashed in his eyes.

"Look familiar?" she asked.

He stared down at the knob, his expression darkening. "This is from my labs." He picked it up, rolling it back and forth between his fingers. "How many armor suits were there?"

"Four. One for each vampire. The mages' spells bounced right off."

"And now Blackbrooke has the armor?"

"Yes."

He pocketed the knob, then began swiping across his phone screen once again. "I haven't been informed of any recent thefts at my labs. Not since the Priming Bangles last month. My security guys are checking the suits now." His phone dinged, and he looked down at the screen again. "Everything is still there."

"Maybe the suits are from someone else," she suggested.

"Maybe." He didn't look convinced. "I'm having security question all the people who work in the lab. We'll find out soon enough." He took another sip of wine, a longer one this time. "What happened after the vampire attack?"

"By then, I wasn't much in the mood for shopping," she said. "I was, however, in dire need of a nap and a shower. And a peanut butter and jelly sandwich."

"I knew that dubious sandwich would find its way into this tale."

"You should really give it a try. You might actually like it," she told him. "I bet Trove's chef could fix you up a nice, pretentious peanut butter and jelly sandwich."

"What is a pretentious peanut butter and jelly sandwich?"

"Oh, I don't know. Maybe they can add some garnish on the side."

"I believe I'll pass."

"Your loss." Shrugging, she took a bite of steak. "Anyway, the stupid centaurs and vampires are the reason I didn't get to buy something nice to wear."

"You're wearing something nice."

Kai's brilliant blue eyes stared at her over the top of his wine glass. There was something very deep—very primal—about the look in them.

"The bouncer let me in at least." She smiled at him. The effect was only slightly diminished by her dropping her fork.

Kai caught it before it hit the counter. "You're doing it again."

"Doing what?"

"Being nervous around me."

Sera didn't have anything to say to that, so she turned

her attention to her steak instead. They sat in silence for the next few minutes while she ate and he watched her eat.

"Do you want the rest?" she finally asked. The only thing more uncomfortable than those tight pants was her full stomach pressing against those tight pants.

Kai reached for the plate as she was pulling away, and their hands brushed together. His magic flared up, gliding past hers. Its whispers were as soft as rose petals, its touch as smooth as honey.

"Sorry," he said, pulling his magic back in. "My magic has been unruly tonight."

She folded her hands together and tried not to think too hard about the fact that he'd apologized to her. Kai Drachenburg didn't apologize. He commanded.

"You're unsettled," he said.

"Nope."

"You are." He slid off his stool, then extended his hand toward her. "Dance with me."

"But we have work to do."

"Dancing first. You need to relax."

Without waiting for her response, he snatched her hand and led her to the dance floor. Raw and heavy, the bass buzzed against her skin. It rippled across her body, leaving goosebumps in its wake. Kai's hands dropped to her hips, the heat of his fingers dissolving through the thin fabric of her pants, flushing through her body. Biting back a shudder, Sera set her hands on his shoulders and concentrated on matching the sway of his body.

He started off slow, his eyes watching her cautiously, as though he thought she might flee at any second. The music sped up, its melody mixing with the bass. Kai's steps grew faster. Harder. He pulled her close, his hands pouring down her back, burning her with languid heat. His cheek brushed across hers, his breath trailing her jaw.

"You look amazing," he whispered into her ear. His words melted against her skin, dissolving like steaming snowflakes.

"I wasn't sure they would let me in at…" He kissed her cheek, and her words crumbled. Every inch of her tingled with magic. His magic. "You're doing it again."

"As I told you before, I'm having trouble keeping my magic in check."

"Why?"

"You know why."

His lips buzzed against her cheek as he spoke. His magic poured across her body like a river of fire, sliding down every curve, climbing every peak. Sera shuddered.

"Do you want me to stop?" he asked, pulling back just far enough to meet her eyes.

Her body protested his absence. Her magic tugged at his, trying to draw him closer. "No."

His blue eyes looked down at her, shining like mirrored glass. He dipped his head and kissed her. It was a light kiss, over almost as soon as it had begun. Even after his lips had left hers, his magic lingered, its teasing touch nuzzling at her restraint.

"Still ok?" he asked.

"Yes."

"Not running away?"

"Not a chance."

"Good."

This time when he kissed her, it wasn't light or soft. And there wasn't much restraint left in either of them. His lips kneaded against hers, hard and urgent, sizzling with magic. That magic dissolved into her, saturating her every pore with fire. She opened her mouth to gasp, and he slipped his tongue past her lips. His hand slid over her butt, tugging her closer. She wanted him so badly that she could hardly think straight.

"Do you want to get out of here?" he whispered into her ear.

"Yes." She gasped as his teeth nuzzled against her neck. "But don't we have a job to do first?"

"About that." He traced his finger down her side. "I might have misled you a tad."

"There's no job?"

"Not really," he admitted. "I asked you here so we could spend some time together."

"So this is a date?"

"It is if you want it to be," he said, watching for her reaction. At this very moment, he looked more vulnerable than she had ever seen him. More vulnerable than he'd looked when Finn had been draining his magic with the Priming Bangles.

"I think…" She cleared her throat. "I think I do want it to be."

Relief spread across his face, trailed by a smile. It wasn't his typical hard and feral smile; it was a genuinely happy one. He kissed her once more, then took her hand, leading her off the floor. They'd only made it a few steps when he stopped abruptly.

"Something wrong?" she asked.

He pulled his buzzing phone out of his pocket, frowning down at it. "Of all the times… Sorry, this will only take a moment." His eyes panned across the screen, his frown deepening. "It appears we have to work tonight after all."

"Oh?" she said, trying not to sound disappointed. Kai

didn't look like he was in the mood for fun anymore anyway.

"Here." He handed her his phone.

The message was only three words long, but those three words chilled her to her core. "Finn has escaped," she read.

CHAPTER NINE
Team Muscle and Magic

THEY HURRIED BACK to the hotel. Kai managed to summon a taxi, for which Sera's feet were eternally grateful. This was the last time in this lifetime that she wore four-inch heels.

As soon as they were inside Kai's suite, he grabbed his computer and sat down on the sofa. A cloud of agitated magic, invisible but potent, rolled out of him, burning the soft fragrant scent in the air. Inside the tall clear vases in the room, flower petals wrinkled and wilted before her eyes. Sera sneezed.

He looked up from his computer, staring across the room at her. "Come here."

She hesitated. "Only if you promise to put your magic away. You're burning the air." She pointed at the vase beside the sofa. "And those nice petals."

"I'm trying to put out half a dozen fires at the moment, Sera. I don't have time to worry about flower petals." He pulled in his magic anyway.

"It looks like you started a few fires of your own," Dal's voice said from the computer speakers.

Sera kicked off her shoes and hurried over to the sofa. As she sat down next to Kai, she waved at the three men staring out from the computer screen. Dal, Callum, and Tony, the guys she'd lovingly dubbed Kai's 'commandos', were as tough as nails and as cool as cats. They weren't just Kai's employees; they were his friends. They'd helped her and Kai take down Finn's revolution. They hadn't survived the ordeal without a scratch, however. Kai had commanded them to take some time off. And yet here they were.

"Hi, guys," she greeted Team Muscle and Magic. "Aren't you supposed to be sitting on a tropical beach somewhere, working on your tans?"

"Nah, we had to give up on that idea. Callum burns horribly in the sun," said Tony, grinning.

"That wasn't sunburn. It was a fire spell," Callum protested, also grinning.

"Sure thing, burning man."

"Sera," Dal said. "How are you doing? How's your training coming along? Is Kai going easy on you?"

"Kai Drachenburg doesn't go easy on anyone," she said, smiling.

The three commandos chuckled.

"I wouldn't be doing her any favors by going easy on her," Kai said.

"Funny. He's always saying the same thing to us," Tony told Sera.

"Right before he blasts us with a tornado," added Dal.

Callum nodded. "Or shifts into a dragon and spits fire at us."

Kai gave them all a cold glare, and the snickers died down. "Tell me what happened at Atlantis."

Tony's soldier mode clicked on. "The prison's security

footage shows a gang of hooded mages popping up in one of the unused storage rooms near Finn's cell, opening the cell with a keycard, then returning to the storage room with him. And then they all just vanished."

"A portal?" Sera asked.

"We think so," said Dal. "But there's no residual magic left."

"How long ago did Finn escape?"

"This morning," Tony told her.

"That's still recent enough, even if they hid the portal." Sera turned to Kai. "You need to get me into that prison. I can break the magic hiding the portal and figure out where they went. We can still catch them."

"You have other things to worry about," he said. "Like the Magic Games. They start tomorrow. You don't have time to go to Atlantis, and you certainly don't have time to hunt down Finn." He looked at the commandos. "Go. Check out the prison. Look for a hidden portal and report back your findings."

"This is foolish," she said as he closed his computer. "You need me there, finding that portal—not here, sitting on my hands."

"You won't be sitting on your hands. You will be fighting in the Magic Games. Once that's done, if you'd like to come work for me, we can discuss my terms."

"Your...terms?" she choked out the words. What was he playing at? "Like what?"

"You'll start by explaining how a first tier mage managed to hide her magic from the entire supernatural community for over twenty years."

She crossed her arms against her chest and frowned at him. "Not everyone."

"And then you'll tell me why," he said.

So he hadn't given up on trying to unearth her secret after all. Maybe that's why he was helping her; maybe he thought that by getting close to her, she'd spill the beans. Nope. Not happening.

"I have no interest in working for you," she said.

His eyes narrowed. "What are you hiding?"

"Why do you want to know?"

"I don't like secrets."

"Neither does your Magic Council," she said. "That's why I'm here. They want to crack my mind open like an egg. The question is why you're helping me. Why not just let them break me? Then you'd know everything you ever wanted to know about me."

He leaned forward as his lips slid back to show his teeth. He looked positively primal. "I don't want to crack your mind, Sera."

"Then put away the dragon fangs. You can't just go around intimidating people into doing what you want. It's not nice."

"But it is efficient." His face went neutral. "I wasn't trying to intimidate you. I was annoyed that you still don't trust me. I meant what I said. I don't want to crack your mind. I want you to just tell me. I know you're not a threat to the Magic Council—well, except maybe that smart mouth of yours—and I don't want them hurting you to figure out what you're hiding. Whatever it is, they don't need to know. But I do."

"Why?"

"People who work for me don't get to keep secrets from me. Not big ones like this."

"Well, then it's a good thing we've already established that I won't be working for you," she shot back.

Kai frowned at her. Seriously, though, what did he

expect her to say to a dumb comment like that? He opened his mouth, as though he wanted to say something, but he just shook his head instead.

"Can we just get back to the crisis at hand?" she said.

He leaned back and closed his eyes. "I'm not sending you to Atlantis. Callum, Tony, and Dal can handle the hunt for Finn."

"They can't sense magic like I can. No one can."

His eyes opened. "Except your sister."

Sera said nothing, afraid to clue him in on the fact that she and Alex were Dragon Born. He was already dangerously close to the truth.

"Alex is your twin," he said. "So she must have powerful magic too. The only reason she's not being called to test in the Games is because Gaelyn is protecting her. He still holds sway over the Magic Council."

"Is he really as old as people say?" Sera said, deflecting.

The hard look Kai gave her told her he wasn't fooled. Not for a second.

"Send me to Atlantis. I'll just take a quick peek at the portal, then come right back." She wiggled her pinkie at him. "I promise."

He ignored her wiggling pinkie. "There's no time for that, and you know it. The Magic Games start in sixteen hours, and we need every second we have to prepare you. Let's start with getting you some sleep. Tired mages make for sloppy fighters."

Sera sighed, suddenly feeling completely exhausted. Exhausted and not the least bit ready for the Games. Maybe she should have let people fight their own supernatural battles for a change today. She just couldn't seem to keep her nose out of other peoples' messes.

"Get some sleep, Sera," he said. "I'll come by at seven tomorrow so we can train."

"Oh, letting me sleep in?" She tried to smile, but her face was too tired. So she just stood and headed for the door.

"Sera."

She stopped in front of the door, looking back at him.

"You are getting better," he said. That was high praise from Kai Drachenburg.

"Maybe. But will it be good enough?"

She opened the door and headed down the hall to the elevator. By the time she stepped into the suite she shared with Riley and Naomi, she felt like a zombie—except maybe a bit more dead. She dropped her purse onto her bed and changed out of her silly club clothes before hitting the bathroom.

When she returned to the bedroom, her phone was buzzing on her bed. She picked it up—and nearly dropped it again. There on her screen was a picture of her and Kai dancing at Trove, taken just a few hours ago. Below the picture were the words, "Look forward to seeing you again soon, Sera. Love, Finn."

CHAPTER TEN
Wake the Dead

SERA DIDN'T SLEEP well that night. Visions of Alcatraz plagued her dreams. Finn stalked the shadows. Globs of semi-solid magic oozed off of him like molten lava, sizzling the ground with tears of malice. As his faceless minions pushed Kai to his knees, Finn stepped into the firelight. With a wicked smirk, he slapped the Priming Bangles over Kai's wrists. The magic chomped at Kai's flesh, and he roared out in pain.

Sera jolted awake, his tormented scream still ringing in her ears. She fumbled for her phone and brought up Finn's message from last night. He was just trying to get into her head, to unnerve her.

He'd succeeded.

She set her phone back on her nightstand, then buried her head under her pillow, drowning out the thump on her door. Was it seven o'clock already? That meant she'd slept for nearly nine hours. It felt more like two. She wasn't getting up. Kai would just have to find another victim this morning.

The knock thumped on her door again, louder this

time. Sera clutched her pillow to her ears. The door shook with the force of explosives—or maybe that was just a really big dragon claw. Kai was so going to pay for this. She was going to pop the wheels off his tank—wait, no, she was going to paint the tank pink. With bright yellow flowers. And hearts. That would teach him.

"Rise and shine, sleeping beauty!"

That wasn't Kai. It was Riley. And he didn't have anything Sera could paint pink. Grumbling, she tossed one of the spare pillows at the door. Hopefully, he'd get the message.

"That's nice," he said. "But I suggest you save your energy for the fight. You'll need it when Kai's throwing you across the fighting pit."

Someone snickered. It sounded like Kai. Sera threw a second pillow at the door, just for him.

"You wanted to have a look at the fighting pit before the Games," Kai said. "Well, here's your chance. We leave in half an hour—whether or not you've had breakfast."

His words echoed in her empty stomach. She groaned a final protest, then dragged her body out of bed. She put on the first sports outfit she could find, not even caring if it was torn or dirty. After a few minutes in the pit with Kai, it would be ruined anyway. She was running out of things to wear, and her attempt at shopping hadn't ended well.

Sera met up with Naomi on her way to the tiny kitchen corner in their suite. Her friend was still wearing pajamas, but she looked more awake than Sera felt.

"Did they pound on your door too?"

"No, but the pounding on your door was loud enough to wake the dead." Naomi wrapped her arm around Sera's shoulder. "How do you feel?"

"Like one of the dead."

"I'll bet." Her mouth kicked up into a smirk. "You look like one too."

"Thanks."

"A good breakfast will perk you right up. Your boyfriend brought over some granola for you."

"He's not my boyfriend."

"Uh-huh, sure."

Sera looked toward the suite's kitchen corner—or rather, away from the knowing sparkle in Naomi's eyes. "What kind of granola?"

"Strawberry vanilla."

"That's my favorite," Sera said.

"And Kai Drachenburg knows it."

Naomi didn't say anything more. They'd reached the kitchen corner. Riley and Kai were already eating breakfast. Her brother's was a bowl of cereal, and the dragon's was a roll stacked full of salami.

"I shouldn't be surprised that a dragon eats meat for breakfast," Sera commented, sitting down beside Riley.

Naomi took the free chair beside her, which put her dangerously close to Kai. Rather than cower before him like basically every other supernatural, she gave him an impish wink.

Kai's gaze remained locked on Sera, like he had her caught in the cross hairs of his rifle. "Perhaps you'd prefer if I'd flown out to the mountains to catch myself a fat sheep or goat to eat?"

Sera blinked. "I hope you're not serious."

"Of course not," he said, taking a sip of his coffee. "Sheep and goats are far too small. I prefer cows."

"You're messing with me because you know my brain's all wacky from not sleeping well last night," she said.

Kai handed her a bag of upscale granola. The bag was pale blue with a gold bow and a label that told her it had come from the expensive organic magic shop inside Magic & 8th Avenue.

"Bad dreams?" he asked as she poured granola into her bowl.

"I had a dream about you," she said.

Riley's spoon clinked against his bowl, Naomi's bagel paused in front of her mouth, and even Kai stopped eating. All three of them were staring at her.

"About you and Finn," Sera amended. "At Alcatraz. He was using the Priming Bangles on you." She cringed. There was no need to mention the flesh-chomping magic or Kai's screams. She was trying hard to forget it herself.

Kai set his coffee cup down. "Sera, the Priming Bangles are where no one will ever find them."

"I know."

"And now that I know Finn's true nature, he won't be able to gain the upper hand again."

"I wouldn't be so sure about that."

She pulled out her phone, swiping to Finn's message before handing it over to Kai. As he read, his magic lashed out, electrifying the air. Ice crystals crackled across the screen.

"When did you get this?" he asked, low and deep. Pure fury burned in his eyes.

Sera grabbed her phone and brushed off the frosty crust with the sleeve of her sweatshirt. "Last night. Right after I got back here."

"You should have called me over the minute you got his message."

"And then what?" she said. "Have you watch over me all night long?"

"If need be."

"I can take care of myself. I'm not afraid of Finn."

"Your nightmares suggest otherwise," Kai said cooly. "The Magic Games start this afternoon. You need to be rested. Your mind needs to be rested." His phone buzzed. He looked at the number. "I need to take this call. Eat quickly, so we can start our training session on time."

As he walked off, Sera stared into her bowl. She felt the urge to not eat, just to show him he couldn't tell her what to do. But no one won in that scenario. Besides, the delectable scents of vanilla and strawberries were a temptation she couldn't refuse.

"Stupid controlling dragon," she grumbled between bites of granola. It tasted even better than it smelled. The sweet flavors exploded on her tongue. The subtle, tingling aftertaste of fairy magic lingered on her tastebuds. It was the best granola she'd ever had.

"Kai's just doing this because he's worried about you," Riley said. "He cares about you. And you care about him."

Sera looked up from her granola.

"Oh, yes," Naomi agreed. "You can see it in the way she looks at him."

"And how is that?" Sera demanded.

"Like you want everyone to leave the room so you can jump his bones."

Sera rested her chin on her hands and smiled. "Don't you have to get ready for work?"

"Yes. Sadly." Naomi took a final bite of bagel, then rose from her chair. "You can borrow some of my clothes if you want. I have a great pair of pants that would show off your butt." Then she winked and disappeared into the bathroom.

"She's a one-way ticket to trouble," Sera commented.

"Maybe." Riley grinned. "But she's right. I know about what happened in that tower on Alcatraz. You can pretend you don't have feelings for Kai, but we both know that's not true."

"So you've decided to play matchmaker?"

"No, but I think you owe it to Kai—to yourself—to give him a chance," Riley said. "Just look at all he's done to help you. And to keep your secret, even though he doesn't know what it is. He's putting himself into a difficult position by helping you."

"How do you know?"

"Because he and I are friends, and we talk."

"Complaining about me, is he?"

"No. He's mentioned that he's worried about you. He knows you're scared of your magic, and he wants to help you. He is helping you. And it's costing him."

"How?" Sera asked.

"I'm not sure exactly. Kai doesn't talk about that part, but I'm not stupid. I can read between the lines. And I've overheard stuff. He's put himself between you and the Magic Council, and they're not happy about it. The Council has a feeling you're special, and they always get suspicious when someone pretends to be human who's not. Most people exaggerate their magic, not hide it."

"I suppose that's true," she said, stealing a glance at the bathroom door. Naomi had turned on the shower in the bathroom, but Sera lowered her voice and leaned in closer anyway. "Riley, the thing is, well, I know you and Naomi and Alex mean well. But I can't really afford to care about Kai." Or kiss him again. "He's dangerous. He sits on the Magic Council, and that means he upholds their laws. My very existence is against those laws."

"I told you he's been protecting you from the Magic Council."

"Because he doesn't know what I am." She dropped her voice to a whisper. "An abomination."

"Sera, you're not—"

"Every supernatural in the world has grown up believing that I am, Kai included. The moment he found out, he would turn me in."

"Kai wouldn't," Riley said.

"I wouldn't do what?"

The shadow of Kai's magic loomed over her—or maybe that was just the shadow of her impending doom. She turned to look at him.

"You wouldn't turn into a dragon in the fighting pit. There's no space," Riley spoke before Sera could. It was a good thing too because she had no idea what to say. She'd probably just have made some sarcastic comment.

"That's not entirely true," Kai said. "The Magic Games fighting pit is very large. There's plenty of room for a dragon."

"Does that mean you will be bringing out the dragon today?" Sera asked him, suppressing a cringe. Fighting elemental mage Kai was bad enough. She was far too tired to fight dragon shifter Kai at this hour.

He looked at her empty bowl. "Are you ready to go?"

"Yes," she sighed, not missing the fact that he hadn't actually answered her question. "I just need to grab my bag."

CHAPTER ELEVEN
The Fighting Pit

THE WORDS 'MADISON Square Garden' loomed over Sera in big, raised letters. Groups of scurrying mages crisscrossed the cavernous lobby, their boots echoing off a pale marble sheet that resembled an ice rink more than a floor. They strung lights and magic from the pillars and railings. They didn't stop as she and Kai passed by, though a few of them did slow down just long enough to scowl at her. Maybe they didn't approve of her clothes. Sera looked down at her pants. So maybe they weren't pristine, but they weren't really *that* dirty. Especially considering that this morning's training session with Kai had been a fifty-stringed combo of some pretty spectacular kickings of her ass. She'd hit the mud more times than a three-legged centaur.

Shuddering at the memory, she folded her giant pizza slice in half and took a bite. It washed all that pain right away.

"I don't think they like that you brought food in here," Kai said.

"They have basketball games here. And hockey games.

And concerts. If they can put up with sweaty guys, hot dogs, and half-empty beer cans, they can deal with my pizza too."

"Perhaps we should have eaten at a proper restaurant instead of ordering from an establishment with one counter and no chairs. Then we wouldn't have needed to eat on the street."

She smiled at him. "The lack of chairs didn't stop you from snarfing down six slices."

"Snarf?" A crinkle formed between his eyes.

"Yes, snarf. You ate them faster than they could make more," she said.

"Magic requires energy. In other words, food."

"Kai, you might as well just admit that you liked the lunch I picked out."

"You're dripping oil," Kai told her.

Sera looked down, catching the golden drop before it hit the floor. She licked her finger clean. "And you're evading."

He stopped and stared down at her. "I don't evade problems, sweetheart. I confront them head on."

"With dragon scales and hellfire?"

"Yes."

Sera snorted and nudged him toward the escalator. Beside them stood a pair of mage security guards who could very well have been professional wrestlers. They acknowledged Kai with a curt nod, then carried on looking big and bad.

"How many of those security guys are there?" Sera asked as she and Kai stepped onto the escalator.

"A lot. The Magic Games attract far too many supernaturals who come solely to get drunk on magic and booze and then start fights with the other spectators. The security guards need to be capable of kicking out any troublemakers."

"I'm more concerned about being kept *in*."

Kai remained silent, as though he didn't know what to say to that. He didn't look surprised, though. Of course he didn't. No sane person wanted to participate in the Magic Games.

Sera stole a final peek at the guards before they were out of sight. "Those two certainly look…capable," she said with a smirk.

Kai looked at her, his face expressionless. Oh, goody. Kai the granite block was back. And he clearly didn't appreciate her trying to lighten the gloom and doom mood.

"Are you ogling at them?" he asked, his tone checked.

"Maybe just a little." She grinned at him. "Jealous?"

"No." He turned to step off the escalator. "You don't even know their names."

They passed the rest of their walk in silence, which was just as well. Every time she opened her mouth, she ended up flirting with Kai. Which she'd already decided was a bad idea. For multiple reasons.

"Here we are," Kai said.

Sera looked down over the rows of seats. At the very bottom, in the middle of the arena, was the fighting pit. Above the fighting pit, a high ceiling loomed, speckled with speakers and lights—and, at the very center of it all, an enormous 360-degree rounded display panel. The screens were blank right now, but they'd be on during the Magic Games. And there would be closeups. Sera frowned at the display panel to let it know exactly how she felt about it.

"Something wrong?" Kai asked her.

"Just thinking about the fact that several hundred supernaturals will be treated to a closeup of the Magic Council's attempt to crack open my mind."

"They won't crack you."

"They cracked you," she said.

"Yes, but I wasn't as stubborn as you are. Just remember everything I showed you, and you'll get through it."

"Do you really think so?"

"That you're stubborn? Yes."

"Funny, dragon. Absolutely hilarious."

"Sera," he said, his tone serious.

Ok, he was basically always serious, but this time he was more serious than usual. And there was something else. A hint of apprehension speckled his magic, like he was about to bring up something he'd rather not talk about. Or that Sera would rather not talk about.

"Yes?" she asked.

"You're worried about Finn."

"I'm worried about what he might be plotting. Have the commandos been able to track him?"

"Not yet. I wanted to call them again for an update," he said. "By the way, they know you call them that."

"Commandos?"

"Yes."

She shrugged. "Well, that's what they are. They can't argue with that."

"They're not arguing. In fact, they like it. They think it makes them sound tough."

"They've survived having you for a boss." She grinned in his face. "Of course they're tough."

"Yes," he agreed, his face unreadable.

"I wonder what Finn is up to," she said.

"We upset his plans. I wouldn't be surprised if he was looking for revenge."

"That's what I'm afraid of."

"You're worried about your family and friends," said Kai.

"Yes."

"Instead of being worried about yourself, of course," he added.

"If Finn wanted to come at me directly, he wouldn't be sending me love messages," she said. "Besides, I have a long history of killing monsters and madmen, and I don't have enough sense to be afraid of anyone."

He grunted in assent. "I've set guards on Riley and Naomi."

"Naomi agreed to that?"

Sera's friend was a tough mercenary. Maybe she wasn't as mean as Sera, but she fought her own battles.

"I selected guards she would approve of," he said.

"Oh." She snickered. "You set Naomi up with some mage eye candy."

"One of them is a fairy."

"Even better." She turned away from the fighting pit to look at him. "You've figured her out then."

"She's not as complicated as you."

"Complex, you mean."

"Do I?"

"Yes," she told him. "Complicated sounds bad. Like I'm a really hard problem you hate to have and loathe even more to face. Complex makes me sound intriguing and mysterious."

The shadow of a sigh escaped his lips. "You're making things overly complicated, Sera."

"And complex?"

"That too."

"Speaking of bodyguards, what did the Magic Council say when you told them a hate group was gunning for them?" she asked. "Are they going to arrange extra protection for themselves?"

"That depends on their own egos," he said, and this time, he sighed for real. "I looked into getting some protection for your sister too."

"Alex can take care of herself. She's even tougher and meaner than I am."

"Even so, she cannot be on guard twenty-four hours a day."

Sera didn't mention that she and Alex had essentially been on guard their entire lives.

"It turns out, though, that she doesn't need protection, not if she's hanging out with the notorious assassin and thief Slayer," he said.

"Oh? Is that his name?"

"Yes."

"Oh, you've met him? What's he like?"

"Competent." Kai packed enough disdain into that one word to crack ice.

She chuckled. "He stole from you, didn't he?"

He glared at her. "With the assassin looking out for her, your sister is very safe. Slayer doesn't fail."

Sera fought the grin spreading up her cheeks. "He failed pretty spectacularly at getting into her underwear drawer."

"I see." He paused. "So I take it your sister isn't sleeping with the assassin then?"

"Not sure. Alex sounds...lovestruck, I guess you could call it. This is the first time anything like this has happened," she said. "Alex has always been so tough.

So…"

The look Kai gave her made her blush, and the words fizzled out in her throat. Kai chuckled.

"Maybe your sister has finally met her match."

"Maybe," she said, returning her eyes to the pit below. "Have your people had a chance to check out that piece of magic-proof armor I gave you?"

"Yes. And its construction is identical to the ones in my lab." Magic pulsed behind each word, deep and hollow. "Security checked again, and none of the prototype armor suits are missing."

"A thief might have broken in and made a copy of the armor specifications."

Kai's magic continued to throb in agitated bursts, his fury hot enough to liquefy metal. "What are you suggesting?"

"Finn got into your storage facility once before. And now he's free again. Maybe he's responsible this time too."

"No." The single syllable pounded like a hammer. "I've since put Finn on the black list."

"The black list?"

"The security system takes extra measures when dealing with the people on that list. No, Sera," he cut in before she could speak. "Based on our past conversations, I am very certain that you don't want to know more about that."

Sera got a flash of that werewolf Kai had stepped on. With audio. She gave what remained of her pizza slice a woeful glance, then dropped it into the nearest trash bin. There was nothing like the memory of crunching bones to spoil her appetite.

"Suffice it to say, I would know if Finn had tried to break into my facility," Kai said. "Plus, the vampires are being controlled by the Blood Orb, which is in the hands of a group that despises all supernaturals. That's the complete antithesis of Finn's cause: the rise of the supernaturals over humanity. The two groups are mortal enemies. They wouldn't work together."

"Both groups would like to see the Magic Council overthrown," Sera pointed out. "The enemy of my enemy is my friend and all that jazz?"

"The enemy of my enemy is *not* my friend," Kai said. "He's rather just another psychopath on an already too-long list of psychopaths to kill."

"You mean, on an already too-long list of psychopaths to capture and imprison so they can face justice for their crimes."

"Yeah," he said, his tone as dry as twice-burnt toast. "Of course." He pulled out his phone. "Now, back to why we're here. I've had a look at your opponents for today."

She glanced at the timetable on his screen. "I'll be fighting Monster Mixer, Blood Brothers, and…Mages of the Universe? Wow. Someone sure thinks highly of themselves."

"Your first match is against the Monster Mixer. They'll throw a series of three different types of monsters at you. You don't know what you're going to get until you're in the pit, but the monsters they use tend to be things like giant frogs, harpies, dark ponies…"

Sera hoped she managed to avoid the dark ponies. Their coats were as bright as sunshine and their souls as black as night.

"…insect swarms, giant sand worms. The purpose of the Monster Mixer is to weed out mages with very weak magic. If you fail, you get dropped down to the lower testing tiers."

"And if I pass?" she asked.

"Then you move on to the Blood Brothers."

"Vampires?"

"Yes, three of them, it says here." He scrolled down the list. "Then the Mages of the Universe. That's another wildcard. You don't know which mage you'll get of the eight listed here. There are two from each of the main combative mage categories: two elementals, two telekinetics, two summoners, and two shifters. At the end of the day, after all the matches are over, they'll evaluate the magic you used today and select your opponents for tomorrow's matches."

"What happens if I don't use any magic?"

"Why would you not use magic?"

"If I don't use magic, then they think my magic is weak and that they don't need to push so hard to crack me."

Kai shook his head. "That trick won't work, Sera."

"We'll see. Surely, they can't make me use magic?"

"No, but you'll annoy Duncan Blackbrooke if you don't."

"The bossy mage I saved at Macy's?"

"Yes, he's the Game Architect for the Magic Games," Kai told her.

Oh, goody. "Why am I not surprised?"

"Forget Blackbrooke. Worry about today's matches. They shouldn't be too hard for you. Concentrate on taking out your opponents and go easy on the battle banter."

"I can do that."

He gave her a hard look.

"What? I can be serious. See?"

He took one look a her 'serious face', then slowly

shook his head. "Let's just get down there and check out the fighting pit. We don't have much time until they encourage us to leave."

She followed him as he jogged down the steps. "Encourage us to leave? Or do you mean kick us out?"

He kept running, not even bothering to answer. Well, that said everything right there, didn't it? Sera scanned the arena. There wasn't a single person anywhere in sight, which was odd considering the hustle and bustle in the lobby. The Magic Games started in an hour, and the arena was abandoned.

"You didn't get permission for us to check out the fighting pit, did you?" she asked him. "You paid those two guards to look the other way. And to keep everyone else out."

"You say that like it's a bad thing."

"The Magic Council would say it's cheating."

Kai didn't appear moved by her words. "What are they going to do, kick you out of the Games?"

He had a point.

"Besides," he added. "When it was their turn in the Games, you'd better believe that every one of them cheated."

"You too?"

"We all did."

She snorted. "Good. I was starting to wonder if the only rule you'd consider breaking was one related to parking."

"Some rules are unjustified."

"Such as the one against parking on sidewalks?" Sera teased, but she couldn't help but wonder if he'd consider the death sentence for the Dragon Born one of those unjustified rules.

There was something encouraging in the smile he gave her as they reached the bottom—something that made her wonder if maybe Alex and Riley might be right. As they stepped into the pit, lights blared to life overhead and a magic barrier blazed up all around them. They walked across the pit, their feet kicking up a cloud of dust. Born of sand and magic, the dusty mist rolled across the ground, hovering just over the surface. When it reached the end of the pit, it dissolved against a fiery magic barrier.

"That's meant to do more than just keep the stands free of sand," Sera commented, watching the veil of fire shift into a web of lightning, then to ice.

The magic shifted every few seconds, so fast that her mind had barely identified the element when it switched again. This game of magical musical chairs was giving her a splitting headache.

"Huh," said Kai, sniffing the air. "That's something new."

"It smells like a car exploded down here. And then someone took a flamethrower to the debris," she added, plugging her nose.

"The barrier is there to keep magic inside the fighting pit," a voice called down from above. "And also any supernaturals fighting there."

Sera looked up the rows of seats. Cutler stood at the top level, smirking down at them. No, at Kai.

"Get yourself caught in a trap, Drachenburg?" he taunted.

Kai glared at him, his magic slamming into the barrier. The flames pulsed, gobbling up his magic like it was candy.

Cutler chuckled. "You're not nearly as scary trapped

inside that cage."

"I'm not trapped."

Kai hit the barrier again with his magic. And again. And again. It groaned under the strain. Fissures crinkled across the frosty face, splitting off chunks of ice. One of those chunks fell into the pit, dissolving into a puff of mist the moment it hit the sand.

Cutler's grin faded. "There's no need to get testy. I'm only trying to help Sera."

"Since when is angering the dragon I'm stuck inside a pit with helping, Cutler?" she demanded, waving her hand toward Kai.

With the barrier's ice magic shattered, he'd moved on to lightning. The entire arena echoed with the clash of magic. It wouldn't be long before Kai broke through the barrier entirely. At which point he'd turn his magic on Cutler.

Dense as he was, Cutler seemed to have realized that too. He began walking down the stairs, his hands lifted in the air. "I *am* trying to help. Don't touch the barrier, Sera. It packs enough charge to knock a mage unconscious." His gaze shifted to Kai. "Even a dragon."

"Oh, really?" Sera said. "Thanks for warning me. Because I was going to step up to the freakishly glowing barrier and lick it."

If her sarcasm inched him in the direction of common sense, he didn't show it. Seriously, pissing off a mage who shifted into a dragon who could—and would —step on him? What was he thinking?

"The barrier isn't the only magic lurking in the pit." Cutler pointed at the cylinders hammered into the ground in clusters. They looked like big metal salt and pepper shakers.

"What are they?" she asked.

"Nothing good," he said. "Various mists come out of the tops. Sedatives, poisons, elemental mayhem. Basically, bad news."

"Ok, I'll watch out for them."

"That's it? You're not going to thank me?" He looked disappointed.

"That depends," she said. "Are you going to try to proposition me now?"

"No."

"Thank you."

"Funny, Sera." A satin smile slid across Cutler's lips. "That's what I like about you."

The lighting sliding across the barrier fizzled out. Another element down. Fire flared up in its place.

"Cutler?" she called up.

"Yes?"

"Kai is almost done eating through that barrier. You should get going."

"But—"

The flames let out a single, ear-piercing crack, then dissolved into steam. Kai's blue eyes, lit up like an electric storm, glared out through the steamy mist at Cutler.

"Ok, fine," Cutler said and hurried back up the way he'd come.

Sera caught Kai's arm as he made to follow. He turned his glare on her.

"Let him go," she said calmly.

Fire-charred steam snorted out of his nose.

"You wanted to call the commandos," Sera reminded him, wiping the soot from her cheek.

Still fuming, Kai took out his phone. His finger had hardly tapped the screen, however, when Sera's phone buzzed in her pocket. She checked the message—and froze.

"What is it?" Kai asked.

"Finn," she said and turned her phone to show him the message: a picture of her and Kai standing inside the fighting pit, the word 'soon' typed out beneath it.

Kai's magic pulsed out. A blast of wind shot out from the fighting pit, rippling up the rows. The seats clapped in protest. High above, the enormous television screen rocked.

Even before the wind had dissipated, Kai was talking into his phone. "Report."

A soft rustle of words hummed out of the phone, but it was too quiet for Sera to hear.

"Put it on speakerphone," she whispered to Kai.

She was surprised when he did as she'd asked.

"...was pretty well-hidden. No sign of the teleportation glyphs," Tony's voice buzzed out of the phone's tiny speaker.

"Told you," she muttered to Kai.

"The team of Magic Sniffers you told us to bring along had better luck," said Tony. "They uncovered the glyphs. Unfortunately, there wasn't enough magic left in them to take us anywhere. It seems Finn's crew cast a magic consumption spell as they fled."

"I thought we'd decided to call them minions," Dal's voice piped up.

"No, *you* decided that."

"Callum thought it was a good idea too."

Kai cleared his throat.

"Sorry," Dal said and fell silent again.

"The magic consumption spell Finn's crew cast ate away at the residual magic," Tony said. "It sped up the magical decay by over ten times. All that remained of the glyphs was little more than a skeleton."

Kai looked at Sera. She sighed. Even if she had been there, she wouldn't have been able to do anything. Finn's minions—yes, she liked the name too—were sneaky. They'd learned a thing or two about covering their tracks since last time.

"Keep looking," Kai told the commandos. "They must have left behind some trace. Question the prison guards. Atlantis is protected by magical barriers that are supposed to keep prisoners in and rescue teams out. Finn's followers couldn't have popped in and out of there without some inside help. Find out who helped them. Do whatever you must to find Finn." Then he hung up.

"You think one of the prison guards helped Finn escape?" she asked.

"Perhaps. Tony, Dal, and Callum will find out."

"I wish I were there, helping them."

"They can handle it. They do this sort of thing all the time. And you have your plate full with the Magic Games."

"I know. That's why I wish I were somewhere else."

"Your magic is erratic," he said, his brows drawing together. "You need to calm down. There's no need to be nervous."

A pained laugh burst from her mouth. "Isn't there? The Magic Council wants to crack open my mind and serve it up to an arena of overly zealous supernaturals." She pointed up at the television screens. "With closeups."

"Sera, listen to me." He turned to face her, setting his hands on her arms. "You will be fine. We're just going to take this one match at a time. Today is only the preliminaries. You are the best monster hunter on this side of the Atlantic. That's all you have to do today: fight. The mind games don't start until later."

"When?"

"Don't worry about it. Just focus on knocking down your opponents."

"Knocking down opponents, you say?" she replied. "I can do that."

"I know you can."

Magic erupted from the levels above, blasting open the doors to the hallway. Security guards flooded inside, pouring down the aisles in a stampede of thumping boots. Every single one of them looked like he'd been built to smash rocks. With his bare hands.

"You're good at talking your way out of trouble, right?" she asked Kai as the guards flooded the fighting pit.

"Of course."

"Excellent. Because I'm only good at *fighting* my way out of trouble."

He grunted in assent, then turned to the guard in front. "I am Kai Drachenburg."

A few of the guards exchanged wary glances and shifted their weight. Apparently, Kai's reputation preceded him.

"I know who you are," the head guard shot back, unimpressed. "And you don't belong in the pit. Come with us." He looked as though someone had just spat in his coffee. A security guard who took his job seriously. Go figure.

"Your response time is abysmal," Kai said as Mr. Serious waved the other guards forward.

"What?"

"We were here for ten minutes before you finally

arrived," Kai told him. "You're supposed to be guarding the arena."

"Yeah, not standing around the water cooler eating donuts and dishing gossip," Sera added.

Kai spared her a brief I-thought-we-agreed-you-wouldn't-be-talking look before returning his attention to the guards. "The Magic Council prides itself on always hiring the best and the brightest. I'm sure my colleagues on the Council would be interested to hear my report on your…unfortunate response time."

Mr. Serious exhaled, some of the wind going out of his sails. "So this was a test?"

"That depends entirely on you," said Kai.

Mr. Serious glanced back at the other guards, then at Kai. He stepped aside. "You can go. The Magic Games will be kicking off shortly." Shifting his gaze to Sera, he pointed at a doorway at the corner of the pit. "Participants need to get to their designated rooms in the backstage area. Spectators and coaches must find their seats in the stands."

"Go," Kai told Sera, then walked around the guards to sit in one of the front row seats. He pulled out his phone. "I'll be right here."

She nodded and headed for the door. Mr. Serious and two of the guards followed her. The others walked up the stairs, spreading to cover every section of the arena.

"You're Serafina Dering," Mr. Serious said. It wasn't a question. "The guys and I have a pool going about how far you'll make it before you crack."

Sera wasn't sure if she should be flattered or worried that he knew who she was. She settled for sarcastic. "How nice." She smiled at him. "You've already lost."

"You don't even know what my bet was."

"It doesn't matter. You bet that I'd break." Panic was throwing a party in her stomach, but she kept her face neutral—and her magic buried deep. "I won't."

"Everyone breaks," he insisted.

"I'm not everyone."

His frown cracked into a sick grin. "We'll see soon enough."

"Is something funny?" she asked, stuffing her bag into the locker with her name taped on it.

"You're up first, peaches," he said and gave her one of those testosterone-charged man slaps on her back. "I bet the guys $100 that you'd make it through the day. Be sure to put on a good show."

CHAPTER TWELVE
Monster Mixer

A ROAR OF applause burst through the open doorway that led to the fighting pit—until it was swallowed whole by a thunderous roar. The beast's war cry boomed out, a shockwave of sound and magic. The ground beneath Sera's feet rumbled and shook.

Light poured through the door, bathing the dark and dusty hallway in streams of red and blue. Ahead, somewhere inside the fighting pit, the beast was scraping its hard feet against the sandy ground. Hooves. It sounded like hooves. That narrowed down the list of possible monsters. Maybe it was a manticore. Or—Sera cringed—a dark pony. She couldn't yet see the beast, but whatever it was, it didn't sound friendly.

She walked toward the light. As she passed through the doorway, the magic barrier buzzed and snapped shut behind her. Inside the fighting pit, a large body was pacing around, its dark silhouette a blurred smudge against the bright background. Sera blinked down hard, and her opponent came into focus.

Her heart stuttered, then took an immediate nosedive

into her stomach. An elemental bull. She had to fight an elemental bull.

Born of magic and rage, an elemental bull looked like a freakishly large bull—with one big difference. Magic, not hair, coated its body. A mixture of elemental magic, these glowing tendrils flared, sizzled, and swayed across the bull's thick back. The beast's dominant element shifted every few seconds, just like the magic barrier surrounding the pit. Green to red to blue to gold, the bull and the barrier were blinking like the lights on a Christmas tree.

Past the magic barrier, the stadium was packed full of spectators. Mages, fairies, and vampires sat in the audience, sporting binoculars and plastic glowing sticks. A few of them were snacking on hotdogs and pizza slices. Even more of them were drinking beer or magical cocktails served by the telekinetics walking up and down the aisles with mini concession stands hovering in front of them.

"Hey, pretty girl!" one of the mages in the audience called down to Sera, waving his beer can in the air.

Beside him, four other guys were singing silly songs and swaying in their seats. And they weren't the only ones. It was barely the afternoon, and at least a third of the audience was already wasted. Kai was right. People came to the Magic Games to do more than just watch the fights.

"Girly!" the drunk mage shouted at her again. "Wanna go out with me?"

He was waving so wildly that the beer can shot out of his hand and smacked against the magic barrier. It dissolved instantly upon impact, but the low moan of dying metal lingered in the air for a few seconds longer.

The bull's horned head whipped around. Its gold eyes found her immediately. It grunted at her, and lightning sparks spilled out of its nostrils. The bull's magic was potent. Musk and magic hung heavy in the air, held inside the fighting pit by the magic barrier. Sera coughed, and the bull gave her an indignant, electrically-charged snort.

"What?" she demanded. "You have to admit that you really do stink."

Sera wasn't sure if the monster even understood her. It was thumping one of its hooves against the ground, kicking up a hell of a sandstorm, but that was just normal bull behavior. You know, before they…charged.

She jumped out of the way of the charging bull, running behind a cluster of those metal mushroom cylinders. Cutler had warned her to stay away from them, but this was the same mage who'd gotten himself stuck on top of the Golden Gate Bridge. Twice. He'd been waiting to hitch a ride with a flock of migrating winged horses that had never come. And no matter how many times he insisted the horses took that path south, they never came. Maybe they didn't even exist. Cutler wasn't exactly the universe's most reliable source of information. Or common sense, for that matter.

So far, the metal mushrooms he'd warned her about hadn't done anything more menacing than look like metal mushrooms, so she was going to take her chances with them. They couldn't be worse than the elemental bull who wanted to skewer her on his horns and fling her bloody remains against the magic barrier.

The mushrooms were sticking too far out of the ground for the bull to run over them. She hoped. The beast hadn't yet slowed its gallop. The ground quaked under its hooves—and its magic. Earth magic, so ancient it rumbled in her soul, was pulsing out of the creature, seeping into the ground. The whole stadium was shaking now.

Just as Sera was starting to worry that the bull's magic would take down the entire building—pouring the broken steel and concrete remains into the train station below—the creature's magic shifted to fire. Ablaze with red and orange flames, it veered away from the metal mushrooms and ran back to the other side of the pit, buying her a few precious seconds to figure out what the hell she was going to do to get herself out of this mess.

Magic. The Game Architect was trying to force her to use magic. That's why he'd sicked an elemental bull on her rather than, say, the Easter Bunny. Or Santa Claus. She'd heard both of them were total pushovers. Though rumor had it that the Tooth Fairy was a biter.

Sera could probably take down the elemental bull with magic. After all, she'd fought Kai in dragon form. But the problem with magic was it's a two-way street. Every time she used magic, it opened a temporary hole in the shield she'd put around her mind. Most supernaturals weren't able to take advantage of this, but a mage didn't get to be the Game Architect by being most supernaturals. Mr. Sadistic Blackbrooke had spent decades cracking open mages' minds. He was experienced, efficient, and just plain evil. Even a split-second hole in her mental shield would be enough for him to wiggle himself into her head.

On the other side of the pit, the bull reared, thumping its icy hooves against the half-height wood wall that surrounded the fighting area. One of the advertising banners hanging from the wall froze solid. The bull thumped it again, and the banner shattered into a million tiny icicles. Then the creature pivoted toward Sera, crunching the ice into the ground. A cloud of wintery air puffed out of its nose.

The metal mushrooms picked that moment to squirt golden liquid at Sera's feet.

She hopped away, avoiding the lion's share of the attack. A few yellow drops splattered her leather boots, but she escaped otherwise unscathed. Of course, her retreat put her back out in the open, well within charging distance. But it was either that or death by mushroom. Golden liquid was pouring out of the metal cylinders, drenching the sand with something that smelled an awful lot like gasoline. She hoped it wasn't magic-infused gasoline. And that the bull didn't run through it while it was on fire.

The bull glared at Sera, blue fire burning in its eyes. It stomped its hooves against the sand, preparing to make another pass. The icy spikes on its back shattered, and tendrils of purple-gold lightning slithered across its body.

Lightning. Earth would be next. The bull's magic was powerful, but its elemental pattern was pretty simple. After earth would be fire. She eyed the growing puddle of gasoline. Fire. She could work with that.

As the bull kicked off into a gallop, a web of sparks pushed out from it. The lightning shockwave shot toward her, frying the air. Sera jumped out of the way, retreating to the other side of the pit. The audience booed and hissed. Still running, Sera gritted her teeth. What exactly did they expect? That she grabbed the bull with her bare hands and tossed it at the barrier?

The bull had made it to another patch of metal mushrooms. They looked dormant at the moment, but who knew how long that would last. Still sizzling with lightning, the bull kicked its back legs, spinning around. Behind the creature, its pink and purple magic crackled like electrical flowers atop the metal mushrooms. The air stank of metal and burning rocks and...earth. The bull's element had changed again.

The ground quaking beneath her boots, Sera hopped up and grabbed the nearest advertising banner hanging from the wall. It looked highly flammable, which was pretty stupid of the organizers considering what went on in the pit. Stupid, but useful. She waved the portable fire hazard at the bull, daring it to come.

It didn't keep her waiting long.

The bull sprinted forward. Every time its hooves hit the ground, a tremor shook the arena. Like a pounding hammer, the quakes echoed through the arena. Fissures cut across the floor, splitting it open. Sand poured down through the cracks. Somewhere across the pit, one of the wooden panels ripped off the wall and hit the dirt. The crowd, which had been so rambunctious just a minute ago, had fallen completely silent.

The bull was almost upon Sera, magic boiling in its green eyes as it rushed toward the banner she was waving. She dashed to the side, whisking the banner away. The bull smashed horns-first into the wall, knocking off a few more wood panels. Sera ran for the cluster of gasoline-gurgling metal mushrooms, zigzagging around the slippery puddles. She held the banner inside the golden geyser, drenching the cloth in gasoline.

The bull was already running toward her again. Wood splinters freckled the emerald waves of magic pulsing across its body. Then, between one step and the next, fiery plumes split across the bull's skin, swallowing the

126

creature. The splinters dissolved, pouring down to the broken ground like ash tears.

Sera tossed the thick banner over the bull's head. An angry, panicked growl pierced the fabric, and the creature veered blindly to the side. The sudden jerk tossed the gasoline-drenched banner off its head. The flame-licked fabric landed in the big golden puddle, setting it ablaze. A moment later, the dazed bull sloshed in too. Fire crackled and hissed, pouring down the bull's body and across the pond of fire.

A frigid breeze tickled Sera's ear, the precursor to the next elemental jump. Blue magic slid across the bull's body and flooded the puddle. The war cries of fire and ice hissed and crackled, the wicked song echoing through the arena. The bull thrashed and sloshed and kicked. Chunks of ice broke off of its body, freezing the gasoline puddle upon impact. Its flames crystalized, the fire had been defeated. But so had the bull. Its legs were frozen to the ground. Sera ran at it, delivering a spinning kick to its side. Ice groaned, and the frozen bull hit the ground, shattering into a million pieces.

The crowd went wild.

Sera glared up at the cameras—and the television screens showing a closeup of her face, smeared with sweat and dirt. And rage. There was a lot of that too. The audience didn't seem to care. They pounded their fists against the seats and cheered her name. Cutler was there, in one of the front rows. Smirking, he threw her a salacious wink. She was considering returning an obscene gesture of her own when a thick tube rose from the ground, and the pit spit out its next delight.

A swarm of hornets shot into the air, their gold and obsidian bodies shimmering like metal. Poisonous magic hornets. Awesome. As Sera watched them swerve and loop overhead, the metal mushrooms behind her began to gurgle.

She stole a quick glance back at them, just long enough to see that they were squirting up globs of dubious purple magic. The globs bounced out one after the other—like an army of suicidal ants diving to their deaths—and splattered the floor. A few drops sprinkled Sera's pants, scorching tiny holes into the fabric and sizzling her skin. She bit back the pain burning across her legs and kept her eyes on the swarm.

They'd turned their final loop downward into a dive headed straight for her. A sting from one of those hornets was enough to knock a mage unconscious. A whole swarm of stings would kill her. What was the Game Architect playing at?

But she didn't have time to think, only to act. The swarm was almost upon her, their fat stingers sparking with magic. She ran straight into the middle of the metal mushrooms, ignoring the bubbling, burning goo that splattered her arms and legs. Their collective buzz drowning inside her ears, the hornets followed her into the mine field. The goo geysers continued to gurgle and spew, smacking the swarm with thick, sticky globs, eating away at its numbers. Sera just kept running. Behind her, hornets and goo smacked against the ground.

The deafening buzz had died down to a murmur. She pivoted around to look down a path of mushy purple goo. What few hornets had survived the goo bombing were stuck inside the translucent purple jelly, wiggling their wings in a futile attempt to escape. She glared down at them and stomped them into the ground.

The crowd roared in appreciation. Sera scraped the

purple goo off her boot before it ate through her sole, then shot the sick bastards in the audience a feral sneer. They pumped their fists in the air and cheered louder.

A soft, feathery melody resonated against the barrier surrounding the fighting pit, filling the arena with its sweet song. The crowd's cheers melted into awed whispers. Sera looked up—right into the eyes of her final opponents.

A pair of gigantic magic dragonflies, each as large as a house cat, hovered above. Their wings, silken and sparkling, hummed out the magical song that had so captivated the audience. Giant dragonflies were beautiful, especially as far as monsters went, but despite their pleasing appearance, they were about as nasty a creature as they came. If you let them get close enough, they'd bite a big chunk out of you.

As the two dragonflies swayed and danced in fluid, graceful loops, Sera reached down her legs. The guards had taken her sword from her, but she still had some knives hidden inside her boots. She slid them out and launched them at the monsters. The blades sank in, but it wasn't enough. The knives were way too small to do real damage to creatures like them.

The dragonflies fluttered past each other, making circles around Sera. She turned, trying to keep them both in her sight, but they'd coordinated their movements perfectly. The soft melody deepened—darkened—as they sped up. One of them head-butted her from behind, the force of its blow knocking her across the pit. She hit the ground, rolling away from the purple puddle she'd nearly smacked face-first into. She hopped to her feet, brushing off the magic-charged sand. Her legs were freckled with burns, she had a singe mark on the front of her shirt, and one of her sleeves had burned clear off. In other words, she was completely pissed off.

Sera reached down and grabbed one of the cylinders that the elemental bull's tremors had unearthed. It was long, awkward, and heavy—but it would have to do. She swung it at one of the dragonflies buzzing around her, knocking the creature at the cluster of electrically-charged metal mushrooms. It smacked against the little lightning rods, its body convulsing amidst screeches and smoke as it sizzled atop the mushroom caps.

Sera turned her back on the dragonfly, walking away from the dying scent of sugar and vanilla icing. The second monster roared and spun around to smack her with its tail. She stumbled back, but before she could retaliate, it bit a chunk out of her arm. It performed a graceful backward loop, trailing the scent of chocolate chip cookies with a helping of delighted chortles.

"Oh, think that's funny, do you?" Sera growled up at it. Her body had blocked off all feeling to her arm, which right now was probably all that was keeping her in this fight. It also meant she'd be in for a world of pain later.

The dragonfly chuckled.

"You are so dead," she told it, peeling her hand off her bleeding arm. Crimson drops flicked off her fingers, splattering the sand.

The dragonfly came at her again. Its mouth opened, showing off two rows of tiny, pointed teeth. Sera swung the cylinder like a baseball bat, knocking the monster at the magic barrier. It smashed against the web of lightning and burst into tiny, dragonfly-bits confetti.

The audience jumped to their feet, their voices raised in cheer.

"You're all a bunch of demented lunatics!" she roared

back at them.

Her words dissolved into the crowd. She wasn't even sure if they'd heard her. And it didn't matter. As the door out of the fighting pit burst open, she clutched her bleeding arm and walked toward it. The pain in her legs and arms was slowly returning. She walked faster. She had no intention of passing out in front of several hundred bloodthirsty supernaturals.

Sera ran for her locker, reached inside her bag, and pulled out a bottle of healing spray. She drenched her body in the stuff, not even bothering about getting her clothes wet. They were ruined anyway.

The bottled magic sank into her skin, flooding her with soothing warmth. The spray wasn't half as effective as a mage's healing spell, but it was enough to keep her conscious. She'd worry about second-degree burns and bleeding body parts later. For now, she had to worry about finding someone to heal her.

"Sorry, peaches," the guard said when she asked to see a healer. "You need to heal yourself. No outside help. Those are the rules of the fighting pit."

"I'm not in the fighting pit, genius," she snapped back.

A muffled sound buzzed from the guard's earpiece. Someone was talking to him.

"Rules are rules," the guard told her.

Sera grabbed her bag—and her sword—and marched off. "Rules, my ass," she muttered under her breath as she headed for the exit sign.

The guard had said he'd bet money on her making it

through the day. It was in his best interest to find her a healer. Unless he was lying about the bet. Or someone had ordered him not to help her heal. Like the Game Architect.

Dizziness rushed through her head, a kaleidoscope of yellow and purple lights dancing in front of her eyes. Sera swayed to the side. She reached out, catching herself on the wall before she smashed into it. Her hand, slippery with blood, slid across the satin-smooth surface, smearing it red.

Sera had reached the exit door. She pushed it open and stepped out into the lobby, blinking back the flood of bright white lights. She staggered out and shuffled across the slick marble floor. The light show in her head had exploded into the grand finale of all migraines. She stumbled over her own feet and fell.

Two arms caught her, powerful and smelling strongly of dragon. Sera blinked back the blotchy lights, and Kai's face came into focus.

"The dragon," she slurred, then blacked out.

She didn't know how long she was out, but it couldn't have been more than a few minutes. When she came to, she was lying on top of a counter in the lobby. The fairy on the other side had retreated to the corner, her face as green as her hair. She looked about two seconds from throwing up. Beside her, her vampire colleague was licking his lips.

A warm, soothing magic rushed through Sera, its silken touch washing away the pain. She turned her head, now that she actually could move it again. Dal was beside the counter, muttering as his hands wove a web of sparkling silver-blue magic across her body. He pressed his palms together, then yanked them apart, dissolving the spent magic.

"Thanks," Sera croaked, trying to sit up.

Dal caught her arm and pulled her up. A wicked grin twitched at his bottom lip. "Does that mean we're even?"

"Sure," she said, returning the grin. "After you've done that another hundred or so times."

He snorted. "There weren't *that* many monsters in the tower at Alcatraz."

"How would you know? You were asleep the whole time," she teased.

"She's back to her normal self," Dal sighed, turning to look back at Kai.

The dragon stood against the wall, his arms crossed stiffly against his chest, his jaw clenched like he'd just bitten down on a piece of iron chewing gum. He looked like he needed to kill something. Now.

"Frowning gives you wrinkles," Sera told him.

Dark scales split out of his wrists, sliding up his arms. Magic boiled in his eyes, setting the dust in the air on fire.

Dal sighed. "Sera, try not to stoke the fire too much," he said, then walked off, dodging the cloud of burning dust flurries on his way out.

When he was gone, Sera hopped down from the counter, landing beside Kai. "Are you all right?"

"Am I...all right?" he grunted, his words scraping out like sandpaper.

"I take it that's a 'no' then."

"You're hurt." He set a hand on her shoulder. It was bare, bruised, and dirty. The strap of her tank top had torn clear off. The rest of the shirt hung in tattered strips. There wasn't enough fabric left to make a bandage.

"It looks worse than it is," she replied with a shrug and a smile.

"You're hurt," he repeated. "And you're asking if I am all right? No, I'm *not* all right. You look like you've been run over by a tank, torn apart by vampires, then burned to a crisp by dragon fire."

"Nah, I only let you burn me, baby."

"This is not funny, Sera," he growled.

"I was very nearly killed. I'm going to deal with that however the hell I want."

"By making snarky comments?"

"Laughter is the best medicine," she said, smiling at him.

He gave her the evil eye. "No, the best medicine is never needing medicine to begin with. You were supposed to use magic against those monsters, not play baseball with them or lure them into gasoline puddles and set them on fire."

"Magic is the window to the soul."

"How poetic," he said drily.

"Every time I use magic, I give Blackbrooke a way into my head."

"You're not going to make it through the Magic Games without using magic," he told her.

"Why not?"

"Because no one has ever done it."

"Maybe no one has ever thought of it," she said. "I am not like other mages."

A deep sigh rumbled in his chest. "Oh, trust me. No one is arguing that point, sweetheart."

"Funny." She planted her hands on her hips and narrowed her eyes at him.

He met her stare, the magic building up in his eyes once more. His magic wasn't burning dust bunnies this time, though. It was rough but fluid, like an ocean tide crashing against the rocks. It rolled against her magic, daring it to come out.

"So," she said, clearing her throat. She pushed her magic down deep inside of her. Here of all places, she needed to keep her magic in check, not nuzzle and nip at Kai's magic. Especially not when the Game Architect was probably nearby with his notepad and an arsenal of mind-frying tricks.

"So?" he asked.

"Blackbrooke. I think he told the guard not to heal me."

Kai frowned.

"You think I'm being paranoid?" she asked.

"No. You're not. Blackbrooke wants to break you. He'll stop at nothing to do it. Especially after you thwarted his first attempt in the pit."

"Nowhere in the rules does it say that I must use magic in the pit. I read the whole book."

"You're right," he said. "And wrong. The Magic Games exist to rank a mage's magic, yes. But the Games have another purpose."

"To crack open a mage's mind and serve it to the hungry crowd."

"No, Sera. Pushing a mage's mind to the breaking point tests your limits, but it also unleashes your potential. Most mages, even the powerful ones, have a lot more magic than they know. The trials of the Magic Games push them so hard that the floodgates open, allowing them access to magic they never knew they had."

"I think I'd rather pass on that little perk," Sera said, waving her hands across her torn and bloody clothing.

Kai picked a shopping bag off the ground and handed it to her. "For you."

"Clean clothes?" Grinning, she peered into the bag. A pair of jeans and a black tank top waited inside. "How did you know?"

"That you'd tear up your clothes in the pit? Let's just say that you have an impressive track record."

Sera couldn't argue with that. Her track record was a graveyard of monster parts and decimated clothing.

"Any chance there are some boots in here?" she asked, poking around inside the bag.

His dark brows drew together. "Did you ruin those too?"

"Well..." She lifted her foot up, showing him the partially dissolved sole on her boot. "Do you think it's salvageable?"

He pulled out his phone and began typing away. "I'm sending someone out for boots."

"While you're at it, could you send someone out for pizza too?" she asked hopefully.

"You're hungry? Again?"

Her stomach groaned.

"I'll see what I can do," he said, typing faster.

"It's all the fighting," she told him. "And running away. And dodging goo-spewing metal mushrooms."

"You wouldn't need to run away so much if you just used your magic." He slid his phone back into his pocket and looked at her. "Aren't you the least bit curious about unlocking your magic?"

Maybe a bit. A teeny, tiny bit. But she couldn't allow them to break her. "Not like this," she said. "If there were another way..."

"In private?" he asked.

"Yes."

"There's a ritual. It pushes a mage's mind to the

breaking point, just like the Magic Games. But it's not a public event. And it's not done anymore."

"Why not?"

"The Magic Council wants to keep these things within their control. Also, there's more money in it this way," he admitted, frowning.

Yeah, tickets to the Magic Games were expensive, and the fees for the participating mages were even worse. Then there was the control factor. The Magic Council was a suite of dictators with a hyperactive case of megalomania and a side order of paranoia. They had to know everything about every supernatural on the planet, and they used their collective magical might to squash anyone who stood in their way. It was a wonder there hadn't yet been a worldwide revolt against them.

Sera grinned at him. "I hope you got me a nice discount on my entrance fees," she said, shaking off thoughts of revolutions. For all she knew, that was what had gotten the Dragon Born into trouble the first time around.

"The Magic Council doesn't give discounts."

"Not even to their own members?"

"No."

"Shame."

"Besides," he said, magic swirling in his eyes. If she hadn't known better, she'd have thought he was feeling a touch whimsical at the moment. "If you pay off your debt too quickly, I'll have no excuse to see you."

"You could always, you know, ask me out like any normal guy would."

"I have a feeling normal guys are too scared to ask you out." He leaned in closer, his breath caressing her cheek, his hand kneading slow, deep circles into her back.

"Probably," she agreed, closing her eyes. Her muscles went liquid.

"Dal didn't heal you completely." His hand lingered on the small of her back.

She cleared her throat—and her head of those treacherous thoughts. "There are some things magic can't heal."

"Sera, would you—" He stopped, his hand dropping to his pocket. "Sorry. Just a minute." He pulled out his phone and read the message on the screen. "It appears that the first picture Finn sent you—the one of us at Trove—was taken from one of the security cameras."

"Oh?"

"And the picture of us in the pit before the Games came from a camera in the arena."

"So, Finn hacked into the security feeds?"

"Magic events and businesses keep their feeds in-house."

"No connections to the outside world?" she asked.

"No, we cannot risk that the human population could get a peek at what we do. They don't understand our world or our ways. Our practices are…"

"Draconian?"

"Necessary," he amended. "Supernaturals are powerful and dangerous. Keeping them in check means no human massacres. And we avoid a war neither humans nor supernaturals can afford."

"I know all about the consequences of misbehaving supernaturals. I hunt down monsters for a living," she reminded him. "So, if Finn couldn't hack into the security feeds from the outside, that means he had to do it from the inside." Dread, dark and dreary, curled itself around her heart.

"Yes," he said, his tone cautious. "But don't panic."

"Who's panicking? I have to worry about the Magic Council's plans to crack open my mind, a plot to a murder that same council using a flock of vampires compelled by an ancient magic artifact, and a magic-high mage with revolutionary aspirations and a cult of brainwashed minions to back him up. Oh, and did I mention that the magic-high psychopath is stalking me?" She laughed like a drunk hyena. "I don't have time to panic."

"Finn is weak. He's only a threat when he's siphoning magic from better mages."

"He has a whole cult of mages to siphon magic from," she pointed out.

"Forget about Finn. He's just trying to intimidate you."

Sera pulled her chiming phone out of her bag. "Well," she told Kai, showing him the phone. "It's working."

On the screen was another message from Finn: a picture of her facing down the elemental bull with the subtitle, "Can't wait to taste your magic again, Sera."

CHAPTER THIRTEEN

Blood Brothers

"THAT'S CREEPY, RIGHT?" Sera said. "I have my own personal stalker."

Kai put on his hard, expressionless face. You could have cut diamonds on that face. Somewhere behind him, the contents of a trashcan caught on fire.

Sera looked down at the hand he'd locked around her wrist, then met his eyes. "You're burning the trash, hotshot."

A cool wind snuffed out the fire, spreading the scents of ketchup and pizza across the lobby. Mmm, pizza.

"You should let go," she told Kai, nodding toward her trapped wrist.

"Why?"

"Firstly, because I don't think gluing yourself to me will prevent Finn from sending me sleazy SMSs," she replied cooly. "And secondly, because the guards aren't going to let me drag you into the fighting pit with me."

He released her wrist. "You're right. You don't have long until your next match. If you fail to show, we'll have bigger problems than Finn."

"The Magic Council's wrath?"

"For instance."

"And you don't have any sway over your fellow Council members?" she asked.

"Over some of them, yes. That's why I've been so busy stocking up on favors. You never know when you might need the support of another Council member," Kai said. "But other than those few small favors, no, I really don't have much sway." He stroked the stubble on his chin. "But I could step on them for you, if you want."

Sera coughed. "You're joking."

He flashed his teeth at her. Shit, was he serious?

"Yes, I'm joking." He chuckled. "But you should have seen the look on your face. Like I'd suggested sacrificing you to a pit of hungry vampires."

"You wouldn't be doing those vampires any favors," she told him. "I bite back."

"Yes, I imagine so." Magic pulsed in his eyes. He picked up the shopping back she'd dropped earlier and pushed it into her hands. "Now get changed. And don't worry about Finn. The commandos will find them."

She cracked a smile. "Do they know that *you* call them that too?"

"No, and I'd appreciate if you didn't tell them. It would go straight to their heads."

"Sure thing," she chuckled.

"They'll find Finn, Sera. You just stay focused on the Games."

"But—"

"No buts. Go." He pointed at the bathroom sign. "There will be a pizza slice waiting for you when you return."

"There had better be," she grumbled, heading for the

bathroom with the shopping bag in hand. The click of her broken boots on the marble floor drowned out the low rumble of her hungry stomach.

A few minutes later, she left the bathroom looking halfway human again. She'd washed the blood, sweat, and sand off her body using a stack of wet paper towels that now lay in a dirty bundle at the bottom of the sink-side trashcan. The new clothes fit. Better yet, they were stretchy enough to not constrict her in a fight. Sera had to give it to Kai's people; they sure knew how to pick out battle-worthy clothes. They also had an ill-conceived sense of humor.

"You need to introduce me to whoever picked out this shirt," Sera told Kai as she rejoined him in the lobby. "I need to thank them personally."

Kai looked from her hard grin to the shirt in question. Black and strappy, it looked more like lingerie than a shirt. It certainly only covered about as much of her as a bra.

"By thank, you mean—"

"Introduce to my sword," she said, turning around once. "I mean, just look at this."

"Oh, I'm looking all right."

She blushed. "This isn't funny, Kai."

"I'm completely serious. Turn around again." His brows peaked. "I need to get a closer look at this travesty."

She punched him in the arm. He didn't even try to dodge the blow. He just looked down at her fist, an amused twitch on his lips. She shook out her throbbing hand. You'd think by now she'd have learned not to punch the dragon.

"This is half a shirt. There's less fabric here than in my ruined top," she said.

"But it's artistically cut."

A growl buzzed in her throat. "You need to fire the person responsible."

His gaze panned up her body. "Actually, I'm thinking of giving him a raise."

So the guilty party was a man. Figured. No woman would have come to the conclusion that it's a splendid idea to fight monsters in her underwear.

"Do you have my pizza?" Sera asked.

He pointed to the counter. "Over there. You'll have to eat it fast. Your next match starts in ten minutes."

"That won't be a problem," she said, swiping up the paper plate. It was already drenched in oil that had slid off the pizza. Mmm. "I'll be done in two."

"Since you defeated the Monster Mixer, you'll be facing the Blood Brothers next, followed immediately by someone from the Mages of the Universe," Kai said as she devoured the pizza.

"Any idea which mage?" she asked between bites.

"No, it's a surprise."

"Goody." She used the napkin to wipe the last of the oil from her fingers, tossed it and the paper plate into the trash, then swung her bag over her shoulder. "Ok, ready."

He tossed her a new pair of boots. "Good luck."

She put them on, grinning at him. "It will be easy."

He didn't return her grin. Instead, he said, "I'll send Edwards out for more clothes."

She wasn't sure if he was teasing her or just being practical. "Aha! Now I have the offending party's name."

"Seven minutes," Kai reminded her.

"Going," she said, hurrying off.

Two guards stood in front of the door that led 'backstage'. They let her pass, their eyes glued to her chest. Maybe she could work with this—distract the Blood Brothers with her new outfit while she kicked their asses. Yeah, that could work. The vampires were a horny bunch. Then she'd just have to do the same with the mage, and she'd be all done for the day. No magic necessary. She smiled as she deposited her bag and sword in her locker, then headed down the hall to the fighting pit.

The guard who'd refused to find her a healer stood beside the open door to the pit, looking big and dangerous.

"I found a healer," she said, giving him a defiant glare.

"So you did." He looked pleased. "And new clothes," he added with a leer. "I'm going to have to pat you down for weapons. You weren't supposed to bring those knives into the pit last time."

Sera sighed and handed him the two knives she'd tucked into her new boots. "Here. No pat-down necessary."

"Sorry, peaches." He set her knives into a box near his feet, then gestured for her to lift her arms. "Rules are rules."

He took twice as long as necessary to pat her down. He was enjoying himself far too much. Whatever. She probably wasn't allowed to break his kneecaps, but she'd think of something else. Something more subtle. Like poisoning his coffee. There was nothing like a case of magical food poisoning to teach you not to grope the Magic Games fighters.

Sera passed through the door, following the scents of sugar and sex into the fighting pit. Shapeshifting vampires. Their magic had a pretty distinct smell. Like a smoker who drenched himself in cologne, the vampires' potent perfume covered most of the blood smell. But only most. As soon as you got close enough, the charade shattered. Sera kept walking. Any minute now…

A tangy, metallic taste tingled her tongue. There it was. Blood. A shapeshifting vampire's magic was as strong as a mage's, but deep down, he was still a bloodsucker. There was no hiding that, no matter how many layers of magic they wrapped around themselves.

The Blood Brothers stood back-to-back at the center of the pit. A spotlight swung toward them, bathing them in crimson light. Their long, black cloaks glittered like crushed rubies, and their emerald eyes, cat-like, glowed out from the darkness of their hoods, meeting Sera's gaze. They turned, their cloaks kissing the ground as they swayed.

The cracks, puddles, and general disarray in the fighting pit had been repaired with magic since she'd last been there. The metal mushroom clusters appeared dormant, but she wasn't counting on them staying that way. The magic barrier around the pit was up. Right now, it was gleaming a particularly sickening shade of green.

"Hi," Sera greeted the vampires.

A cool breeze cut through the pit, swirling up wisps of sand. It knocked the hoods off the two vampires. Their faces were hard and gaunt; their skin cast green in the barrier's eerie light.

"I'm Sera," she said, trying again. "And you are?"

They watched her in silence, their eyes screaming hunger. Some crazy vampires starved themselves before a fight. It made them stronger and meaner. The *really* crazy vampires starved themselves, then consumed a single drop of blood just before the fight. Such was the recipe for an all-out bloodbath. Sera hoped these two vampires were only normal crazy, not really crazy.

"Stop chatting and fight!" shouted someone—likely drunk—from the crowd.

"Rip off their heads!"

"Pull out their spines!"

"Fry their brains on that barrier!"

Sera rolled her eyes. "Fools," she muttered under her breath.

The vampires still hadn't moved, as though they were waiting for something. For her to cut her own throat and throw herself at their feet maybe. *Not damn likely.* She rolled her shoulders back, stretching out her arms. The vampires remained as stiff as statues.

"Fine," she told them. "I'll just have to come to you."

She didn't even make it halfway to the vampires. They disappeared into a cloud of purple mist. The mist gurgled and bubbled, pouring down to the ground like a gaseous waterfall. Sera couldn't see. She could hardly breathe through the stench soup of rotten fruit and animal droppings. A shrill cry pierced the purple veil. Bats.

She'd no sooner had the thought when a squadron of the creatures broke through the fog, diving straight for her. She rolled out of their path, and they shot over her head. A deep, primal growl roared out of the mist, followed a moment later by a big, silver wolf. *Hello, vampire number two.*

The wolf snapped at her, trying to tear itself a mouthful of her flesh. So much for distracting the vampires with her feminine wiles. Sera kicked it in the face, her new boots doing their job nicely. The wolf flew across the pit, swallowed up by the mist.

The wolf's blood brother screeched again. The bats were coming around for another pass. Sera turned and ran, following the strongest magic in the pit to its source: the barrier. The mist was so thick that she couldn't see the glowing curtain of magic, but she could feel it. She stopped when she was a few feet from the edge and turned her back to it. The bats screeched another time. They were close—so close that the vampire's pliable magic rippled across her skin. She still couldn't see a damn thing.

On instinct, she ducked. A gust of fluttering wings rushed over her and smashed into the barrier, which gurgled and gushed. The light show of clashing magic from the collision was finally enough to pierce the fog. Dozens of glowing green eyes pulsed, and then there was a vampire at Sera's feet. His cloak was torn and his skin tie-dyed with black scorch marks, but he was still breathing. He'd gone into a deep sleep to regenerate his body. He'd be napping for a while.

A howl split through the fog, shattering it. Tiny purple shards rained to the ground, then dissolved against the sand. The wolf was standing only a few feet away. He ran forward, closing the distance in a few bounds. He brushed past Sera, ignoring her, and prodded the sleeping vampire with his paw. His head snapped up. As his eyes met hers, a sneer slid across his snout, exposing two rows of pointy teeth.

Sera shrugged. "He was the one who flew into the barrier. All I did was duck."

The wolf's snarl swallowed the chorus of chuckles from the audience. Bands of silver-tinted magic curled around his body, morphing him back into a vampire. Sera blinked. No, make that two vampires. He'd magically cloned himself. Fantastic.

The vampire and his clone charged. Since Sera didn't have a death wish, she ran. Vampires were strong, fast, and had the personality of a grizzly bear with a bad rash. If she'd had her sword, maybe she could have taken them. Maybe. But she didn't have a sword. And thanks to Gropy the Guard, she didn't even have her knives. What she did have was—Sera looked around the pit—sand? Lots of sand. A magic barrier the vampires weren't going within spitting distance of. And a few clusters of inert metal mushrooms drilled into the ground. Why couldn't they at least make themselves useful and spit out some sticky liquid? Burning goo? Anything? They'd been perfectly content to squirt all sorts of weird shit at her earlier today.

The vampires were gaining on her. Her ingenious plan to run for her life obviously wasn't working, so she darted into the mushroom cluster, zigzagging between the cylinders. The vampires followed, with every stride gaining ground. The stench of boiling blood singed her nose and turned her stomach.

The final cylinder in the cluster loomed before her, taller and skinnier than all the rest. It looked more like a flagpole than a mushroom. She didn't question why; she just jumped. Her hands closed around the pole, her momentum swinging her around. Her boots slammed against the vampires, kicking them onto the mushrooms. Their heads thumped against the rounded tops, and they went down. As they hit the ground, the clone flickered out. Sera swung off the pole and landed beside the real vampire.

"Top marks for the dramatics, Dracula," she said, staring down at his sleeping body. "But I've been fighting supernaturals with a drama queen complex since I could pick up a sword. It takes more than a few cheap magic tricks to best me."

The crowd exploded with applause. Beer cans and glowing sticks shot up into the air. A few of them hit the magic barrier and sizzled to ashes. The whole arena smelled of blood, adrenaline, and magic. But most of all, it smelled of victory.

If only it could have lasted.

CHAPTER FOURTEEN
Mages of the Universe

SERA STARED UP at the rows of spectators. Riley was there, right beside Naomi. They met her eyes with dual grins and tossed confetti up into the air. The guy sitting behind them got a mouthful of it, but he dropped his fist-waving as soon as Naomi turned to give him a coy wink. Cutler was in the front row, as always, but Sera had learned to ignore his leers by now. She had a bigger problem, and that problem was stepping into the fighting pit.

The mage walked across the field of sand, grainy particles crunching beneath her stilettos. Yep, she'd worn five-inch heels to a magic fight. Vixen-red stilettos. Sera would have laughed—if not for the supercharged aura clinging to the mage like a pair of leather pants on a hot summer day. Her magic roared and snapped, an avalanche of shooting stars and cosmic debris. A telekinetic. She smelled of lemon grass and insanity.

The magic barrier rippled like a flag in the wind. Whatever the mage was doing to the barrier, it didn't like it. Ridiculous shoes or not, she was going to be a problem. A big problem. She was a first tier telekinetic, and first tier telekinetics were always completely out of their minds. Like Cutler. Sera stole a look at her crude coworker. An intense look was on his face, like he was cataloging every move that she made. When he noticed she was looking at him, he pulled out his phone and snapped a shot of her, a devilish grin spreading to the corners of his face.

Metal screeched and groaned, and the audience fell silent. The metal mushrooms in one of the clusters erupted from the ground, a veil of sand and broken wires spilling down from them as they rose into the air. The telekinetic's arms were raised high above her. As she met Sera's gaze, a smirk curled up her thick lips.

The swarm of metal mushrooms shot forward at Sera like a round of torpedoes. Metal hummed, a song as beautiful as it was deadly. Sera took off running, hoping to avoid the barrage. The mushrooms changed directions and followed her.

"Stupid telekinetics," Sera muttered as she ran faster.

She grunted as one of the cylinders knocked against her back, but she managed to stay on her feet. Barely. The mushrooms hit almost as hard as a vampire. Sera angled for the telekinetic. She had to end this fast. She couldn't withstand too many more hits—preferably none actually, but she didn't think she was going to be that lucky. The mushrooms looked pretty intent on pummeling her into oblivion.

Sera didn't make it far before a second cluster of metal mushrooms burst out of the ground and joined the hunt. Sera's muscles were on fire and her lungs screamed for air, but she didn't stop running. Sweat trickled down her face, smearing her vision.

"Use your magic," the telekinetic said. Her words bounced off the barrier and echoed across the pit.

Sand exploded under Sera's feet, blinding her. While she was busy rubbing it out of her eyes, one of the mushrooms collided into her side. The force of the spelled cylinder shot her at the magic barrier. In just a few seconds, she was going to be a bug on that windshield.

She reached down, grabbing for the wood-panel wall that surrounded the pit. Her fingers slipped, failing to get a grip, but it was enough to slow her down. She pushed out her legs, slamming her boots against the barrier, all the while praying that the soles were thick enough to hold up. She kicked off the barrier, rolled in the air, and landed in the sand, the scent of burnt leather singeing her nose.

The telekinetic frowned at her and sent her metal minions in for another pass. Rage building up inside of her, Sera ran toward her. She held back the rage—getting angry would only make her lose control of her magic—channeling the energy into her run. She zigzagged through the mushroom swarm, pushing through the pain whenever one of them hit her. She just had to get to the mage, and then this would be all over. The woman looked like a total pushover.

Sera reached down to the ground, snatching up the long pole she'd used in the previous fight. As she slid through the final flying mushrooms, she swung the pole. It hit the telekinetic in the stomach, and she doubled over. Sera swung a swift followup blow to her opponent's back. The telekinetic hit the dirt, and all her cylinders fell out of the air.

"See?" Sera said, poking the mage with the toe of her partially-melted boot. "Just like I said. Total pushover."

The audience cheered, stomping their feet loudly. Sera

tossed the pole to the ground and walked out of the pit.

A shopping bag was waiting in front of Sera's locker when she got back to it. Kai must have had the guards bring it back here. She silently thanked him, then headed off to the bathroom. Her clothes were trashed—unsurprisingly after those last two matches—and her boots were even worse. The soles had nearly melted off. It was a wonder she'd been able to run with them on. Now that no one was looking, she allowed herself to limp to the bathroom.

It took a long, hot shower and a whole bottle of body wash to scrub off all the dirt and blood. It took even longer to tend to the myriad of cuts and scratches afterward. Her wounds screamed and burned when she doused them in antiseptic spray; they weren't particularly fond of the bandages either. A healer could have fixed her right up in minutes, but Sera hadn't bothered to ask the guard again for one of them. She imagined that after her spectacular display of no magic in the evening matches, the Game Architect was fuming. He'd have told the guards to just let her bleed.

So that left Sera to tend to herself. She forced herself to work slowly and thoroughly, even though all she wanted was to get the hell out of there. She was supposed to meet Kai for dinner, and she had no intention of arriving at the restaurant dirty and bloody. Her stomach gurgled.

She was positively famished. She pulled on the piece of fabric masquerading as a skirt and headed for the lobby. By the time she got there, it was dark outside, and Kai was nowhere in sight. She wasn't surprised, considering how late she was, but she couldn't help but feel disappointed.

"Hey, Sera!"

She turned to find Naomi walking toward her. She was wearing a black dress that hugged her curves and gold heels with tiny charms dangling from the ankle straps. Her makeup was perfect and her hair glittered as gold as her shoes. She looked like a supermodel. Sera, on the other hand, looked...well, at least she was clean. She'd gotten most of the sand out from under her fingernails. The trick was to cut the nails short.

"Hot date?" Sera asked her.

"Hmm?" Naomi looked down at her own outfit. "Oh, this. No, not a date. Riley and I are going to catch some dinner at the hotel, then we're hitting the clubs. I'm going to find *him* a hot date." She tapped her fingers together with mischievous glee.

"What does my brother think about your plan?"

"I haven't told him, but why would he complain? It's a grand idea. Everyone has been so tense lately with the Magic Games and everything else going on. We need to unwind." She glanced at the sword strapped to Sera's back. "*You* need to unwind." She turned, her eyes panning across the lobby. "Speaking of which, where's your boyfriend?"

"You realize he's not actually my boyfriend, right?"

Naomi's eyebrows lifted. "Does *he* know that?"

"Of course."

"I wouldn't be so sure about that."

Sera didn't know what to say to that, so she changed the subject. "Where's Riley?"

"He already headed back to the hotel."

"Maybe he caught wind of your plan and is hiding,"

Sera said, smiling.

"No, he went back because I told him I wasn't taking him clubbing the way he was dressed. I picked out something much better for him to wear when I went shopping before work this morning."

"So that's what you were doing while Kai was introducing me to his dragon."

Naomi grinned.

"Did that sound dirty?"

"Maybe just a little."

"I meant while we were training this morning. He didn't pull any punches."

"I know what you meant," Naomi said, wrapping her arm around Sera's shoulder. "So, if the dragon isn't here, how about you join me and Riley for dinner?"

"I was supposed to have dinner with Kai."

Magic sparkled in Naomi's eyes. "Ah." She grinned wider. "Like a date."

"More like an after-battle refueling."

"Sounds romantic."

Sera snorted. "Well, Kai's not here. I took too long getting myself cleaned up and changed after the fight. I guess I'll just refuel with you guys then."

"No." Naomi shook her head. Her shoulder-length locks swayed, singing like chimes in the wind. "You should find him."

"I tried. He's not answering his phone. Or he's just not answering my calls. Maybe he's annoyed with me because I didn't use magic in the pit."

"Sera, if he were annoyed with you, you'd know it. Kai Drachenburg doesn't ignore. He confronts."

"I... Yeah, I guess you're right."

"Of course I am." Her arm still wrapped around Sera,

she walked toward the exit. "So, here's what I'm thinking. You're good at tracking magic, right? It shouldn't be too hard for you to track Kai's magic. I bet it's potent enough to light up New York."

She wasn't wrong about that.

"Ok, I'll give it a shot," Sera agreed.

She reached out with her magic, searching for Kai's distinctive aura, that mix of spice and dragon. That magic that ignited the air and crackled with power raw and ancient, power that hit hard and took no prisoners. She found his trail almost immediately. It was hard to miss. No one's magic felt quite like Kai's.

"He went this way," Sera said, pointing down the street.

"Great." Naomi released her shoulder, then linked her arm in Sera's. "I'll walk with you as far as the hotel."

'As far as the hotel' wasn't more than a couple minutes. Naomi gave her an encouraging wave, then disappeared into the building. Sera continued walking, following Kai's trail down the sidewalk. She turned at the next block, then stopped. His magic had led her to the doorstep of the Empire State Building. Two mages stood on either side of the entrance doors. Guards, no doubt. They gave Sera a cursory look, then waved for her to enter.

Inside, soft mood music played from tall speakers, meshing well with the lobby's warm browns and golds. The ambience was lavish, and the dressed up mages standing about nibbling on appetizers and sipping wine even more so. Sera had walked right into the middle of a gathering of the magical elite.

Thankfully, she was too insignificant for anyone to pay her any mind. She slipped through the crowd gathered in front of the door, muting her steps as best she could. The last thing she wanted was for them to wonder what a nobody mage with a big sword was doing crashing their exclusive gala. What was she even doing here? As soon as she'd seen all those tuxedos and evening gowns, she should have turned and left. This gathering—or whatever it was—was even less her scene than Trove. At least at Trove, they'd been playing the same trashy music she listened to.

Sera tapped the elevator button, ducking inside as soon as the doors opened. Kai was somewhere up there. She'd felt that much. But which floor? She looked up. Kai's magic whispered to her from the 86th floor, humming against her lips. She closed her eyes and let the heat wash over her. It wasn't as potent as being next to him, but it was enough to throttle her pulse into overdrive. And the closer the elevator got to the 86th floor, the stronger the feeling got.

Sera folded her hands behind her and pushed her treacherous magic back inside of her. More and more, she was beginning to think she should never have gone looking for Kai.

The elevator doors opened. As soon as she stepped out, another aura tugged at her, tingling her nose. It was a mage—and a first tier mage at that—and there was something familiar about it. Like she'd felt it before. But where? And when? Her matches today had fried her brain, making it basically useless at conjuring up any thoughts beyond the basest instincts. *Eat, fight…*

Sex.

Sera stopped. *Wait, what?* She shook that loose wire in her head.

That's no loose wire. That's me, genius, the voice in her

head snickered.

It hadn't spoken to her for a while—long enough, in fact, that she'd begun to think she'd just imagined it. Well, except that Alex had told her to listen to it. What did her sister even mean? Only crazy people listened to the voices in their head.

The voice had gone quiet again. Sera continued following the two magic trails toward the Observation Deck. As she closed in on the source of the magic, she could hear two men speaking.

"She defeated all her opponents today," one of them said. His words were crisp and precise, but there was a hint of reproval in them.

"She's good." The second speaker was Kai.

Sera peeked around the corner. Past the stairs, in the middle of the tight room, he stood with none other than Blackbrooke, the Game Architect.

"She did it without magic."

"She's good," Kai repeated.

"Kai, surely I do not have to remind you that the point of the Magic Games is to test the boundaries of a mage's magic, *not* to let them show off how well they can fight without magic." A suspicious wrinkle formed between his eyes. "What is she hiding?"

"You've grown paranoid in your old age, Duncan. Not everyone is hiding something."

"I've always been paranoid. It's served me well over the years," he replied. "And, yes, everyone is, in fact, hiding something. I've cracked hundreds of minds in my tenure as Game Architect."

"You were cracking minds long before that."

"Yes, well, we all have our own special talents. Mine is extracting secrets. And I can tell you without a shadow of a doubt that Serafina Dering has a big one."

Kai said nothing.

"She's twenty-four years old. She should have gone through the Magic Games years ago," Blackbrooke continued. "I've looked into her records. She's been tested by magic detectors before. They always came back negative for magic."

"Interesting."

"Interesting? You think this is funny, Kai?"

Kai shrugged. "Your reaction sure is."

Blackbrooke's face went as red as a hellfire demon. "It takes a very powerful mage to fool a magic detector. I can count the number of mages in the world who have done it on one hand. You are one of them."

"I did it just to prove I could, not because I had any nefarious purpose. What can I say? I was young and bored."

"Did you teach her how to fool the detectors?"

"I have known Sera for all of one month."

"Is that a denial?"

Kai's sigh rocked his whole chest. "Yes, it's a denial. What's the matter with you? Did you take a shot of that fizzy blue liquor they're serving below?"

"No…ok, yes. It has a delightful flavor, like magic dancing the samba with my tastebuds." His eyes drifted up, a content smile settling on his lips. It lasted only a moment before he cleared his throat. "But that's beside the point. I didn't have enough for it to muddle my mind."

"You could have fooled me."

"This newfound sarcasm doesn't suit you, Kai," Blackbrooke said sternly. "It's an unfortunate habit you've picked up since you started gallivanting around with that mercenary."

"Do you have a point to all this, Duncan? Or are we just up here to enjoy the view?" Kai checked his watch.

Blackbrooke frowned at him. "Don't tell me you have something more important to do than ensure the security and sanctity of the Magic Council."

"Sera's alleged secret, if it even exists, is not a threat to the Council," Kai said. "And, yes, I do have something more important to do than play paranoia. I'm supposed to meet her for dinner."

"That there is the whole problem. Don't you see?" Blackbrooke waved his hand around, his movement clumsy and awkward. He really was drunk. "You're a powerful Sniffer yourself, Kai. Better than those enchanted artifacts we use as magic detectors. You can detect even a weak mage from a block away."

Kai's eyes narrowed. "And?"

"And your mercenary is not a weak mage. You must have known she's powerful from the moment you met her, no matter how good she is at hiding her magic," he said. "You knew and didn't tell the Magic Council."

"I was always getting distracted by her sword."

"You were distracted all right, but not by her sword," he snapped. "I never would have expected such egregious behavior from you, Kai. You've changed."

"You sure haven't."

"I should think not." Blackbrooke straightened, as though the implication of change felt like an army of fire ants crawling across his skin. "Our order is an ancient one. Your duty to the Magic Council is far more important than your latest conquest."

"Sera is not a conquest. She's a person," Kai growled, his magic buzzing in the air. "I brought her here to be tested in the Magic Games. She's done her duty. And so have I."

"Just see to it that you do," Blackbrooke replied with a haughty twitch of his head.

Something in that twitch got Kai's back up. His magic went from buzzing to electrifying. "Leave her be, Duncan. There's no need to treat her differently than any other Magic Games participant."

"As you said, she's special."

The determination in his tone should have worried Sera—someone on the Magic Council had made it his own personal project to rip her mind apart until he uncovered her secret—but she couldn't worry about that right now. The air popped with the lust and blood of hungry minds and even hungrier magic. Vampires. A whole lot of vampires. They were close.

Sera turned, scanning the area for them, but they weren't anywhere in sight. Realization smashed into her like a wrecking ball. They weren't inside. They were outside, cloaked by shadows.

She sprinted up the stairs into the indoor Observation Deck, ignoring Blackbrooke's bemused expression as she passed him and Kai. Drawing her sword as she ran, she beelined for the door that led to the outdoor deck. A vampire was already there. He looked just as bemused as Blackbrooke, so she must have surprised him while he'd been lurking there. Lurking? The thing was, common vampires didn't lurk; they attacked in a fit of bloodlust. Someone was controlling this vampire, just like someone had controlled the gang of bloodsuckers at Macy's yesterday. There were more vampires here too. Sera could feel them outside, also lurking.

She swung her sword at the vampire. He crumpled to

her feet, his head sliced right off, but another one had already taken his place. The other vampires jumped at the windows, their fists pounding like an army of synchronized hammers. The glass began to buckle and crack under the strain of their collective supernatural strength.

"Keep Blackbrooke back! Away from the windows!" she shouted to Kai. "They've come to finish the job!"

Her second opponent proved not quite as headless as his predecessor. He ducked the sideways slash of her sword, then kicked out, knocking her back into the room. As she touched down, the windows shattered, and a river of broken glass rained into the room. The vampires swung inside, each one landing in a crouch. There had to be a dozen of them. The wind howled at their backs, the city lights casting eerie halos around them.

Kai had pulled Blackbrooke behind him, but another batch of vampires had broken through. They were flooding into the room, their movements crisp and efficient. Before Sera could intercept, two of them had grabbed Blackbrooke. Kai was too busy fighting the others to stop them as they chomped down on the mage's neck. She rushed in like a child on a mission to scatter some pigeons. Unfortunately, vampires weren't pigeons. They continued to feast on Blackbrooke's blood. Only when Sera's sword had punctured their monstrous hearts did they finally stop drinking.

She crouched down beside Blackbrooke. "What kind of mage are you?"

He didn't answer. His lips twitched, and panic poured out of his aura, flooding the room. The vampires paused to sniff the air. Feral smiles broke out on their lips, and they snarled in appreciation. Blackbrooke's fear was pumping them up.

"Hey, stop that." Sera slapped his face. "Snap out of it. We need some help."

Blackbrooke hugged his knees, his eyes wide. He was in shock. Sera shook her head and rose to her feet.

"He's a healer," Kai told her, smashing the vampires with a blast of wind. One of them flew through the broken window and tumbled off the side of the building.

"In other words, not very useful in a fight."

"Not really," he said. "Afterwards maybe."

So the sadistic mind behind the Magic Games—the man who tormented mages until their minds broke, then roasted their secrets on a spit—was a healer. Talk about irony. Blood dripped down Blackbrooke's neck, but he didn't even put up his hand to stop it. Or try to heal himself. He seemed to have forgotten he even had magic. He was the broken one now.

"Fine. He can make himself useful later by healing my sore muscles." Sera waved her hand, putting up an ice barrier between the three of them and the vampires. "You think you can shoot more of those guys out of the building?"

"There are too many of them to worry about precision right now, Sera." Kai hit the vampires with another gust of wind. "This is pure brute force."

"Your favorite flavor," she said, grinning despite the dire situation.

He looked at her, his eyes pulsing with magic. "One of them."

She couldn't say why, but there was something about the way he looked at her as he said it that made her blush. "Ok." She could hear more vampires coming. She could feel their vile magic streaming down the side of the building. "Ok, so Mr. Snivels there is useless. How about some backup?"

"I've messaged the commandos."

"How ever did you do that while fighting two dozen vampires?" she asked in shock.

He shrugged. "Multitasking."

Ok, there was *definitely* something naughty in the way he looked at her that time. But rather than contemplating what other things he could multitask, she cleared her throat and asked, "When will the commandos arrive?"

"They're five minutes out," said Kai. "We just have to hold off the vampires for that long."

Sera looked at the solid wall of vampires staring out from behind her ice barrier. Their fists pounded at the ice.

"Five minutes, you say?" Sera laughed weakly as the vampires shattered her wall. "No problem."

CHAPTER FIFTEEN

Web of Magic

THE VAMPIRES MARCHED forward, moving like a group of coordinated soldiers—not like common vampires. The blank obedience in their eyes was downright eerie, far worse than their usual bloodthirsty crimson gleam.

"Any chance the mages downstairs would care to lend us a hand?" Sera asked Kai.

"Doubtful."

"I'm getting the feeling that your fellow Magic Council members aren't as hands-on as you are."

"True. And even if they wished to help, it wouldn't be a very good idea. They might all be the vampires' targets."

"So are you," she reminded him.

A dangerous look gleamed in his eyes. "I can take care of myself."

"Just try not to take out the whole building. I hear skyscrapers are expensive," she teased.

His lips curled up in a deliciously feral grin, and the look in his eyes went from dangerous to deadly. "I'll try to remember that."

Sera looked back at Blackbrooke, who was still sitting on the ground, muttering to himself as he rocked. He was so out of it that Sera didn't think he'd noticed the magic she'd performed earlier. And he certainly wasn't in any condition to go spelunking through her mind.

"Can you put up a fire barrier to stop them?" Sera asked Kai, pointing at the encroaching vampires. Sure, Blackbrooke was off in his own world, but there wasn't any need to tempt fate. Her magic was about as reliable as an old car engine.

Kai arched a single eyebrow at her but performed the spell anyway. A wall of flames burst out of the floor in front of the vampires. Vampires had a mortal fear of fire. Any other ones would have at least recoiled. These vampires walked right through the fire. The flames slid off their bodies.

"That's new. Isn't that spell supposed to burn them all to a blackened crisp?" Sera asked Kai.

He frowned. "Yes."

"They're not even wearing armor," she commented, looking out at the vampires. They were dressed in normal street clothes, not the fancy armor the vampires from yesterday had been wearing.

"A mage is protecting them from the flames," Kai said. "Probably the same one who's controlling them."

Sera looked at him, surprised.

"I'm not blind, sweetheart. Anyone can see that those vampires are not acting normal. They are being controlled. By a mage. It takes a mage to use any of the Orbs. The only way for a human to use them is if the Orbs have already been saturated with magic."

"You can see the magic controlling them?" Sera asked, looking at the web of crimson sparkling strands that coated each vampire.

"No, I can't." He looked from the vampires to her. "Can you?"

"Yes."

"Can you break it?" he asked.

"Maybe, if I can get in close enough."

The last of the vampires had stepped through the flames. They weren't moving very fast, but they didn't look like they'd be easy to stop either.

"Their targets are you and Blackbrooke," Sera told Kai. "You could turn into a dragon and fly away with him while I distract them."

"That would be contrary to your earlier request."

"Which one?"

"The one not to break the building. There's not enough space in here for me to shift into anything large enough to carry Blackbrooke. And," he added with a growl. "I'm not leaving you here to fight off several dozen vampires alone."

She shrugged. "They don't want me. They'll probably just run off after you fly away with Blackbrooke."

"But not before they tear you to pieces."

"I'm offended at how little faith you have in my monster-slaying skills," she joked. "I've fought at least as many giant caterpillars as there are vampires here."

"This isn't the same, and you know it. These vampires are controlled and protected by magic. And I'm not amused by your ill-advised attempt at humor, Sera," he added with a scowl.

Before she could answer that scowl with snark, the vampires finally charged. They ran toward Blackbrooke, but Kai pushed out his hands, blasting them with a gust of wind that sent them back through the fire barrier. So the spell protected against fire but not wind. Interesting. Sera supposed it made sense. The amount of magic required to protect a few dozen vampires against fire was enormous; the amount needed to protect them against all the elements was probably impossible.

One of the vampires had dodged the windy shockwave. As he tried to jump over Kai, Sera caught hold of his ankle and yanked. The vampire smacked against the floor. Still holding onto him, Sera extended her magic, tugging at the protective film coating his body. The spell ripped with a resounding snap. She pulled him up and kicked him into the fire. This time, he did burn. The magic controlling the vampire popped, and screams poured out of his mouth.

Sera wrinkled her nose, trying not to inhale the smell. "Kai, throw another one at me."

Kai shoved one of the vampires he was fighting in her direction. She shattered the protection spell and hurled him into the fire too.

"Taking them out one at a time sure is tedious," she told Kai after the sixth time.

His hands were full fighting off four vampires, but he managed an amused snort.

"Are you having fun?" she asked.

"I always have fun fighting with you, Sera." He froze a vampire into an icy pillar, then swung around to strike another in the arm. Bone cracked and snapped. The vampire's arm hung limply at his side.

"You snapped that vampire's arm like a twig," she gasped, incredulous. Vampires were too strong to break like that. At least, she'd always thought they were.

"There's a trick to it," he said, rolling his shoulders back. He pushed his hands out, frying another vampire on a bolt of lightning. "I can show it to you sometime."

"Somehow, I don't think it would work as well if I tried it," she said.

He was wearing one of his trademark black t-shirts, the fabric so taut that it showed off every muscle in his chest. His arms, exposed by his short shirt sleeves, weren't bad to look at either. The muscles were defined but flexible. Maybe he did werewolf-curls with his biceps. She quickly averted her eyes, before this little fantasy went any further. Drooling wasn't particularly useful in a fight. Neither was being distracted.

"Sera?" he said. Something in his tone told her this wasn't the first time he'd tried to get her attention. So much for not getting distracted.

"Hmm?" she asked.

"You said you can see the magic controlling them. Do you think you could break the spell?"

"I'd need to touch them to do it." She grabbed a vampire, shattered his protection, then fed him to the flames. "Which means going through them one by one, just like I've been doing with the fire protection spell on them."

"It has to be one spell that connects them all," said Kai.

She concentrated on the vampires—and on the magic controlling them. "Yes, it is," she said, looking out at the field of glistening crimson strands that connected the vampires together. "Even if I can break it, I'm not sure that I should. We'll be surrounded by a bunch of blood-crazy vampires in a rage."

"They won't be working as a team," Kai said, evading two vampires' coordinated punches. "That's easier."

Three more vampires rushed forward, tackling him to

169

the ground. Five more followed. He was being overrun. She couldn't even see him anymore.

Panic pulsing through her, Sera grabbed the nearest vampire. Magic shot out of her. It smashed against him, blasting apart the protection spell. Her magic hit him so hard that it broke the force controlling him too. It pulsed through the web of gold and crimson strings connecting the vampires, melting the magic. The web snapped, and the magic unraveled. The vampires stopped. For a few seconds they didn't move...then several dozen eyes turned toward her, blazing red. Beads of saliva dripped from their fangs.

Drenched in bloodlust, they rushed her. They'd be on her in seconds. Sera didn't have time to worry about consequences. She had no choice. She had to risk bigger magic. She reached for her magic, drawing on the power of fire.

Nothing happened.

The vampires were getting closer. At the last moment, they turned, running for Kai instead. They ran over him like a swarm of beetles. Sera screamed out, fear and rage igniting her magic. Every single vampire caught on fire at once—then they exploded.

"What was that?" Blackbrooke gasped. He stumbled to his feet, gaping at Sera.

She pushed past him, throwing vampire parts aside on her way to Kai. He was on the ground—unconscious, bloody, and torn. And he wasn't breathing.

CHAPTER SIXTEEN
Healing Magic

SERA'S HEART WAS crashing inside her chest. She slapped Kai's face, trying to wake him. He couldn't be gone. He just couldn't. Tanks had shot at him, and he'd said it only tickled. First tier mages had thrown their worst at him, and he'd merely sneezed.

She pounded her fists against his chest. He didn't move. Didn't breathe. Magic boiled inside of her, melding with despair.

"You're not getting out of our deal so easily," she told him, pounding his chest again. "I killed dozens of monsters for you. You're going to help get me through the Magic Games." She pounded him a third time, tears streaming down her cheeks, lightning exploding out of her hands.

Kai's body spasmed. His eyes shot open, and he jumped to his feet, shaking beads of lightning off of his body. "Are you trying to kill me?! Don't you ever do that again," he growled.

"I thought you were dead," she said, slouching with relief.

"It takes more than a few vampires to kill me." He looked around, his eyes widening when he saw the vampire parts everywhere. "How long was I out?"

"Half a minute or so?" She hadn't been keeping track of time. She'd been too busy punching him to life.

Kai glanced over at her. "I don't feel any more of them coming. Thankfully. Your magic is like catnip for monsters."

"And dragons?"

"Yes."

Wow. "I was just teasing."

"I know. And I was serious." He stared at her, his gaze snagging on the hemline of her skirt. Magic ignited in his eyes.

"You're appreciating my clothing again, aren't you?"

"No, I'm appreciating *you*. The clothing is merely enhancing my appreciation."

"I'm going to throw that Edwards fellow responsible for these outfits into the fighting pit," she grumbled. "And, just for the record, the vampires didn't come here for me."

Before she could start pointing fingers, the commandos rushed into the room. Their eyes panned across the battlefield, taking in the dead vampires. The rest of them couldn't have looked much better. Sera's clothes were torn and bloody. Again. How long had her new clothes lasted? Half an hour? Less? Geez, that had to be a new record. She sure had rotten luck when it came to clothing. And monsters. It was a good thing the hotel didn't run out of hot water for showers.

"It looks like we missed the party," Tony commented.

"Boss, you must have really been pissed off this time," Callum said, picking up a vampire hand.

Kai gave them a dark look. The commandos looked away.

"It wasn't him," Blackbrooke said, standing. His beady eyes snapped to Sera. His finger shook as he pointed it at her. "It was her."

Dal snorted. "Oh, it all makes sense now. Sera has an uncanny ability to make messes."

"But not clean them up," Callum added, grinning.

It was Sera's turn to shoot them a dark look. Unfortunately, it didn't have the same effect as Kai's had. Maybe because she couldn't make magic pulse in her eyes. Tony gave her a manly slap on the back along his way to check on Blackbrooke. Callum and Dal exchanged chuckles, then began to deal with the mess she'd made.

Kai left them to it, joining Sera by the window. He stopped beside her and folded his arms across his chest. She looked at him. Blood was dripping down his arms, splattering his shoes. She turned and moved in for a closer look. His chest was bleeding. His arms were bleeding. Hell, every corner of his body was bleeding.

"You're injured," she said.

"I'm fine."

"You were dead. You're not fine."

"I wasn't dead," he said. "I was regenerating."

"You're full of shit, Kai."

Satisfaction slid across his face. "You were worried about me."

"Of course I was worried. A dozen vampires swarmed you. They tore at you." She shuddered at the memory. "You weren't breathing."

Humor danced in his eyes. "I've been swarmed by many dozen vampires and survived."

"This isn't funny," she snapped at him. "This is no

time for jokes. You nearly died."

A chuckle rumbled deep in his throat. "But I didn't. And you always find time for jokes."

"This is different."

He brushed his hand down her face. "You were really that scared?"

"I was petrified," she told him. "I thought you wouldn't wake up."

"That jolt of lightning you gave my heart could have woken the dead."

His eyes met hers, the look in them so intense that they seared her soul. His magic lapped against hers like the tide at midnight. She closed her eyes, letting it wash over her. His hand had moved to her lower back. It began to knead loose a cluster of tense muscles that had been bothering her all day. Suddenly, just as a soft gasp brushed past her lips, he dropped his hand.

"Take Mr. Blackbrooke back to his hotel. Stay with him until his security arrives," Kai called over her shoulder, presumably to the commandos.

When the footsteps had grown distant, Kai looked down to her. "The vampires went straight for Duncan. They didn't seem interested in either of us."

"I noticed that too," she said, disappointed that he didn't resume his massage. Her back felt like it had gone through a trash compactor, then been fed to a flock of seagulls. "Why do you think that is? If the people controlling the Blood Orb are targeting the Magic Council, wouldn't they be after you as well?"

Kai looked around, like he expected the villains in question to be hiding in some dark corner nearby. "Come with me. We need to talk somewhere less exposed."

By the time they reached the hotel, most of Kai's wounds had healed. And by the time they stepped through the door to his suite, there wasn't a scratch on him. It must have been nice to have turbo-charged dragon healing.

Even though the wounds themselves were healed, blood still clung to his body like warpaint. As soon as they were inside, Sera rushed to the kitchen sink and filled a bowl with warm water. She carried the bowl and a stack of white towels over to the table. Why did hotel towels always have to be white?

Because they don't expect their guests to use them to wash their battle wounds, said the voice in her head.

Sera mentally hushed it and turned her attention to Kai. "Sit," she ordered.

To her surprise, he obeyed. That didn't stop a smug smile from tugging at his mouth.

"Something funny?" she asked, soaking the first towel in the water.

"You're cleaning my wounds."

"You don't have any wounds. They're all healed," she replied. "I'm cleaning the blood left by your former wounds."

"There's blood on you too." He pointed at her arms.

"I think that's your blood actually. From when I was jolting you awake."

He caught her hand and tugged gently, until her arm was in front of his nose. "Yes."

"You can smell your own blood?"

"Yes." He inhaled deeply. "My blood and a touch of your essence."

She gave him a puzzled look.

"Your sweat, Sera. I smell your sweat mixed in with my blood."

"Oh. Well, I was fighting and…" She pulled her arm away. "Whatever." Why was she even defending herself? He knew people sweated during a fight, especially a fight to the death against dozens of vampires. "Well, I'm glad you find my sweat funny," she finished, frowning at him.

"I don't find your sweat funny. I find your scent invigorating."

Danger! Danger! warned the voice in her head. Or was that just her normal thoughts?

"Oh," she said. "Then why were you smiling?"

"I was amused by the futility of this." He indicated the growing stack of blood-stained towels. "It would make more sense for me to step into the shower and wash all the blood away there." Magic boiled in his eyes, tart and tempting. "You could join me."

"No." She dunked the next towel into the bowl. "There will be no showering. And no joining." She wiped the towel across his arm, focusing her eyes on the blood she had to clean. The blood and nothing else.

They didn't say anything more for the next few minutes. His eyes were probably doing that magic-pulsing thing, but she wasn't looking. She had employed the tunnel-vision defense. She saw nothing but blood and torn clothing and bloody torn clothing, none of which could possibly be the least bit tempting.

Finally, she was finished. She carried her pile of bloody towels and her big bowl over to the kitchen sink and dumped them in. She probably should have called the cleaning staff to come get them, but she wasn't in the mood to answer questions about the bloody towels. Maybe Kai was right. Maybe he should have just taken a shower. Alone. Not with her. And especially not with soap sliding over naked flesh.

Sera shook her head, trying to exile the images. Her mind was so far in the gutter, that she couldn't even see the light anymore. She needed to stop fantasizing about Kai naked. And her naked with him. She washed the blood off her arms, then walked back to the table.

"Ok, so I guess I'll be going," she said, keeping her gaze locked on the empty space over his right shoulder.

"We still need to talk about the vampires," he reminded her.

"Oh? How about tomorrow? When we're rested." And not fresh off an adrenaline high. Adrenaline highs only ever led to doing stupid, reckless things. "It's been a long day. I should stretch out some before bed." She reached her arms behind her back, pulling them against each other. Something popped and pain shot up her neck. She cringed.

"You're injured," he said.

"No, I'm fine. Just a few pulled muscles and some sore spots. Between today's matches and our fight with the vampires, my body is finished. Dal was too busy sweeping up vampire bits to heal me. And Blackbrooke ran off before I could make him do it."

"Make him?"

"You know, sit on him and yank his arm behind his back until he agreed to heal me," she said.

"I can do a bit of healing myself," Kai told her. "And you don't even have to sit on me." He smirked. "Unless you want to."

"That's ok," she said, trying to keep the panic out of her voice. "You're still too weak."

He caught her hand as she stood. "I'm a mage who

turns into a dragon and steps on monsters. I can handle a few pesky vampires and still have enough power left to heal you."

He got to his feet, and before she could say another word, he was behind her, massaging her back. Soothing magic eased out of his fingertips. Her muscles relaxed into a pool of hot liquid mush, melting under his touch. His hands worked her back in deep, powerful strokes, kneading the tense magic out of her. Her magic slipped away, drifting lazily until it met his. And then it sizzled.

"Sera," he said, his voice deep and husky.

"Mmm?"

"Is that an issue of Mages Illustrated in your bag?"

Her eyes snapped open. She looked down at her sports bag. Sure enough, an issue of Mages Illustrated was peeking out of the top. The issue with him on the cover. Topless. Her liquid muscles tensed again.

"Naomi," she grumbled.

"Pardon?"

"She's been teasing me with this magazine for weeks now. She must have stuffed it in there this morning." Sera was happy her back was to him so he couldn't see her burning face. Mortification didn't even begin to cover how she felt right now. If they'd still been in the room with those piles of vampire parts, she'd have hidden herself under one.

"I see," was all Kai said. His tone was neutral. Without seeing his face, she couldn't tell how he felt about this—and she was too embarrassed to look at him.

"I don't, uh…stare at that picture or anything…" Though she couldn't claim she didn't ogle at the real thing. "…not that it's not a good picture of you…um…" *Stupid, stupid, stupid.* She cleared her throat. "This isn't going quite as well as it did in my head."

He snorted.

"So, those vampires, you say?" she asked. The best cure for mortification was to change the subject. Immediately. "Why do you think they went after Blackbrooke and not you?"

"Perhaps he was just the easier target. Or perhaps he is the target and not the entire Magic Council."

His hands hadn't stopped massaging her back, not even when she'd stumbled through that weak explanation of the magazine. Her muscles were starting to relax again.

"Why him?" she asked.

"He is the Game Architect," Kai replied. "The one who makes our mages stronger. The Convictionites might see his continued survival as a threat."

"More so than the dragon who could wipe out their entire organization in a single swoop?"

"They are too big. I couldn't do it in a *single* swoop. Maybe two or three," he added, a smile carrying through his words.

"And so modest too."

"You were the one who claimed I could do it in a single swoop."

"I was teasing."

He paused. "You do that a lot."

"Yes."

"Why?"

"Maybe I like you," she said, turning her head to give him a silly wink.

"Sera."

The seriousness in his voice stilled her next teasing remark. She turned around all the way, facing him. The look on his face was almost as painful as it had been when

Finn had slapped the Priming Bangles on his wrists and sucked out his magic.

"I like you too," he finally said, the back of his hand brushing her cheek.

She'd known he was attracted to her, but when he said he liked her now, it sounded like this was more than just him appreciating her body.

"And that hurts you?" she asked cautiously.

"Watching you in the Games is…unsettling. I don't wish for you to be hurt. In body or mind. The Magic Council is digging into your past. They are determined to figure out why you've been hiding your magic."

"They?" she asked. "But not you?"

"I don't care what you are." His finger traced up her arm. "I only care who you are. And you aren't a threat to them."

"I overheard your conversation with Blackbrooke." She caught his hand, intertwining her fingers with his. "I know you've been trying to protect me from them."

"I brought you here," Kai said. He sounded disgusted with himself.

"You didn't have much of a choice. Neither of us did." She sighed. "The world isn't big enough that I could hide from the Magic Council, not once they found out about my magic. And they would have come for you if you'd tried to help me."

"Let them come," he growled, agitation pulsing through his magic.

She leaned in, rising to her tiptoes to whisper into his ear, "Thank you. For all your help. I know I let my sarcasm get in the way, well, pretty much always, but I wanted you to know I am grateful for your help. I wouldn't have made it this far if you hadn't helped me control my magic. Well, kind of control my magic."

"You're better at it than you think," he told her, his breath dissolving against her cheek. "Your magic is strong. And the stronger a mage's magic is, the more difficult it is to control it."

"Thank you," she said again, kissing him lightly.

As she pulled back, their eyes met. He traced his finger along her shoulder and down her arm. He paused when it reached her hand, lingering on her wrist. His eyes never left hers. They watched her closely as he slid his magic across hers, nudging it gently. She gasped. Smiling, he brushed it against her again, this time with a little extra push. His mouth swallowed her second gasp, and he pulled her closer. His hands, lips, and magic worked in unison, massaging her body in slow, sensual strokes.

"Kai," she moaned.

His hands slid across her back, under her top. He peeled the torn garment off of her and tossed it to the floor.

"I was disappointed when our date was cut short the other night," he said, his lips teasing her ear.

"So was I." She reached around him, alleviating him from the burden of his ruined shirt too. A smirk tickled her lips. "All we got to do was dance."

"You dance beautifully." His gaze intensified. "You are beautiful," he added, his fingers teasing her through her lace bra.

Heat flooded her, rushing over her breasts, licking her skin as it cascaded down her body. His magic danced lower, sliding down her sides, down to her hips. His hands followed in its wake, burning the skin already taunted by magic. Slipping his hand under her skirt, he caressed her inner thigh in languid strokes, slowly inching upward. One of his fingers brushed against her panties. He stopped, and her breath caught in her throat.

"Only if you're ready," he said, looking her in the eye.

She resisted the urge to grab his hand and put it where it belonged. "Of course I'm ready," she said, her voice thick and rough. *Oh god, what am I doing?* "I've been ready since you massaged me."

He kissed her lips, her jaw, her neck. "I've been ready since you first strolled into my life, that badass mercenary with a big sword and even bigger mouth," he whispered into her ear. His magic crashed into hers, flooding her body.

"What are you doing to me?" she gasped, the heat between her legs growing.

The corner of his mouth drew upward, his smirk cocky and even a bit mischievous. Her head spun, dizzy from the rush of his magic. His magic's touch was feather-soft but daring. It teased every dip and curve of her body, leaving her squirming for more.

"Touch me," she pleaded, her breath stuttered.

"No."

"No?"

His smirk grew more devilish. "I'm having way too much fun," he said and poured more magic across her body.

"Fine," she growled, picking up the broken pieces of her self-reserve. "But two can play at that game."

She uncurled her magic toward him. She started at his neck—teasing the skin in soft, light ripples—then his shoulders. As she slid her magic lower, kissing the ridges of his sculpted chest, she went deeper. She saturated him inch by delicious inch. His muscles grew taut under her caress. His magic flared up, engulfing her. His scent, potent and thick with masculine spice, burned against her like hot ice.

"Sera," he growled, nipping her lip.

He tugged roughly at her skirt, pulling it and her panties off. His hands had forgotten his earlier refusal to touch her. One slid around her butt, gripping her hard. The other slipped between her legs, his fingertip tracing her curves. Fire flooded her, hot and liquid. It collided with her magic, rocking her whole body. She rubbed her body against his, moaning in frustration when the brush of denim against her thighs reminded her that he was still dressed from the waist down.

"Too many clothes," she muttered, fighting with his belt.

Finally, she got it loose. She hooked her fingers under his clothes, lowering into her knees to slide them down his legs. As she rose, she kissed her way up, in slow, languid strokes. He groaned, deep and primal, like an ancient predator. Like a dragon. His hands reached down to catch her, pulling her roughly into his arms. He carried her off toward the bedroom, his kisses impatient, his hands bold. They reached the bed, and he lowered her onto it with surprising gentleness considering the fervor of his caresses.

"Are you sure?" he asked. He was kneeling on the mattress beside her, looking down upon her, but he hadn't climbed onto her yet. From the strained look on his face, it was taking every shred of willpower not to do so.

"What would you do if I said no?" she teased, tracing her finger down his rigid stomach.

"Curse you as an evil temptress," he growled, his eyes rolling back as he suppressed a groan. He caught her hand before it could venture lower, then looked at her, his eyes serious, if not throbbing with desire. "Then go take a cold shower. With lots of ice. Maybe summon a blizzard while I'm at it."

"Well, we couldn't have that. Frostbite is nasty business, even for a dragon. You could lose a toenail—uh, talon."

Then, smiling, she gave his arm a tug, pulling him onto her.

CHAPTER SEVENTEEN

The Tunnel Vision Defense

WHETHER FROM KAI'S healing massage or the other sort of massage that came afterward, Sera woke up the next morning feeling refreshed. She felt more refreshed, in fact, than she had since that pinecone-scented mage had showed up on her doorstep nearly a month ago to inform her that she'd been entered into the Magic Games—and, oh, by the way, participation was not voluntary.

She rolled over on the bed. Kai wasn't there, but he hadn't been gone long. His pillow was still thick with his scent. Sera grabbed it, pressing it to her nose and inhaling deeply. Her toes might have curled a little.

Diffused sunlight shone through the billowy curtains, a gentle breeze rippling across the soft fabric. It was still early—she glanced at the clock—just not early enough. All she wanted was to nestle into the soft sheets and sleep, but soon she'd have to wake up. She had to get to the Magic Games. In less than two hours, she'd be facing down her next opponents. She only hoped it wasn't vampires again. She was sick and tired of vampires.

Extending her yawn into a stretch, Sera rolled up. She could feel Kai in the next room. His magic was taut and alert, like it usually was. Except for last night. She teetered between a smile and a blush. She'd made Kai lose control, made his magic do things she'd never felt before, made him utter noises that she would give anything to hear again.

Despite his confident—ok, arrogant—demeanor, he'd turned out to be a caring lover, as attentive to her needs as he was concerned about his own. In fact, nothing seemed to arouse him more than her own pleasure. And he'd experimented with that—thoroughly. By the time they finally went to sleep, he'd pushed every button in her body, including ones she hadn't even known existed.

"Calm down," she whispered to herself, trying to push down the heat pulsing through her body as she remembered what he'd done to her. His hands. His lips. His tongue.

She pivoted away from the door, beelining for the bathroom. And the shower. This was no time for her raging libido.

A few minutes later, she was clean, dressed in a fluffy bathrobe, and thinking only chaste thoughts. Ok, scratch that last one. But she was *trying* to think only chaste thoughts. When she got to the fighting pit, the battle would smack the remaining giddiness out of her. Hopefully not literally.

She turned the doorknob and stepped out into the living room, nearly tripping over a bag of clothes in front of the door. She snatched it up and backed into the bathroom to get dressed. New clothes kept appearing out of nowhere—like magic.

When she emerged the second time, Kai was sitting

on the sofa, talking on his phone. From the half of the conversation that she could hear, it sounded like the commandos were on the other end. Kai turned to look over the back of the sofa. He met her eyes and waved her over. She approached, encouraged by the fond look in his eyes and by the scent of hot blueberry pancakes.

"Check in with the other Magic Council members present for the Games. So far, the vampires have only gone after Blackbrooke, but that doesn't mean he's their only target. They *all* need extra security," Kai spoke into the phone.

He looked up at Sera and pointed at the breakfast tray on the coffee table. In addition to a stack of blueberry pancakes—lightly dusted with powdered sugar—there was a large glass of milk. Mmm.

"Look, I don't care what they claim, Callum," Kai said impatiently. "The fact is that a magic hate group is in possession of a magical artifact that can control vampires. They are using this power here, in New York, to target a prestigious member of the Magic Council. They aren't just going to give up. And Sera is far too busy jumping through Duncan Blackbrooke's Magic Games hoops to save his ass again, let alone babysit the entire Magic Council contingent here. Tell my esteemed colleagues that they can either get some added security or get dead."

As Sera sat down next to him, she could hear the buzz of one of the commandos speaking.

"Yes, you can quote me on that," Kai said and hung up the phone. He set it on the table, then turned toward her. "Good morning, Sera. I ordered you some breakfast while you were in the shower."

A warm flush spread across her cheeks as she remembered the thoughts that had necessitated the shower. "Thanks," she said. "I love pancakes."

"I know." The look in his eyes made her blush again, as though he were saying, "I know what else you like."

She grabbed the plate, focusing on the pancakes. Her tunnel-vision defense hadn't held up long last night, but maybe it would work this time. As she slid the fork into the first pancake, Kai leaned over to kiss her on her head. She jumped a little, and the fork tumbled from her fingers, bouncing against the plush white carpet. She stared down at the blueberry-stained spot and groaned.

"You look forlorn," Kai said.

"Between the bloody towels and the blueberry carpet stains, the hotel manager is going to blow a fuse." She cringed, imagining hotel manager parts and pieces raining down on the lobby. "Do you have any idea how many monsters I have to kill before I can pay off those damages?"

"It's just a few towels and a tiny stain, Sera."

"And the mutilated remains of the hotel manager."

"I wasn't aware that he was dead," he said drily.

"He will be after he sees this mess."

"Is it possible that you're overreacting?"

She wiped down her fork, then cut into the pancakes. "I'd never admit to that." She ate her way through the first pancake, then, realizing she was being rude, held out her fork to Kai.

He shook his head. "I already ate."

"What did you have?"

"A roll with salami."

Of course. "No sheep? Or goats?" she added with a smile.

"The kitchen was fresh out of grass-fed quadrupeds."

She snorted, and milk shot out of her nose.

Thankfully, it didn't get on him. "Sorry," she muttered, patting her face with a napkin. "Geez, that was really attractive."

"You're always attractive," he told her. "Even with milk shooting out of your nose." He leaned down to kiss her on the head again, watching her closely the whole time, like he was afraid she'd bolt.

"Still here," she told him with a smile.

"I was…concerned," he said. "The last time I kissed you, you dropped a fork and proceeded to plan out the murder of the hotel manager."

"Hey, I didn't plan his murder," she protested, dipping a piece of pancake in some milk that had spilled onto her plate. "I only said he'd explode when he saw the mess I'd made. And I didn't drop the fork because you kissed me."

His dark brows lifted. "Oh?"

"I dropped it because you kissed me while I was thinking salacious thoughts, and I, uh, felt guilty about that."

He studied her face for a moment, then said, "Tell me."

"Tell you what?"

"I want to hear more about these salacious thoughts. Was I naked? Were you? And what were we doing?"

"We're always naked in my thoughts. And doing, um, things."

He lifted his hand to her neck, caressing the sensitive skin. It slid down, tracing her collarbone, then disappeared beneath her top. His fingers kissed her breasts, his lips tickled her jaw.

"Like this?" he whispered, his words grazing her ear. Her skin tingled with goosebumps.

"For instance."

She tried to concentrate, to think through the fog clouding her mind, but he was making that impossible. His hand stroked the inside of her thigh.

"I liked it when you were wearing a skirt," he said, his voice strained.

"I could do it again."

"Yes." His hand slid under her top, his fingernails massaging her skin. His other hand moved up her thigh, rubbing her through the stretchy fabric of her sports pants. His magic whispered across her skin like a warm summer breeze.

She moaned, deep in her throat, losing a grip on her plate. Kai caught it one-handed before it hit the ground. He shoved it hurriedly onto the table, then returned that hand to her back. He tugged her shirt up, lifting it over her head.

"Kai," she protested, her words nearly dissolving before they left her lips.

"Hmm?" His voice buzzed against her bellybutton.

"We'll be late for the Games."

"Plenty of time," he said, kissing down her stomach. His tongue teased the waistband of her pants.

Oh, to hell with it! She grabbed hold of his shoulders and pushed him down onto the sofa.

"Your pancakes are cold."

Sera looked at Kai, who was leaning leisurely against the puffy arm of the sofa. Deep breaths purred inside his chest, and he returned her glance with a satisfied smirk. He did look a tad guilty about the pancakes, though.

"They're fine," she assured him, taking a bite. "Just as good cold as hot."

"And you?"

"Sorry?"

"Are you fine?" he asked.

"Yes." She leaned in to kiss him, a smile on her lips. "Though maybe a bit too relaxed to fight any monsters at the moment."

"So basically you'd like me to work you up into a frenzy, then unleash you on the monsters?"

"You wouldn't dare," she said, poking him in the chest.

He kissed her finger. "I would dare a lot of things, sweetheart."

"The Magic Council—"

"Forget them," he said. "This has nothing to do with them."

"Blackbrooke was on your case about me, and that was before we slept together. He would have an aneurysm if he found out about us."

"Let him. I don't care what he thinks."

"Could he pull you as my coach?" Sera asked.

Kai said nothing. But his silence told all.

"That's what I thought. We can't tell him, Kai. We can't tell *anyone*."

He looked at her. "Do you trust me, Sera?"

"I trust you to have my back in a fight," she said, smiling. Her smile died on her lips as a cool, expressionless mask slid across his face.

"That's not what I mean." He expelled an exasperated sigh. "After all we've been through, you still don't trust me. Not really. Not completely."

"I..." She opened her mouth, ready to lie, but

decided he deserved better than that. "I don't trust easily." Her secret was too dangerous. She looked up from her clasped hands, meeting his eyes. "And neither do you."

"That's true. I don't trust easily," he agreed. "But you're not a very good liar, Sera. I see right through you, through that hard and tough exterior. You're sweet inside. Gooey even."

"Gooey?" she said, coughing.

"You heard me, Miss Badass Mercenary. I know you, and you're no revolutionary. Whatever secrets you're keeping locked away inside, they don't make you a threat to the Magic Council. The Council has nothing to fear from you until the day they go after someone you care about. You fight hard for the people you love."

"Yes." She skewered a piece of pancake onto her fork. "I do."

"Good. You'll need that fighting spirit today at the Games."

Sera's phone buzzed across the table. She ignored it.

"Are you going to get that?" he asked.

"No."

"Care to elaborate?"

"No."

He folded his hands together and stared at her. Sera lasted about two seconds beneath the dragon's stare before she cracked.

"There's no point in checking. I already know who it is. One of my two stalkers."

"There's another one now? Besides Finn?" His face betrayed no emotion, but the bolt of magic lightning that blew up the toaster on the counter behind him was pretty much a dead giveaway.

"Technically, Finn was the second," she said, picking

up her phone with a heavy sigh. "The first is Cutler. He keeps messaging me, asking me to go out with him."

"Let me see that."

"No." She sat on the phone, then, before he could do so much as arch an irked eyebrow at her, she said, "I have this hunch about Cutler."

"That his parents are bribing the Magic Council with large sums of money to keep him out of a mental institution?"

"No." She stopped. "Wait, huh? Is that true?"

"Sadly, no."

"So you were being playful?"

"Roar," he said, his face deadpan as he clawed the air like a kitten.

Sera snorted, thankfully this time without milk in her mouth. "Ok, my hunch. I've been running into Cutler everywhere since we arrived in New York. Macy's, Trove, the fighting arena…"

"All the places that the photos Finn sent you were taken," Kai finished for her.

"Yes."

"You think Cutler is working for Finn," he said. "That he's one of the mages in Finn's cult of crazy."

"Cutler sure fits the bill for crazy," she pointed out.

"Hmm." He grabbed his phone off the table. "I think I'll have a chat with Cutler."

"It's just an idea. He could have nothing to do with Finn," she said. "Maybe he's just engaging in normal stalker behavior."

"As opposed to criminal mastermind minion stalking behavior?" He looked up from his phone. "If this is your way of dissuading me from talking to him, it needs work."

"Just promise me you won't open your chat with Cutler by tearing his arms off."

"Of course," he said. "I never open interrogations—er, chats that way. You can't start by going straight for the big guns. You need to build up to it."

"Kai!"

He snickered. "Kidding. I don't tear people's arms off. You let me worry about Finn and Cutler. You concentrate on the Games."

Sera's phone buzzed beneath her butt. She grabbed it and flipped the case open—and immediately wished she hadn't. It was another message from Finn. She showed Kai the picture on the screen, one of her fighting the vampires in the Empire State Building last night.

A moment later, her phone exploded.

CHAPTER EIGHTEEN
Black Magic

SERA STOOD UP, looking at the broken remains of her phone strewn across the living room. Then she turned to Kai, gaping. "You blew up my phone," she said quietly.

"I apologize," he said. At least he looked guilty about it. Mostly just fire-breathing, devastation-wreaking angry, but also a little guilty. "I'll get you another one."

She plucked the melted SIM card from the ground. "I'll need another one of these too."

He swiped a few things across his phone screen, then looked up at her. "You'll have a new one before we leave the hotel."

"This happens a lot, doesn't it?"

"On occasion."

Yeah, right. It probably happened every time he lost his temper. Dragons were a moody bunch. And yet, she couldn't resist teasing him.

"How many phones have you gone through this month?"

"One or two."

She poked the fire again. "I've had the same phone for

years."

"I find that surprising considering your hobbies."

"Verbal sparring with dragons?" she muttered under her breath.

"I heard that," he said. "And no. I meant your other hobby: hunting down monsters." His eyes hardened. "Without magic."

"Hunting monsters isn't a hobby. It's a paycheck. And it was magic—your magic, to be precise—that broke my phone. *Not* a monster. My phone survived many years of my magic-free monster hunting lifestyle. What it didn't survive was my new lifestyle with a certain dragon-shifting mage."

"So I'm part of your lifestyle." His magic grinned. Yes, grinned. Magic could grin, even if its master was stingy with the smiles.

"Yes," she said.

She could have denied it, but that wouldn't have been fair to either of them. He was a part of her life now, as much as Naomi was. The question was, could she trust him? She'd known Naomi for years, and she still hadn't told her that she was Dragon Born. It wasn't exactly a prime conversation starter. In fact, it was more like a conversation ender. And then, ten seconds later, agents of the Magic Council would storm the room.

"So, as someone who is an acknowledged part of your life, you wouldn't mind if I'm concerned for your wellbeing?"

"I guess not," she said slowly, wondering where this was going.

"Finn is stalking you. He's obviously obsessed with you."

"He's not my type."

"This isn't funny, Sera."

"No," she agreed. "But there's nothing we can do about Finn right now."

"I have already done something. I've called in some extra security to protect you."

"Like bodyguards?"

He nodded.

"That's not concern," she told him. "It's meddling. With a side helping of jealousy. What are these bodyguards supposed to protect me from? From someone taking a picture of me? Finn hasn't done anything more than that and send creepy stalker messages."

"Yet," he said. "I don't like it. Finn is up to something. The first thing he did after breaking out of prison was start stalking you. And Cutler, whether or not he's working for Finn, is insane himself."

"I thought I was supposed to worry about the Games, not Finn or Cutler. Your words. Not mine."

He nodded. "Precisely. Which is why I'm sending some of my guys to guard you. So you don't have to worry about those stalkers while you're busy with the Games. For once, don't be stubborn. Let someone take care of you."

"Your security guys should be taking care of Blackbrooke and the Magic Council mages. The vampires are targeting them. No one is targeting me. All I have are two weirdos annoying me with sleazy messages."

"Sera—"

She plopped down on the sofa beside him. "I'll be fine."

"What if you're wrong? I can't just leave you unprotected."

"I've been fighting monsters since years before I met

you. I assure you I can take care of myself."

He watched her for a few moments, silent, calculating. Finally, he spoke. "No. I don't buy it. Finn is up to something. Something big. He wouldn't be sending you messages for no reason."

"Kai," she said calmly, touching his hand. "Finn is a psychopath. Psychopaths do all kinds of things for no reason."

He frowned. "Is that supposed to make me feel better?"

"I guess not."

"You need to keep your mind in one piece, no matter what Duncan throws at you in the Games," he told her.

"I thought you didn't think I could do it."

"I didn't say that. I only said no one ever had." He clasped her hand. "But you aren't like anyone I've ever met."

"Kai, I…I don't know what to say."

"Well, that's a first."

She punched him in the arm. She didn't put too much power behind it—hitting dragons gave her bloody knuckles and bruised bones—but she couldn't leave that comment unanswered.

"You can't watch your back the whole time, Sera. Not if you want to beat Duncan at his own game."

He had a point. The more things she had to worry about, the easier it would be for Blackbrooke to break her mind. And the most important thing was to keep the Magic Council in the dark about her forbidden origin. She could stomach a punch to her pride if it meant preserving that secret.

"Fine," she said, climbing over to sit on his lap, facing him. "*You* can stay with me. Send your guards to babysit someone else. I want the very best."

"Hmm."

Stroking his ego was a dirty trick, but she wasn't above dirty tricks. If she was going to have a guard on her, she at least wanted someone who wouldn't fall to pieces in the heat of battle. Kai was someone who made other people fall to pieces. He was the logical choice. And that had nothing to do with the fact that he was nice to look at.

The voice in her head snorted.

"Ok," Kai said, watching her. Maybe she got glassy-eyed when she was talking to herself. "I'll talk to Duncan about letting me into the backstage area. You drive a hard bargain."

"Thanks to my spectacular powers of persuasion."

He snorted. "Stubborn woman."

"That's what you love about me," she said, kissing him. "That and my uncommon wit. Admit it."

"I can think of a few other things." He returned the kiss, his hands stroking her thighs.

Someone tapped out three crisp, professional knocks on the door. Kai cursed.

"Your commandos are here," Sera said. She could feel their magic humming on the other side of the door.

"Yes."

Sera slid off his lap and walked toward the door, grabbing her sports bag along the way. When she opened the door, Callum's brows lifted in surprise. Behind him, Tony grinned and nudged Dal in the arm. Dal winked at her. Great. So much for keeping her and Kai a secret. Sera stood there, trying not to look like she'd just been caught with her hand in the cookie jar. Apparently, she failed because Dal winked at her again. Kai wasn't helping matters. He walked up behind her and set his hand on the small of her back, his magical aura growling like an overly protective dragon. The commandos took a collective step back.

"Oh, for heaven's sake! Save it for someone who's actually a threat, Kai," Sera said.

Then she resettled her bag on her shoulder and squeezed out of the doorway. As she passed Tony, he handed her a new phone. It was identical to her old one. She blinked. Twice. Even the case was the same, pink engraved with flowers and bees. She swiped past a few screens. All her contacts were there. So were her messages and photos. Everything was exactly where it was supposed to be. It was magic. Black magic.

"Should I be concerned that your people were able to break into my account so easily?" she asked Kai as they walked down the hall.

"No. My people are competent."

Behind him, Callum was smirking at her. So *he* was the tech wizard.

"Besides," Kai added. "It's not hard to guess a girly password like 'PinkLily'."

Lily was the name of Sera's scooter, and she was pink. She also sparkled.

"Girly?" Sera coughed.

"You are very feminine," Kai said calmly.

"I'll just go get my sword and you can repeat that, dragon breath."

Kai chuckled, and the commandos joined in. Sera glared at them, but that only seemed to amuse them more.

A few minutes later, they were walking across the hotel lobby. Naomi was standing at the reception desk, flirting with the staff. When she saw Sera, she swiped a cookie from the plate on the counter and hurried over.

"For you," she said, handing Sera the cookie. It was chocolate chip and the size of at least three regular cookies.

Sera took a bite. "Thanks," she replied, and she meant it. The cookie was soft and fresh. The chocolate chips were still gooey. There was enough sugar in there to kill most mortals, but Sera didn't care. She would die happy.

Naomi grinned as she watched her take another bite. "Come on." She linked her arm in Sera's and walked faster, putting some distance between them and the guys.

"Where's Riley?" Sera asked.

"He'll be along soon. He slept in this morning. Last night's field trip to Trove was a little too much excitement for him."

Sera stopped in her tracks. "Don't tell me monsters attacked."

"No." She pulled Sera along. "But he did have a few too many of those magic cocktails."

"I still can't believe you brought him to Trove," Sera said. "Do you know what goes on there? Did you have a look at what those mages were doing on the dance floor?"

"Oh, we saw *that* all right. It was really hard to miss." Naomi's eyes twinkled—then shifted green. "I blame the cocktails they serve there."

"Those same cocktails that Riley had?" She sighed. "You got my brother drunk!"

"Of course not. He is perfectly capable of getting drunk all by himself."

"Did you at least find him a date? A nice girl preferably. Who doesn't do unseemly things on the dance floor."

An impish smile tugged at Naomi's glossy pink lips. "I've heard about a few unseemly things you yourself were doing on that dance floor."

Sera blushed. "How?"

"Talked to the bartender. Apparently, he knows your dragon. I heard you two practically set the sprinklers off with your magic."

"I…" She cleared the frog from her throat. "That's not even true."

Naomi squeezed her arm. "Good for you. You deserve to let your hair down once in a while."

"Riley," Sera reminded her.

"Oh, right." Naomi smirked at her. "He danced with a few women, but his heart wasn't really in it. It was disappointing actually. He loosened up after a few drinks, and later the two of us danced a bit together. And then there was more drinking and…" She tapped her cheek thoughtfully. "Then we sat at the bar and made fun of all the weirdos in the club."

"Not to their faces, I hope."

"No, but they wouldn't have noticed anyway. They were all too wasted."

"So, basically, you got my brother drunk and then flirted with him," Sera teased.

"Sera, I flirt with everyone."

"Yeah, I know. Just go easy on Riley, ok? He can't handle a woman like you."

Naomi sighed. "None of them can, honey." Her wistful look flipped to devious. "But enough about me," she said, her voice dropping to a whisper as she stole a glance back at Kai. He and the commandos were far back enough that they couldn't hear. Probably. "You didn't come back to our suite last night, young lady." She wiggled her finger sternly at Sera, but the amused twinkle in her eyes ruined the effect.

"Vampires attacked," Sera said.

"Oh, did they now? The *whole* night?"

"They attacked Duncan Blackbrooke."

"The Game Architect?"

"Yes. And he's completely worthless in a fight. Kai and I had to fight off all the vampires ourselves. And there were dozens of them."

"How did you defeat them?" Naomi asked.

"I blew them up."

Naomi blinked, then cleared her throat. "All of them?"

"Not all. We burned a few before that. Then they were swarming Kai. I freaked out and set them all on fire and then...pop. The vampires exploded."

Naomi chewed on her lip. She looked like she didn't know what to say. She finally settled on, "Wow."

"Kai got torn up pretty badly, so I brought him back to his suite."

A wicked grin spread across Naomi's face, displacing the shock. "You sure must be a good nurse."

"Huh?"

Naomi wiggled her eyebrows. "I've never seen the dragon in such a good mood before. He actually looks..." She winked at her. "...relaxed."

Sera turned her gaze forward. The tunnel vision defense worked against mischievous, teasing fairy friends too.

Naomi dropped her voice further and whispered. "I can't believe you slept with Kai Drachenburg. Ok, I can believe it but, wow. Just wow." Her hand tightened on Sera's shoulder, squeezing her closer. "And?"

"And?"

"And spill the beans. I want to hear details."

"He's right behind us," Sera hissed through gritted teeth.

"Ok, you don't need to say anything. From the way you're glowing, it must have been good. Your eyes just had an orgasm. Eye-orgasm."

"There's no such thing."

Naomi smirked at her. "Oh, sure there is. And your eyes just had one."

There was no point in arguing with fairies about things like these. And Sera had bigger problems to worry about. They'd reached Madison Square Garden.

As they entered the lobby, Naomi released Sera's shoulder and fell back to flirt with the commandos. Kai moved forward to walk beside Sera. He didn't say anything to indicate that he'd heard her conversation with Naomi, but he wasn't a very expressive person. Sera studied his face, trying to see this relaxed look Naomi had mentioned, but he just looked serious. No, not just serious. Vexed. Magic cracked and sizzled across his body, snapping in tight, agitated coils. And Sera had just seen why: Blackbrooke was walking straight for them, a contingent of security guards at his back.

"He looks upset," Sera commented to Kai.

"What happened last night after the vampire attack?" Kai asked the commandos.

They closed around him as one smooth, coordinated unit.

"We brought him back to his hotel," Tony told him.

"He was still too much in shock to heal himself, so I did it," said Dal.

"Then we stayed with him until his extra security

came," added Callum.

In other words, they'd acted professional and competent. Blackbrooke had no reason to be pissed off with Kai. Except the look on his face said he was exactly that. He stepped into their path and marched up to Kai.

"We need to talk," he said to Kai but looked at Sera.

They followed him to the side. He led them to a large potted plant, then spun around and glared at them, his eyes screaming murder.

"What game are you playing at?" he demanded, fuming and red-faced.

Kai stared back at him, his face unreadable. "I don't know what you mean," he said calmly.

"This woman," he growled, pushing his finger in Sera's face. "She is not what she seems to be."

CHAPTER NINETEEN
Fighting Magic with Magic

THE FIRST THOUGHT that rushed through Sera's head was that Blackbrooke had figured out she was Dragon Born and had come to sentence her to death. The second thing that hit her wasn't so much a thought as it was a feeling of complete panic coupled with the intense urge to flee. Before she could succumb to this urge, he spoke again.

"I saw the magic she did to those vampires last night." He was talking to Kai, like she didn't even matter here. "She's a Magic Breaker, a Sniffer, an Elemental, and a few dozen other things. That's not magic you can just hide under the rug, Kai. Mages aren't born like that every day, especially not mages from an unknown dynasty. What family are you from and why are you hiding it?" he demanded of Sera. Oh, so apparently she existed after all. "Did they kick you out? Disown you?" His eyes narrowed to tiny slits. "Are you a criminal?"

Kai stepped forward, cutting him off. Even though he'd probably done it to protect Blackbrooke from getting a well-deserved thump on the head, there was something incredibly romantic about the way he put himself between them.

"Say nothing," he whispered to her, then turned his icy glare on Blackbrooke. "As stated by Article 1, Section 22 of the Supernatural Decree of 1993, a mage may at any time sever ties with his or her dynasty without fear of persecution from said dynasty or the Magic Council. Also," he added, a growl buzzing on his lips. "It's really poor taste for the mage representing the esteemed position of Game Architect to engage in idle gossip. Enough with the baseless accusations, Duncan. If she were a criminal, we'd know about it. Leave the gossiping to your sister. She, at least, doesn't muck it up."

Blackbrooke let out an indignant huff. He looked like he'd just swallowed a swarm of his magic wasps.

"Sera is here, going through the Games as ordered," Kai continued, ignoring Blackbrooke's huffing and puffing. "She isn't doing anything wrong. And she saved your life, Duncan," Kai cut in quickly, before Blackbrooke could even open his mouth.

Blackbrooke pressed his lips together, even more sour-faced than before.

"Now," Kai said. "Let us pass. Sera needs to prepare for her first match of the day. It starts in half an hour."

Like oil over asphalt, a sick grin slid across Blackbrooke's face. "There's been a change of plans. Her match starts in ten minutes." He turned that oily smile on Sera. "Congratulations, you've been upgraded."

The front pouch of Sera's bag buzzed. She tried to ignore it.

"Aren't you going to check that?" Blackbrooke asked.

"I'd rather not. I haven't had the best luck with SMSs lately."

His eyes hardened. "Ms. Dering, check your phone."

With a heavy sigh, she dug into her bag and pulled out her phone. "It's from the 'Magic Games'. Sounds like a pleasant fellow," she added with a smirk she didn't feel.

"You really should be taking this more seriously, Ms. Dering. The Magic Games are a long and glorious tradition."

When she didn't respond, he frowned. Maybe he'd been expecting a few oohhs and aahhs. Or a parade of elves to march through the lobby, their voices raised in song.

"In other words," he said, standing poised and pretentious. "More magic, less sarcasm. Your smart mouth won't help you in the pit. Especially not now." He didn't cackle maniacally, but he sure looked like he wanted to. Maybe maniacal cackling wasn't posh enough for him.

"Kai," she said, showing him her new fight schedule. "It's completely different. My opponents aren't even the same as before."

Kai glanced across the screen, his magic crackling like shifting ice. "What's the meaning of this, Duncan?"

"Honestly, Kai, I don't see why you're surprised," Blackbrooke said. "After the magic she demonstrated last night, surely you don't expect us to let her just waltz through the lower tiers of the Magic Games." His delighted gaze shifted to Sera. "She's special. And special mages need special challenges. To figure out her magic, we need to push her. We need to crack her," he added with a wistful smile. He looked like his birthday had come early. And Christmas. And a few dozen other holidays too.

"This isn't a challenge," Kai said, scanning the

timetable. His head snapped up. "It's a full-scale assault. These are some of the top-rated mages in the world."

"Not all. *You* are missing from the lineup, Kai," replied Blackbrooke, looking like he'd love nothing better than to remedy that.

Sera hid her hands behind her back, squeezing them together. If Blackbrooke found some way to make Kai fight her in the Games, she'd be screwed. It took everything she had—every shred of magic, every punch, every trick—just to hold her own against him. She couldn't fight him and protect her mind from Blackbrooke too.

Kai glanced at her, then back to Blackbrooke. "I cannot fight Sera. It is against the rules of the Games."

When he reached over and took her hand behind her back, she squeezed it in appreciation. If her heart hadn't already stopped at the beginning of this conversation, it would have stuttered in relief.

"Yes, yes. You're right." Blackbrooke's face crinkled, the lines writing out the story of his displeasure. "As her coach and sponsor, you cannot be compelled to fight her. However, if you truly care about her, you will agree to do it of your own volition."

"I guess I don't really care about her," Kai said, glancing sidelong at Sera. His magic tickled hers.

She struggled to keep a straight face as she looked up at Kai and replied, "I knew it all along. You only agreed to help me so I'd have to kill monsters for you."

"No one decapitates monsters like you do, baby."

Sera choked down a snort—mostly.

"Oh, yes. How amusing," Blackbrooke said drily.

Kai nodded toward the door to the backstage area. "Sera, let's go."

Blackbrooke pushed out his hands, blocking him.

"Move," Kai said, giving him a look that could have frozen lava.

"You're not allowed back there."

"I'm going." He pushed his phone in Blackbrooke's face. "Look at this."

Sera looked too. A slideshow with all of Finn's messages to her was playing on Kai's screen. Of course he'd copied them to his phone.

Blackbrooke's eyes went wide as he watched the slideshow. "Finn sent all of these?" He glanced over at Sera. "To her?"

"Yes, your lost prisoner is coming for Sera." He paused, and the room grew so silent that time stood still. "I'm not going to let that happen."

"Well, Kai, to be fair..." Blackbrooke's nose scrunched up, repulsed yet embarrassed, like he'd vomited in his own beard. "Finn wasn't really *my* prisoner per se."

"I delivered him to Atlantis." Kai stepped forward, his massive figure casting a dragon-sized shadow over Blackbrooke. "Gift-wrapped." He took another step, practically running him over. "You were the one they called in to rehabilitate him. Now, I ask you this." Pointing at the photos, his voice dropped to a near-savage growl, "Is he rehabilitated?"

Blackbrooke buckled before the dragon's ire, his muscles twitching, his cool and clam demeanor scrambled. "Go. Just go with her." He stepped aside, waving Kai through. "Keep her safe. She's obviously an asset."

Kai set his hand on her shoulder, nudging her toward the entrance.

"Just one thing, Kai," Blackbrooke's voice called out

before they disappeared through the door.

They looked back at him.

"You are not to interfere with the testing," he said, his tone more confident now that Kai wasn't breathing fire down his neck.

Kai nodded, then swung the door shut behind them. They headed down the long corridor. A melody of thumps and roars, peppered with pain, groaned through the open door of the fighting pit at the end, echoing down the hall.

"It sounds like someone is setting off bombs in there," Sera commented.

Kai made a noncommittal noise.

"So Blackbrooke is an ass, but it turns out he's not completely unreasonable," she said.

"Mmm."

Sera tried again. "I'm thinking of fighting the next match topless. What do you think about that idea?"

This time, he stopped—and turned his angry dragon eyes on her. "That would be unadvisable. You do not need to pick up any more stalkers."

She smirked at him. "I was just checking to see if you were listening to me."

"I always listen to you, Sera. I just don't always have something to say. I haven't got your gift."

"You mean my mouth."

"Oh, I've got that, sweetheart."

He did a quick visual scan of the hall to make sure they were alone, then turned toward her. He kissed her once, slow and easy, his hand lingering on her chin long after the kiss had ended. Her skin tingled from his caress; her blood surged with magic.

"You're distracting me," she managed to croak out.

He stepped back, shaking out his shoulders. Apparently, she hadn't been the only one distracted. She liked that. She liked it a lot.

"Your opponent is called Weather Wizard," Kai said, his momentary distraction over.

Sera made a concentrated effort not to comment on the mage's name, even though it was practically begging to be mocked.

"He's a first tier mage, his elemental magic ranked number twelve in the world," he continued, an added edge in his voice. He'd probably guessed what she was thinking. "Fighting him will not be easy. It will require some extra finesse. Most elementals can only control one element. Some can control two. Only a select few can manage more than that. Even most first tier elemental mages cannot summon all the elements."

"I know this already," she said, motioning for him to fast forward. "Get to the good stuff. Tell me how to defeat him."

"Best him at his own game."

"Best him at his own game?" she repeated. "But I don't even know what I'm doing. And he's apparently the grandfather of the elements."

"You can summon all the elements," he said.

"And? So can you."

"Remember what I said about mages with the ability to summon every element."

"That they're all first tier mages."

"Precisely."

She didn't know what to say to that, so she settled for nothing.

"You're a first tier elemental," he told her. "A very strong first tier elemental."

"I figured as much after I blew those vampires to bits last night."

"I have never seen anything like that."

She winked at him. "That's because you dozed through that part of the fight."

"Sera."

"Sorry, I'll be good now," she promised, folding her hands together in front of her.

"You can do this," he told her. "Weather Wizard can summon all the elements, but so can you. You can counter him. Remember how we practiced stringing spells together?"

"Vaguely. Kai, my head is mush." She raised her hand to her forehead. "I'm not sure I can fight him with magic."

"You have fought me with magic many times before."

"Yes, but…well, I still have so little control over it."

"You did fine last night against the vampires," he reminded her.

"That was a matter of life or death." Though, come to think of it, so was this. "When the vampires swarmed you, I panicked. And you helped me in that fight too."

"I'm here now." He took her hand, giving it a squeeze.

"I'm afraid," she admitted. "Afraid to use my magic. Afraid to let my guard down."

"Just use a little magic. You don't have to blast every bit of magic you have. And there's no need to make your opponent explode. In fact, it's probably better if you don't."

"My gauge is broken. My magic is basically on or off."

"I know you can do it," he said, squeezing her hand again.

A mage stepped out of the pit, his steps wobbling as

he passed through the door into the hallway. His clothes looked even more trashed than Sera's had yesterday. He limped down the hall toward the locker rooms, trailing crimson drops.

The guard waved Sera forward. Kai gave her a stiff—presumably comforting—nod as she turned to face her fate.

She entered the pit, looking up. The stands were packed full, the audience jumping and shouting in excitement. She could see them. She just couldn't hear them through the magic barrier. A wall of thick, solid ice magic, it was thick enough to block out all sound, yet transparent enough for the audience to see everything that went on in the pit. Blackbrooke must have been expecting powerful magic to fly in this match. Sera tried not to feel too daunted by that. Fear would only make it easier for him to crack her mind.

She walked across the sandy ground, her footsteps echoing against the magic barrier. Her opponent, Weather Wizard, was at the other end of the pit, standing posed like a Greek hero of old. A cluster of teenage girls sat in the stands close by, giggling and fanning themselves with every ripple of his golden mane in the magically-charged wind. Oh, boy.

Despite his pretty boy appearance, Weather Wizard was dangerous. She could feel it in the magic that crackled in the pit, the magic of a first-tier elemental mage with an appetite for destruction and the power to sate it. But he wasn't even the biggest threat in there.

Twin lines of fairies stood along two facing sides of the pit, a web of their magic linking them together, allowing them to work as one. As Sera neared her opponent, the fairies began to chant. Their magic flared up, curling around her. Suddenly, between one blink and the next, the fighting pit was gone. Instead, Sera was standing in a field, high up on a mountain.

CHAPTER TWENTY
Weather Wizard

LONG, FROST-CRUSTED grass glistened in the pink-orange light of the setting sun. A frigid breeze whistled across the grass and bit at Sera's cheeks, pecking her fingertips with frozen kisses. She couldn't see the fairies anymore. She could, however, see Weather Wizard—and he was smirking at her.

"Lost lamb, lost lamb, run along home," he taunted in a sing-song voice. He was hoarding crazy like it was going out of style.

Sera sighed. Couldn't she—just for once—fight someone who still had all his marbles?

Behind Weather Wacko, funnels of twirling snow flurries spun like icy cyclones. Coils of magical blue-white light glowed against his skin, the living tattoos slithering across his arms. His magic tasted like dry ice and felt like brain freeze.

His pale eyes still locked on Sera, his aura still emanating insanity, he slid his tongue along his lower lip. The ground rumbled beneath Sera's boots. She jumped aside just in time to avoid being impaled on the frozen stalagmite that burst from the grass. She hopped again, narrowly missing the second stalagmite. Then a third. A fourth. One after the other, they erupted. Sera broke into a run.

"You cannot run," her opponent laughed. "Magic is the answer. The *only* answer."

Blackbrooke had fed him that line. Hell, Mr. Sadistic had probably—no, make that definitely—told them all to do whatever it took to force her to use magic. Fine, then. If they wanted magic, she'd give them magic. She danced around an ice cone and ran at Weather Wizard. If she could just get a hold of him, she'd slam a bolt of lightning straight through his heart. If it had woken Kai from near death, it could take down this mage. And it wouldn't even require much magic. Win-win.

Sera was nearly within grabbing distance when a beastly screech roared above her. A dragon. It swooped in, talons slashing. She dropped and rolled. The dragon took up position above the mage, its massive wings beating the air like a drum. It looked…real. It wasn't one of those fiery forms of a dragon that some mages could summon, those illusions woven together by magic. The dragon felt like primeval earth, like forgotten magic and immortality. Its aura shook the very fabric of magic itself.

"It's not real," she told herself, even as she ducked to avoid the swipe of its mighty fist.

She was too slow. The dragon's claws slashed her arm, sprinkling the ground with her blood. The frosty grass sizzled as the crimson drops hit it, her blood eating away at the ice—and then at the grass below. Sera could only stare at the blackened ground in shock.

"It's just an illusion," she said, less sure this time. She looked up at the dragon looping through the air. "All of it."

Magic slammed into Sera, blasting her across the field. She smashed hard into a frozen stalagmite, then dropped. Ignoring the painful protests from pretty much every part of her body, she pushed off the ground.

Weather Wizard's laughter echoed through the field, lingering in the air, heavy with magic and contempt. She couldn't see him. She couldn't see anything through that confounded blizzard he'd summoned. Nor could she see the dragon, but she could hear its dreadful, blood-curdling screeches. It sounded hungry.

Fear and anger blended inside of her, drawing her magic out of hiding. Her hand shot upward, and magic blasted out of her. Twirling as fast as a tornado, the funnel snapped out, cutting through the blizzard. Ropes of blue-green magic wrapped around the dragon's legs, binding it. The beast roared and thrashed, but she held on. In one rough tug, she plucked it from the sky.

The ground shook as the dragon crashed down. Light flashed, blinding Sera. She blinked back the purple blotches and looked down. The dragon was gone.

In his place was Kai. He lay sprawled on the ground, wounded. Blood gushed out of his body, pouring out all around him. She rushed to him. She pressed her hands to the biggest gash on his chest, trying to stop the bleeding. But it wouldn't stop. None of them would stop. He was dying.

Magic slammed her down to the ground. Weather Wizard stepped through the blizzard's icy veil, his raised hands glistening with liquid crystals. He blasted her again, even before she could move. Ice poured through her body—ice and pain. She stumbled to her knees, but the hammer of his magic pounded her down again. She reached out, taking Kai's hand. They were both drenched in blood. They were both dead.

Get up!

Can't, she told the voice. *Hurts.*

Sissy.

I killed Kai.

It's not real, the voice told her. *Look at the fairies.*

For a moment, Sera could see them. They stood on either side of the field, chanting and swaying. Then they faded out. She looked at Kai. He'd grown transparent, if only slightly.

Move, badass! Move!

Sera pushed off her hands. As her feet hit the ground, Kai faded completely. She looked around for Weather Wizard. She didn't see him anywhere. She could hear his sinister laughs through the whistle of the whirling blizzard, but the sound was just echoing everywhere, bouncing off the magic of the snow spell.

You know what you have to do.

Sera nodded. She stretched her hands out to her sides, slowly waving them upward until they met over her head. She clapped them together, then slapped them down against her thighs. Flames blasted out of her, swallowing the blizzard. The snowflakes fizzled away. Steam dripped from the air, thick and warm. Beneath her feet, the grass was black. Her spell had torched it.

The mage stepped through the mist, coils of magical purple-gold light slithering across his skin. Lightning tattoos. The wet air hissed and hummed. Magic buzzed against Sera's skin. The mage's magic was building to a crescendo.

Thunder boomed overhead, swirling the clouds into a thick stew. A storm was brewing. Weather Wizard reached up, extending his hands high into the air with dramatic flourish. Lightning shot down. As it hit his hands, he pushed them out, shooting the magic at Sera. She drew a circle in the air in front of her—a magic shield that sparkled like crushed pink diamonds. The mage's lightning hit her shield, then bounced off, slamming hard into his chest. He flew back, tumbling head over heels in a crooked loop, then hit the ground with a magical, resounding thump. The impact knocked him out cold.

Sera lowered into her knees, reaching down. She dug her fingers into the blackened earth, reaching out with her magic-breaking power. The charred grass dissolved into black oil, the fairies' magic fighting back. She pushed harder, ripping at the illusion without mercy. It let out a final, pitiful protest, then shattered, raining down all around her like the remains of a broken mirror.

Magic gurgled and hissed. The pit faded back in. Sera stood at one end; her opponent lay unconscious at the other. As the final strands of the illusion washed away, all the fairies fainted as one and fell to the ground.

CHAPTER TWENTY-ONE
Secrets and Fairy Dust

SERA WALKED OUT of the fighting pit, waiting until she was out of the cameras' sight before allowing herself to limp. Her feet hurt. Her arms hurt. Every part of her hurt, most especially her head. The fairies' illusion magic had given her a massive hangover that wouldn't be going away anytime soon. Even the soft buzz of the hallway lamps drilled at her battered eardrums.

Kai was waiting in the hallway, a dark smudge against the brightly-lit background. Sera rubbed the Fairy Dust from her eyes. Her vision slowly cleared. The moment his face came into focus, she nearly ran right for him. But she held back.

She'd used magic in front of hundreds of people. In front of Blackbrooke. Had it been enough to allow him a glimpse inside her head? Everything was just so messed up. She wanted nothing more than to throw her arms around Kai and allow him to soothe her worries away. *All* of her worries. But he didn't know all of her worries—her secrets—and she couldn't tell him. She choked back a pained laugh. This would never work. How could she be in a relationship with someone she was constantly lying to?

When she saw the look in his eyes, though, she forgot about all that. All the lies, the omissions, the gloom and doom—for this one moment they didn't exist. He reached out to touch her shoulder, his caress gentle, his magic warm and soothing. She threw herself against him, squeezing him hard to make sure he was real.

"I thought I'd killed you," she muttered against his chest. "Your blood was on my hands." She glanced down at her palms. There was blood on them, but not his. It must have been her own.

He wrapped his arms around her, drawing her in close. "It was just an illusion," he said, his soothing whispers melting against her ear. "This is what they do in the Games, try to break a mage's mind. Twenty-six fairies. Duncan wasn't holding back." His smile was ferocious. "But you held up. You beat their magic. You beat Weather Wizard. And kept your mind together."

"How do you know Blackbrooke didn't crack my mind?"

"Oh, trust me, you'd know. And so would everyone else. If he'd cracked you, you wouldn't have walked out of that pit without assistance." He kissed her forehead. "And you wouldn't have the wherewithal to come up with silly questions."

"I'm not sure I have much wherewithal left in me," she said. "And I forgot all about stringing spells together."

"It doesn't matter."

He hugged her tightly to him, the hard ridges of his body as comforting as any soft and plushy teddybear. No, *more* comforting. A teddybear couldn't fight monsters with her. A teddybear didn't have her back. Kai did. He always had.

"Kai," she said, glancing up at him.

He met her eyes, the look in them making her heart race.

"I thought you were dead." She brushed the back of her hand across his jaw. She wanted to kiss him so badly it hurt. "You said earlier that I don't trust you. Maybe I didn't. But I do now. I want to tell you…" She took a deep breath. "…everything."

He watched her, his magic crackling against her, growing hungrier by the second. He snapped it down. "Sorry. When you stayed in the pit so long, I grew concerned. My magic is still tense."

She fiddled with the collar of his shirt. "I like it."

Magic pulsed in his eyes, temptation battling reason. He reached toward her face—then dropped it. It seemed reason had won.

"You've just been through a lot, Sera. As much as I want to believe this is you speaking, I suspect it's the Fairy Dust." His chest sighed against hers. "Fairy magic is quite potent. It muddles the mind like nothing else."

"Stop it." She frowned at him. "You're ruining my revelation. I am not high on Fairy Dust. I'm just tired of not trusting anyone. Some people are worth trusting." She leaned into him, teasing his lips with hers.

"Sera," he said, his growl buzzing against her neck. "Don't tempt me."

"Why not?"

"Blackbrooke."

The name was like a glacial shower. Her shoulders slumped, and she took a step back.

"He has spies everywhere. And if they find out about us, Blackbrooke will remove you as my coach."

"Yes," he said, his eyes following the pair of guards who were coming down the hall. One of them was the helpful fellow who had refused to heal her yesterday. His comrade looked equally friendly.

Sera leaned back against the wall behind her, feigning casual and relaxed. Kai stood opposite her, his arms folded over his chest, his magic rumbling like he meant business. The two guards passed between them on their way to the pit. They shot her and Kai suspicious glowers but didn't say anything.

When they were gone, Kai spoke again. "I don't want to fight you in the pit."

"Of course not." She shot him a playful wink. "You wouldn't want to lose in front of all those people."

The corner of his lip quirked up. "Your snark appears to have recovered."

"It never left me."

"Hmm."

"It takes more than a few fairies to muddle my mind."

"It's not just the fairies, Sera. Right now, your magic is all over the place." He lifted his hand, freezing the protest on her lips. "Don't even try to deny it. I can feel the erratic beat of your magic. You usually do a better job of containing it. It's the strain of the Magic Games, Finn, and the armies of vampires. Once that is all over—once we're back home and you've had at least one night of decent sleep—if you still want to share your secrets with me, I'll be there."

"Are you always this stubborn?"

"Yes," he said. "It's a dragon thing. Deal with it."

"Oh, don't worry. I know just how to deal with dragons."

"Yes." His magic smoldered. "You do."

"Oh, for Pete's sake! I meant with my sword."

"I didn't."

She threw her hands up in the air. This conversation wasn't going anywhere.

"Come on," Kai said, setting his hand on her back. "Let's get you some lunch. You need to replenish your magic before your next match."

"Pizza?" she asked hopefully.

"I was thinking we could try something different."

"Different as in other-than-pizza different?"

"Yes."

Hmm. "Why?"

"Because you can't always eat pizza," he said.

"Sure you can. There are more than enough kinds of pizza to keep even the biggest glutton busy for months. Thick crust, thin crust, square, circle, mini pizzas, pizza bagels, pizza cookie—"

"Pizza cookie?"

"It's a thing," she assured him. "A type of dessert."

"It sounds awful."

"Yum." She grinned. "Now, where was I? Ah, yes. Red sauce, white sauce, cheese, extra cheese, red tomatoes, yellow tomatoes, sun-dried tomatoes. Mmmm. Pepperoni, mushrooms, peppers, corn, pineapple—"

"Bananas?"

"No." She pretended to retch. "That's just gross. Then there's New York Style, Chicago Style, Italian Style, California Style, and, best of all, Wizard House Pizza Style. Pizza is versatile. It's practically its own food group."

"Except that it's not," he said.

"Merely a technicality. When I'm elected Empress of the Universe, that will all change."

"Empress of the Universe?" he asked as they set off down the hall.

"Yes. Right now my platform hinges on the pizza referendum, but I'm sure I'll come up with a few more gems. I figure I've got the 18 to 25 demographic in the bag."

He glanced over at her, the expression of complete and utter bewilderment a welcome change to his usual hard and confident dragon face. "You are a very peculiar woman."

"Of course." She nudged her shoulder against his arm. "I thought you knew that already."

"I'm beginning to know it in new and unexpected ways."

They walked a few more steps in silence, then Sera said, "Kai? I'm worried about my upcoming match. That last fight was intense. The fairies went straight for the jugular. It's like they knew exactly what they needed to show me to get under my skin. And the mage...well, let's just say the fight seemed engineered to force me to use my particular abilities."

"The whole Magic Games are engineered. You heard Blackbrooke earlier. He's figured out your abilities. Now he wants to test them to see how deep your magic runs. With each match, he's learning from your responses."

"To make harder tests?"

"Yes."

"This is all going downhill fast."

"You can do it, Sera. And I'll help you. The good news is you only have to get through one more fight, and then you've completed all the required matches."

"That doesn't sound too bad."

He scrolled past a few things on his phone. "We'll

discuss strategy over lunch. I have your final opponents here: the Summoning Sisters."

Sera abandoned her despair long enough to snicker. "Another stellar name. It's like we're trapped inside the world of professional wrestling."

"It does often feel like that," he agreed, though without the snicker.

"And Blackbrooke is staging it all. This whole thing with him being attacked by vampires…"

"Yes?"

"Attacked by vampires when I just happened to be there. Twice," she continued. "I wonder if that was all staged too. He must have known I was hiding my magic, right? What if he set up the vampire attacks so he could test my abilities in ways he couldn't within the rules of the Magic Games—at least not until he could hone in on my flavor of magic and design challenges with a better chance of breaking me? The first time was a bust, and when I got through the first day of the Games without using magic, he decided he had to do something. So he went bigger in round two. More vampires. And someone cast a spell to make them immune to fire. Only a mage could have done that, not some magic hate group of humans. What if that mage was one of Blackbrooke's people?"

"Interesting theory. There are just two problems with it."

"Oh?"

"Ego and cowardice. Blackbrooke is too self-absorbed to lower himself by serving as vampire bait, and he's too much of a coward too."

"It all depends on how much he wants to break me," said Sera.

They'd reached the door to the lobby. As they passed

through, Sera's phone dinged. The cursed thing was practically on a timer. She glanced at it just long enough to see that she'd gotten another message from Finn. It was a picture of her from her match against Weather Wizard. The delay between taking the photo and sending her the photo was shrinking every time. What had started as hours, was now down to minutes. Like a countdown. But a countdown to what?

"Sera?" Kai asked, looking back.

She'd stopped just past the door but rushed to catch up to him. "Promise not to flip out."

"About what?" he asked, his face cool, cautious.

"And not to blow up my phone."

His aura went from cool and cautious to fire and brimstone. "Finn sent you another message, didn't he?" He held out his hand. "Let me see."

Sera handed him her one-hour-old phone, hoping she wasn't signing its death sentence by doing so. But Kai just mailed himself and the commandos a copy of the message, then handed it back to her. A few seconds later, his own phone rang.

"Dal, you get the photo?" he said. "Good. I want you three to figure out where in the arena it was taken from." Then he hung up.

"You could have at least said pl—" She stopped, a pitiful groan escaping her lips. "Shit."

An army of vampires had just burst into the lobby, moving with quick, fluid ease. A web of magic coated each vampire's body, as taut as the leash on a rapid dog. Led by an unseen master, they moved to surround a cluster of mages.

"Members of the Magic Council," Kai said. "Every single one of them."

"We just can't catch a break, can we?" she sighed.

He shook out his hands, warming up his magic. As his eyes locked on his targets, a deadly smile slid across his lips. "What would be the fun in that?"

What indeed.

CHAPTER TWENTY-TWO
Dying Blood

"AT LEAST THE Council members have bodyguards," Sera said—then, remembering Kai's phone conversation she'd overheard earlier, added, "Though I suppose you didn't give them much of a choice."

"No." He packed enough explosive force behind that single word to take down a mountain.

"You're really scary sometimes, you know."

Fire slid down his arms, licking at his fingers. "Good."

One of the vampires spontaneously combusted.

"Ok, now you're just showing off," she told him, drawing two of her knives. "But at least we know that these vampires aren't fireproof."

He glanced at the knives in her hands, then met her eyes again. "How do you want to play this?"

"You're asking me?" She almost choked on the words. "You, Mr. Bossy Pants?"

"I prefer dragon breath," he replied, amusement tugging at his lower lip. "But, yes, I'm asking you. We're a team."

She grinned at him. "And I'm in charge?"

"Let's not push it, Sera."

"Ok." She snickered. The lobby was full of vampires, but she just couldn't help herself. "There are too many vampires. How about you shift into a dragon, and I herd them over to you so that you can step on them?"

"A fantastic plan."

"I knew you'd like it."

Kai's magic exploded in a flash of light, and then the man was gone. A dragon stood in his place, towering over the mages and vampires. It was a good thing the lobby had a high ceiling, or his shift would have taken down the roof. Obsidian-black with a dark blue-green sheen to his scales and wings, Kai was stunning—a deadly firestorm of magical might, yes, but stunning just the same. His eyes, blue as an electric storm, locked on his first targets: two vampires trying to fight their way past the bodyguards protecting a female mage with jaw-length scarlet curls.

"Try not to step on the good guys," she reminded him.

Kai snorted, and flames shot out of his enormous dragon nostrils, pouring down over the vampires. The scents of burning timber and cinnamon filled the air, spicy and sweet. His eyes panned across the lobby in search of new targets. He settled on a nearby trio of vampires. As he raised his enormous foot, Sera dashed off to find some targets of her own. Sure, the plan had been her idea, but that didn't mean she needed to see him crunch vampires. Or hear it. She cringed, even as she reminded herself that blowing up vampires wasn't any less messy than stepping on them.

She ran between two vampires, striking out with her knives as she passed. As the blades sank into them, she poured fire magic into the wounds. The vampires burst into flames, then fell to the floor, dead. Sera pulled on the fiery magic crackling atop the two monsters, twisting and molding the flames together to form a protective barrier that separated the mages from the vampires. Three vampires made a run for the mages as the barrier was going up. The fire barbecued one of them. The other two got through, but she trusted that the half dozen bodyguards could deal with two measly vampires. The other—Sera counted—twenty-three vampires she and Kai could handle. Maybe.

She ran toward the next group. She'd promised to herd vampires, so that's what she was going to do. And fast. Before the vampires' master wisened up and realized that he had her and Kai outnumbered over ten to one. If they all charged her at once, she wouldn't be able to stop them. Luckily, vampires weren't too bright. Or, apparently, evil vampire masters. And, besides, they were too busy trying to get at the mages.

Taking a trick from Kai's arsenal, Sera blasted the vampires with a wave of wind magic. Despite how easy he'd made it look, a wave of wind was a hell of a lot trickier to control than a ball of wind. Hers didn't shoot as straight as she would have liked. Vampires flew into the air like scattered leaves on the breeze. Half of them ended up at Kai's feet. The dragon grunted in appreciation, then lifted his foot for the stomp.

Sera was already running back toward the barrier. Some genius vampires had decided that if they couldn't go through the fire, they'd just go *over* it. They were tossing each other up in the air. Two had already made it. Another three were on their way over. Sera wound up a ball of wind between her hands and let loose. It smashed against the barrier, igniting it. Flames shot up into the air and bathed the vampires in fire. She blasted the remaining ones, smacking them into the fiery wall.

"Good," Kai said from behind her. There was a smudge of ash against his cheek, but otherwise he looked as human as a dragon shifter possibly could. "There's something very beautiful about the way that you fight." He lifted his hand in the air, and her wall of flames turned to smoke. The mages on the other side looked relieved—and sweaty. "You have more control over your magic than you give yourself credit for."

"Thanks, I—" Something was tugging at her magic like a fish on a hook.

"What is it?"

She stared down at the nearest vampire. His hand was twitching, a final protest before death took him. The magical web—the power of the spell binding him—was unraveling, but it hadn't vanished completely.

"The trail of magic controlling the vampires. I can follow it," she told Kai, running off after the unraveling threads. "This will take us to the vampires' master." If she could get there before the magic completely disintegrated.

"I'm coming with you," Kai said, running up beside her.

"And the Council members?"

"They're all fine. The commandos are with them. Where are we headed?"

"Down." She sucked in a deep breath. "Red line."

Penn Station sat below Madison Square Garden, and that's where their criminal mastermind was. Or had been. The trail was fading fast. She'd have to be faster. She sped up, zigzagging between bustling passengers.

"That way!" she said and ran for a train, trusting him to follow.

He did better than that. He cleared the way. One look at him, and the unflappable New Yorkers scrambled out of the way. Sera and Kai squeezed onto the train as the doors were closing.

"Where is this vampire master?" he asked.

Sera reached out with her magic, trying to get a bite on the unraveling thread. She slouched in defeat when she found it.

"He's not on this train. He caught the one before us. We'll never catch him now."

"We will."

That was all Kai said before he took off down the aisle, heading for the front of the train. It was harder for the passengers in here to scramble out of the way, but they made a solid effort. Kai's magic was pounding off the walls, echoing like the beat of a great dragon's wings. It was so loud that it dwarfed the pitiful thump of Sera's heart.

"Can you tell where he is?" Kai asked her, breaking through he door to the driver's cabin.

"He just got off at Central Park," she said over the driver's stuttering protests.

"You're running late," Kai told the man. He plopped a stack of money onto the dashboard. "Skip every station until Central Park."

The driver's eyes darted from Kai to the bundle of bills. His indecision died a spectacular death in the face of avarice. He went on the intercom to rattle off some bullshit excuse to the passengers, then sped them along their way to Central Park.

The train had barely stopped when Sera and Kai sprinted out. They took the stairs in running bounds.

"There," Sera told him as they ran down the tree-lined

path. She pointed at the hooded figure framed against the watery backdrop. He was running too. But he was slower.

"Are you sure?" Kai asked her.

"Yes, he reeks of vampire."

Kai sniffed the air, then nodded. Apparently, that was good enough for him. "What kind of mage are we up against? I can't get a fix on his magic."

"Neither can I. The stench of vampire and all the magic being kicked up by the artifact he's carrying is putting up too much interference."

"The Blood Orb."

"You can feel it too?"

Tendrils of elastic lightning sizzled up his arms. "Yes."

The mage threw something against the pavement. Glass smashed and magic exploded. A web of purple glyphs appeared on the path ahead, then a portal swirled to life. The mage reached into his pocket and pulled out a red glass orb roughly the size of a tennis ball. The Blood Orb. He tossed it through the portal.

Before he had time to jump in after it, though, Kai snapped his lightning magic out like a whip. The electrified cord latched around the man's leg, and Kai tugged, tripping him to the ground. The portal flickered out.

"Can we go through?" Kai asked as Sera kicked the ground where the glyphs had just been.

"No, this portal was different. Shorter. We can't reopen it."

"Then we'll have to get what we need from him," said Kai.

Their mastermind was flapping against the lightning rope, trying to get it off his ankle. As Kai walked toward him in slow, deliberate steps, Sera circled around and cut him off from the other side.

"The Convictionites stole the Blood Orb. Why is a mage working with an organization that wants to wipe out his own people?" she called down to the man at her feet.

His head snapped up, and he met her eyes. "You are not my people," he growled, his magic lathered with hate. And crazy. There was a lot of that going around lately.

Kai gave the lightning whip a tug, tightening the noose, and stopped beside Sera. "I know him. He works in one of my labs."

The ruffled mage gave Kai a defiant—if not scared shitless—glare.

"Let me guess," Sera said. "The lab with the magic-proof armor."

"Yes."

"Well, at least we know now where those disagreeable vampires who interrupted my shopping trip got their accessories." She looked at their traitor. "What did you do, make a copy of the schematics?"

He lifted his chin in the air. "I don't have to answer your questions."

"But you do have to answer mine."

It wasn't the volume of Kai's voice that made the mage cringe. It was the way his magic amplified it, bouncing it off the massive body of water behind them. Flocks of panicked birds took to the air and fled the scene.

"Unless, that is, you would like me to give you a firsthand demonstration of how I deal with traitors."

"I know all about your reputation for demon magic, Drachenburg," he spat. "And you can't hurt me." The nervous tinkle of his magic betrayed his false fortitude. "I am chosen. I was born of magic, evil and monstrous, but

I shall be redeemed. I will kill the other monsters. All the other monsters."

Kai remained unimpressed. "What else did you steal from me?"

"The heavens will open up and rain down death upon your kind!"

"If you don't stop spewing nonsense and start answering my questions, *I* will rain down a thing or two on you."

"Death first!"

"That can be arranged," Kai assured him, stepping forward.

Sera caught his arm. The look he gave her could have wilted metal, but she only smiled right back at him. "There's no point, Kai. He's one of them. A Convictionite. Can't you see that he's been completely brainwashed?"

"I don't care what they washed." Sparks shot out from the lightning whip, sending the mage into convulsions. "I'll wash it right out of him."

"I think it's too late for that. This…hatred, whatever it is, it's a part of him. I can feel it pulsing through his magic. It's decades old. You can't separate out something that's always been there."

Kai killed the light show. "You're saying he was born this way?"

"I'm saying he was raised this way. The Convictionites must have gotten him early, when he was just a young boy. A baby maybe. He is as much a Convictionite as the rest of them are."

"Except he's a mage. And they hate mages."

She shrugged. "Since when did people make sense? Maybe you should let me talk to him." But when she tried to approach the mage, Kai moved to block her way. "Honestly, Kai. What do you think he can do to me? You have him pinned down. And I'm not a delicate snowflake."

"More like a snow beast," he grunted.

She showed him her teeth. "Keep talking, dragon."

He met her stare. "Fine. Talk to him. But if he doesn't behave, I'm going to eat him."

"You don't eat people, Kai."

"No, I don't." He rubbed the stubble on his chin. "Fine, I'll just think of some other way to kill him."

"You can't kill him," she said. "He might know something we can use against the Convictionites. We need to take him back for questioning."

"I thought you weren't amenable to my method of questioning."

"I'm not. You have anger management issues."

"I'm managing my anger just fine, sweetheart," he told her, a hard grin cutting across his face.

Nearby, a gust of wind rocked a tree, stripping it of all its leaves. A pair of lovers out for a walk jumped back in alarm as they were nearly buried beneath the leafy waterfall pouring down from the tree.

Sera gave Kai her best mega-bored look. "A little early in the year for fall, isn't it?"

He said nothing.

"Ok, then." Sera crouched down beside the mage. "Hi, what's your name?"

"Die, demon bitch!"

"That's a nice one. Shall I call you 'Mr. Demon Bitch' or just 'Die' for short?"

Shockingly, the mage didn't burst into laughter. From the way Kai was glaring at him, though, she didn't have long before he burst into flames.

"You've been planning this for a long time," she said.

"Huh?" the mage asked, clearly puzzled.

"This undercover operation. Drachenburg Industries doesn't hire just anyone. You needed an in. Connections. Those take years to forge."

"I went to school with Finn Drachenburg, dragon boy's cousin. He got me the job as a lab researcher in exchange for me agreeing to spy for him."

Sera didn't press him further. As long as she didn't ask him direct questions, he seemed to get around to spilling the details anyway. It might be part of his mental conditioning. Maybe the Convictionites had programmed him not to answer questions in case he was ever captured.

"So you're a double agent," she said. "That must have been difficult, fooling your coworkers in the lab. Fooling Finn."

He snorted. "Supernaturals are stupid and arrogant. None of you ever suspected a thing."

"I'm curious how you made it through the Magic Games without the Council ever learning your secret." She gave him a crooked smile. "I'm going through the Games right now, you see."

"I never went through the Games. I'm a non-combative mage," he said. "But even if I had gone through them, I wouldn't have cracked."

"You sound so sure of yourself. The Game Architect prides himself on his ability to crack anyone."

"Duncan Blackbrooke?" He sneered. "A spineless and spent old man. Did you see how he fell to pieces when I sent the vampires after him? Pathetic," he added with disgust.

"The other Council members were equally frightened

when you sent vampires after them."

"Yes. They're all pathetic. They will fall easily." He glared at Kai, hatred pouring over his eyes. "That one we're saving for last. The great dragon." He sneered. "He will fall. They will all fall. And when they do, the tight control they've woven around the supernatural factions will break. Mages, vampires, fairies, even the otherworldly...they will begin to fight one another. And humans will be caught in the middle."

"Humans will die."

"By the millions," he said with relish. "And then the survivors will turn to us, begging us to fix the problem they cannot. And we will." Magic, sick and twisted, raged in his eyes. "We will."

"He's insane," Kai said. "Clearly. Let's get him back to Duncan. After what this traitor has put him through, I'm sure he'd be more than delighted at the prospect of scraping his mind for secrets."

The mage closed his eyes and began to mutter.

"What's he saying?" Kai asked.

"Um...magic and blood, something-something..." She leaned in closer. "...flame to fire, earth to stone—"

Kai jerked on her hand, yanking her away from the muttering mage. And not a second too soon. Blood burst out of Mr. Crazy's chest in a hundred tiny sprinklers, hissing against the lightning web holding him.

"Death to abominations," he gurgled out. His chest heaved, then he went completely limp.

Sera gaped down at the fresh corpse, trying hard not to dwell on his final words. Death to abominations. She knew he meant supernaturals in general, not her—and that he was insane anyway. But that didn't change the fact that according to the laws of the Magic Council, she was just that. An abomination.

"That wasn't a recipe for cookies, I take it," she said.

"No." Kai came up behind her and folded his arms around her. "That was the Dying Blood spell. A kamikaze spell. It uses the caster's magic to turn his own blood poisonous. If a single drop had gotten onto your skin…" He was holding her so tightly that she could scarcely breathe.

"I'm fine," she assured him, reaching up to squeeze his arms.

"I'm not." His magic quaked. "He killed himself and tried to take you with him, Sera."

"Yeah, that's because he's nuts."

His deep chuckle buzzed against her neck. Sera could have stayed there forever, snuggling up to the dragon, but unfortunately…well, life happened. She took Kai's hand, kissing it once before putting her big girl pants on again.

"So, then," she said, looking down at the corpse. "Do you want to carry the body or shall I?"

CHAPTER TWENTY-THREE
Magic Burgers

THERE WEREN'T MANY sure-fire ways to get New York to stop and stare, but carrying a dead and bleeding mage to the street curb was one of them. And they didn't just stare; they gawked. There was a good amount of finger-pointing too.

"There isn't some regulation against carrying corpses in public, is there?" Sera whispered to Kai as she watched one of the nearby pedestrians tap out something on his phone that looked suspiciously like '911'.

"Shouldn't you know something like that? I figured that was your area of expertise as a monster hunter."

"Are you teasing me?" she asked as a black van stopped in front of them. Their ride had arrived.

Kai opened the trunk and pushed the dead mage inside. "Of course not. That would be unprofessional."

She smirked at him as they took their seats. "So is the blood on your shirt."

"His chest is full of holes. It's basically impossible to transport someone in that state without spilling at least a little blood."

They'd waited the necessary fifteen minutes for his poisonous blood to go inert again before trying to move him. Deadly or not, the mage's blood was still messy.

"Or without spilling a lot of blood." Sera hitched her thumb back toward the trunk. "He's bleeding out all over."

"Don't worry. I'm sending the cleaning bill to the mages we rescued from the vampires," Kai said.

"Wow, you're sure storing up a lot of favors."

"Yes."

"I fought the monsters and helped take down the bad guy too. You get a gazillion favors. What do I get?"

"I'm buying you lunch."

"You were going to do that already."

"Then I'll just have to think of something." The look in his eyes promised massages—well, massages and a whole lot of other things that she wasn't going to think about with Kai's people in the front seat.

A few minutes later, the van slid to a stop. Kai hopped out, picked up the body from the trunk, and headed toward the entrance to Madison Square Garden. Sera followed him. Everyone gave them a wide berth.

"It's not over, you know," she said as they walked inside. "The Convictionites still have the Blood Orb."

"Isn't your sister working on the Convictionite problem?"

"Apparently."

"Then I think the problem is in good hands."

"But you don't even know Alex. How can you say that?"

"I know you," he said. "And Riley. Tenacity runs in your family."

They'd reached the Games lobby again, so the time for

small talk was over. Blackbrooke was there, snooty and dignified in his custom-cut suit. The mages Sera and Kai had saved from death by vampire were there too, standing in a cluster surrounded by Magic Games security personnel. Their clothes ruffled and singed by fire—oops —they looked considerably less dignified than the Game Architect.

"Pass me the body," Sera muttered to Kai as they crossed the lobby.

He raised a quizzical eyebrow but did as she'd asked. Sera carried the body, which was a lot heavier than the mage's scrawny figure suggested, over to Blackbrooke and dumped it at his feet.

"What is *that*?" Blackbrooke asked, turning up his nose at the bloody body.

Sera snatched the white silk handkerchief from his breast pocket and used it to wipe the blood from her hands. "That there is your criminal mastermind, the mage who was controlling the vampires using the Blood Orb." She tossed the handkerchief back to Kai, so he could use it too. "It turns out he's a brainwashed Convictionite agent who planned to murder the Magic Council in the hopes of starting a war between supernaturals and humans. We thought you could scrape his mind for secrets."

Blackbrooke blinked.

"Yeah, that was the plan anyway before he committed magic suicide," she said. "Now we've just brought him here so you can clean up the mess."

Appalled, Blackbrooke's eyes shifted from her to Kai. "Is she always this impudent?"

"She saves it for special people."

Blackbrooke frowned at him. "You have blood on

your shirt."

"Do I?" Kai looked down. He dabbed the bloody handkerchief once against his sleeve, then tucked it back inside Blackbrooke's pocket.

"This isn't funny," Blackbrooke said, his magic freckled with indignation.

"Sure it is. You just haven't figured it out yet." Sera turned to Kai. "Lunch?"

He nodded. "What would you like?"

"At this point, as long as I don't have to kill my lunch myself, I don't really care."

Kai picked hamburgers for lunch. It was a cute place around the corner called Magic Burgers. It was clean, colorful, and didn't smell like vampires. What more could a girl ask for?

"This is good food for replenishing magic," Kai said as they waited for their food to come.

"Pizza is plenty good for that," she teased, raising her voice to be heard over the lunch-hour bustle. The sizzle of grilling meat. The pop of deep-fried potatoes. The hum of the milkshake machine. The clink of plates and glasses.

He shook his head. "You're just going to have to trust me."

"Oh?" She leaned against him.

They were sitting side by side at the booth rather than across from each other. That was because neither one of them could stand to have their back to the door. Yes, that was totally messed up—and yet comforting. It was nice to be with someone who understood. Someone who was just as paranoid as she was.

"Between the fighting pit and the vampires, you've expended massive amounts of magic today," he said. "You need to trust my experience in this area. I know the most efficient means to recharge."

"Let me guess. Meat."

"Yes."

She laughed. She was still laughing when the waitress came to their table, her arms stacked with plates. Most of them were for Kai. Magic Burgers had a legendary burger called 'the Emperor', two thick beef patties on a kaiser roll stuffed with grilled onions, honey pickles, sliced cherry tomatoes, and spinach. It was so big that half the people who ordered it couldn't even finish it. Kai had ordered three. Crazy dragon.

Next to the parade that was Kai's lunch, Sera's single plate of a standard burger with fries felt…small. On the other hand, she had a milkshake, which was worth at least two burgers.

"That's a lot of food," she commented, nodding at his burgers.

"That's a big milkshake."

"Yes."

She picked up a fry and dipped it into the thick, liquid ice cream. The shake was lumpy—just as it should be.

"There are two straws," she told Kai. "The waitress must have thought we're on a date."

"We are."

Hmm. "Do dates with you always involve killing monsters before sitting down to eat?"

"No."

"Good."

"Sometimes the monster-killing happens after the

meal," he said.

She snorted. "Well, as long as it doesn't happen *during* the meal." She rolled the second straw across the table to him. "Want to share?"

"You're offering to share your milkshake with me?" Kai asked, picking up his second burger. Wow, he was fast.

"Yeah, it's a big deal to me too," she teased.

He peered over the top of the tall glass. "It's liquid dessert."

"Yummy."

"I don't know, Sera. A milkshake? Drinking that might ruin my image."

"As a badass dragon?"

"Yes."

"If any stuffy mages make fun of you, I'll show them my sword," she promised.

"You'd show them your sword anyway. You enjoy making them uncomfortable."

"Who me? No, you must have me confused with some other mercenary. I am always completely professional."

"Oh, really?" He snatched one of her fries and ate it. "Before the end of the first day I'd hired you, you hit me in the head."

In retaliation for the fry theft, she stole an onion from his plate. "That says more about you than it does about me. And, besides, you were being a first class jerk."

"Which is why you then kissed me?"

"I suffer from chronic poor judgment."

But not poor taste. She slid her hand up his arm, following the rigid contours of his muscles. One of Kai's people had been ready and waiting at Madison Square

Garden with fresh shopping bags of pristine clothes. Her excessive wardrobe changes were starting to become something of a joke amongst the commandos. This time, Kai had needed one too, but no one dared tease him about it. Sera had been almost disappointed when he'd returned from the bathroom wearing a new shirt. The old one had been so damaged that she'd kind of hoped he'd go around without one for a while.

"Shall I take it off now?"

Sera blinked at him. Shit. Had she actually said that aloud? She needed to stop getting caught up in her own thoughts.

"Nah," she said, hopefully casually. "That group of women who have been checking you out since we entered the restaurant would probably faint."

He glanced across the room at the women in question. They burst into giggles. One of them began to fan herself. Sera distinctly heard the words 'Mages Illustrated' buzzing over their table.

"You have fans," she commented.

He grunted. "I never should have agreed to pose for that dirty magazine."

"Mages Illustrated isn't a dirty magazine. It's a respected publication with thought-provoking articles and features."

"I'm surprised you got through that sentence without bursting into laughter," he said.

"So am I." Now she laughed. "Oh, look. There it is." She cleared her throat. "Why did you agree to pose for the magazine?"

"Technically, I didn't agree."

"You lost a bet, didn't you?"

"Yes." He looked like he wanted to punch something.

Or someone.

She chuckled. "Just think of it this way. You made the world's female population very happy."

His head snapped toward her, his eyes alight with magic. "Including you?"

"Uh…well…that is…"

"You have the magazine too. I saw it."

"I told you already. That was all Naomi's doing. She gave it to me."

"And you never looked? Not even a peek?"

His hand traced her brow, his touch feather-soft. He leaned in, his mouth so close she could practically taste it. She felt herself arching toward him, daring him to kiss her. His eyes were intense. Penetrating.

"Maybe just a tiny peek," she admitted.

"I thought so." Then, with a smirk, he tucked a stray strand of hair behind her ear and pulled away.

"You're a bad man," she growled at him, her heart thumping.

"The worst."

"When I get back to my room, I'm going to set that magazine on fire."

"Please do."

"I might set you on fire too," she added.

"Interesting."

She threw up her hands. "Bah, dragons!"

"Was that supposed to be an insult?"

"Yes!"

"That's not very professional of you."

Neither was sleeping with him. Simmons would pee his pants if he found out about that. She was pretty sure 'do not have sex with the clients' was buried somewhere in her Mayhem contract. Sera didn't say this to Kai. She didn't say anything. That was probably smarter than her usual method of just shooting off the first sarcastic comment that came into her head.

"For the record, Sera, I do think you're more professional than most mercenaries I've met. And you actually care about people, not just the money. Even if Bethany Harrower thinks you're an evil she-devil."

That ridiculous purple poodle lady again. Sera would never be rid of her.

"Did she tell you that?" she asked.

"Not me personally. She's been spreading it around her circles."

Which meant every mage of consequence in the world—anyone from a distinguished magic dynasty—knew what the old lady thought of Sera. Bethany Harrower was a mage socialite of the highest order.

"I don't know what wild tales she's spreading, but what happened was all on her," she said. "That micromanaging granny mage was the one who nearly got herself—and me—killed. She jumped into the middle of my battle with her garden gnomes because she could not stand back and simply let the professionals she'd hired actually do their job. Do you have any idea how hard it is to play bodyguard and monster exterminator at the same time? Of course I told her off for being a moron."

"Rumor has it you did a lot more than just tell her off."

"Ok, I showed her my knives," Sera admitted, adding quickly, "But just the really small ones. I didn't want to give her a heart attack."

"She claims she was traumatized for life."

"And you believe her?"

"No. Bethany also said the same thing when she saw

her first pair of hot pants."

"Hmm," she said, amusement tugging at her mouth. "Maybe I should have worn hot pants when I went to kill her gnomes."

"Then you might really have given her a heart attack." His serious face dissolved into wicked bliss. He leaned in and whispered into her ear, "But I wouldn't mind if you wore them the next time we went monster hunting together."

"I don't know." She gave him a crooked smile. "You'd have to make it worth my while."

"I'll bring muffins."

"Sold," she said immediately. "But only if they're blueberry."

"I think that can be arranged." He wrapped his arm around her, his hand brushing against her thigh. Magic dripped out of his fingertips, oscillating to every corner of her body.

She slapped his hand away. "Stop that. I'm still mad at you."

"Does that mean you won't be setting me on fire later?"

"It was supposed to be a threat, something that sparked fear in your heart." She frowned. "Not something that you're looking forward to. You've ruined it."

"How about if I shriek and roll around on the floor in agony?"

"Do you even know how to shriek?" she asked him.

"I can roar."

She shook her head. "Forget it. I'll think of some other way to get back at you."

He kissed her cheek. "Let me know if there's anything I can do to help you with that." His second kiss brushed past her lips. "In the spirit of cooperation."

She returned his kiss, catching his lower lip between her teeth. She gave it a rough tug. He groaned into her mouth, his tongue finding hers, his hands clutching her hips beneath the table.

"Nice try, but that wasn't a shriek or a roar," she said, pulling back, teasing his mouth.

He growled in frustration.

"Getting closer."

"You are a wicked woman," he hissed against her lips.

If Sera's phone hadn't chosen that moment to buzz against the table, she didn't know what would have happened. No one had kicked them out of the restaurant yet, but they were about ten seconds away from indecent exposure. She pulled back from him, fumbling for her phone. Her head was still spinning from that kiss. She was making out with Kai. In public. With tables full of people all around her. What the hell was the matter with her?

"I blame the Games. They're messing with my head," she muttered.

"What's that?" Kai rested his arms atop the back of the bench. His posture said relaxed, but his magic was as intense as a speeding train. It pulsed in slow, intense beats, pounding against hers. She might need to slap him again—and herself while she was at it.

"Nothing," she replied, checking her phone. Another message from Finn. Great.

"You're frowning."

"Am I?"

She looked up at Kai. He was frowning too. His magic surged, going from intense to enraged. Frost crackled and spread down her milkshake glass. Inside, her liquid dessert was fast approaching solid ice block territory.

"If you ruin my milkshake, I'm going to make you order me another one," she warned him.

Her glass hissed, released from his arctic spell.

"That's better. Now, let's just ignore Finn and go back to…eating."

Kai was already dialing the commandos. The man just couldn't help himself. "Tell me where the photo of Sera in the pit was taken from," he spoke before any of them could.

"…looked around," came Tony's voice from the other end. "…one-fifteen…front…first five rows…"

"Find him. This is getting ridiculous," Kai snapped, hanging up.

For the next five minutes, he devoured his remaining burgers. She watched. She nibbled on her own burger and dipped a few fries into her milkshake, but she wasn't feeling very hungry.

"You should eat," he said finally, wiping his hands down with a napkin. "You'll need your strength."

She took a bite of the burger and a long slurp of milkshake.

"I think you might be right about Cutler," he said, watching her closely. "He was sitting right where one of Finn's photos was taken from. Maybe I should have a few strong words with him."

Sera reached up, catching his hand as he stood. "Wait."

"Let go, Sera," he growled. "I need to kill something."

She believed it. His magic crashed and churned, the beginnings of a storm brewing behind his eyes.

"Don't do that," she said. "If Cutler is a part of all

this, confronting him will only tip him off. And if he isn't, attacking him will get you into trouble with his mother. Melinda Spellstorm can summon entire herds of unicorns. That woman is scary."

"You think this is funny?

"No, it's very serious," replied Sera. "Don't confront Cutler. Watch him. Use him to find Finn."

"Hmm." He began writing out a message to the commandos. "Since when did you get so level-headed?"

"It's all part of my new and improved super professionalism."

At least that elicited a response from him, if only a slightly amused grunt. "Ok, Ms. Professional. How about you finish your lunch so you don't pass out the moment you step into the fighting pit."

"Your confidence in me is inspiring," she said, taking another long drink from her glass. After all, nothing went better with doom and gloom than milkshakes.

CHAPTER TWENTY-FOUR
The Summoning Sisters

"ALL THREE MEMBERS of the Summoning Sisters are rated amongst the top ten summoners in the world," Kai said as they walked down the now all-too-familiar hallway.

Something big lay at the other end, and it wasn't puppy dogs and daisies. It was the pit. The Pit of Insanity, the Destroyer of Dreams, the Breaker of Mages. If they'd had more time, Sera could have thought up a few more apt descriptors, but time was short. It was always far too short. In five minutes, she was going to be trapped inside that pit of a thousand titles, too busy to think up cutesy nicknames.

"The Summoning Sisters can summon just about anything, so be on your toes," Kai continued. "And there will be fairies again. I'm guessing stronger ones and more of them. Duncan's mortal failing is his obsession with outdoing himself."

"I can think of a few more mortal failings," she muttered under her breath.

She knew he'd heard, but he didn't let her words

derail him. "The fairies will try to mess with your mind, feeding you illusions both beautiful and terrifying. They're not real. Remember that."

She shrugged off his hand. "I'll be fine. If the fairies annoy me too much, I'll snap their wings off."

"Sera—" Something hummed. "I want you to know —" He looked down and growled at his pocket.

"Your pants are buzzing," she told him.

He cursed.

"Maybe you should answer that."

He dug his phone out, glancing at the screen. "I have to take this call."

"Be my guest."

He lifted the phone to his ear. "Drachenburg."

A voice—a woman's voice—spoke from the other end. Kai turned and walked off down the hall, out of earshot.

"He's a fickle beast."

Sera pivoted around. Cutler stood inside the open doorway that led to the pit, leaning one hand against each side, pushing just hard enough to flex his muscles. Sera suppressed a groan. She didn't have time for this shit. Not now. Not ever.

"How did you get down here?" she demanded.

"I walked across the pit."

"And the guards just let you?"

He shrugged. "I bribed them."

Of course.

Cutler looked past her, down the hall where Kai was talking on the phone.

"Do you think his other girlfriend knows about you?" he asked, his face the picture of innocence.

"It's probably his mother. Or a cousin."

"Her voice sounded…" His mouth curled up. "…sultry."

"Then why don't you go flirt with *her*. All you have to do is snatch the phone from Kai's hand."

"There is no try, beautiful. If I want something, I take it." He snapped his fingers. "Just like that." A rose, blood-red and as big as a kitten, floated toward her. "And right now, I want you."

"Sorry, not interested."

The rose dropped into her hand. There was obviously something wrong with his hearing—or his head.

"Have you ever made love with a telekinetic?" he asked, his voice as smooth as hot honey.

No, but I've kicked one in the head.

"It's an unforgettable experience." He eyes flashed. "I could bathe your body in pleasure."

Sera coughed, choking on the building narcissism in the air.

"We could do it suspended in the air."

What girl could say no to a romantic line like that?

"Or I could just strip you naked without ever lifting a finger."

Sera snapped her hand to her shoulder, pushing up her sliding sleeve. "Keep your hands—and your magic—away from me," she said, deep and low, letting the menace simmer in her throat. Just like the dragon.

Smiling, Cutler lifted his hands in the air, then tucked them behind his back. Magic flickered in his eyes like a rogue lightbulb.

She sighed. "What do you want?"

"To talk to you," he replied.

"So talk. And make it fast. My match is about to start."

"Sera…" His gaze darted past her shoulder. Whatever he saw there washed all color from his face.

She glanced back. Kai was coming down the hall. Every time his foot touched down, the floor shook. Rage, pure and undiluted, boiled inside his electric blue eyes, which had Cutler locked in their crosshairs. Magic lashed out from Kai like a whip, snapping and hissing as it electrified the dust in the air. The door to the pit quivered and quaked—then ripped from its hinges, smacking the ground with a resounding thump.

"Watch yourself out there," Cutler said, giving her arm a soft pat before turning tail and escaping into the pit.

Kai stopped beside Sera, his steps surprisingly light and springy for someone who had basically just set off an earthquake in the hallway. "What did he have to say?" His eyes, still seething, followed Cutler's progress across the pit.

"Nothing much. He just came by to hit on me." Sera shrugged, aiming for indifferent.

Kai punched the wall, crunching concrete. Obviously, she needed to work on 'indifferent'.

"I'm fine," she assured him.

She rubbed the dust from her eyes, wishing that she'd never even brought up her suspicions about Cutler working for Finn. It had accomplished nothing except to make Kai grouchy. And they probably weren't even true. Cutler, plotting and scheming for Finn's evil organization? Unlikely. He couldn't plot out anything more complicated than his next clubbing ensemble. And he couldn't scheme his way out of an unlocked room. Cutler was harmless. Crude—but harmless.

Inside the pit, a gong echoed.

"That's ominous," she commented as the crowd's voices cheered and stomped.

"Are you ready?" Kai asked her. The angry light in his eyes had gone out.

"Se-ra! Se-ra! Se-ra!" The voices poured through the doorway; their stomps shook the stands. Apparently, they liked her. Or at least liked the way she brutally took down her foes.

"I'm ready," she told Kai, taking a step toward the pit. She threw a playful wink over her shoulder. "I'll be right back."

"I'll be here," he said, planting himself in the doorway.

She nodded, then entered the pit.

Sera's opponents stood on the opposite end, three female mages positioned in a wide triangle pattern. The one at the front wore a black leather crop top with long, bell-shaped sleeves made of red chiffon; they rippled in the magical breeze wafting off the magic barrier that surrounded the pit. Her pants were also leather, the bottoms tucked into her knee-high boots. The heels on those boots looked hard enough to hammer through a vampire's skull.

Her 'sisters' were dressed…well, differently. The mage to her right wore a long and fluffy white gown that strongly resembled a wedding dress. A veil draped from the sparkling tiara on her head. She even held a bouquet of flowers in one hand. Oh, boy.

The third summoner wore a skin-tight fuchsia bodysuit with a thick gold zipper down the front. She had it unzipped halfway to her navel, exposing shimmering bronze skin. There wasn't a tan line in sight. A big pink-and-white lily was tucked behind her ear, and her long, dark braid hung over her shoulder like a whip.

A row of fairies lined three sides of the pit. They were dressed like Tinker Bell's entourage, the kaleidoscope of garish colors and fabrics making Sera's eyes bleed. Their magic, thick with sugar and seduction, lapped at her like a gentle tide, singing like the ocean at sunset. She could feel them nudging her defenses, trying to find a way into her mind. They were still only teasing. Only playing. As soon as the match started, the sweet lie of their illusion would crumble into dust. They'd tear at her with everything they had.

Ahead of her, the three mages were smirking like they had some grand secret. Whatever it was, they didn't care to share it. They shot monsters at her instead. A glittering silver cloud rolled across the pit at Sera, a storm of stampeding ponies carrying it forward. Their thick bodies, coils of tightly woven magic, glowed like crystal. Their galloping hooves thundered against the sandy ground.

Sera reached for the magic of earth, ancient and unchanging. It thumped through her like a pounding drum, its beat starting slow but growing louder—heavier —as she pulled it up. It burst through the ground beneath the ponies, shattering their bodies into a million crystal shards. The arena pulsated with magic, and the crowd fell silent.

Sweat dribbled down Sera's face. Every inch of her skin was sticky and hot. Her head felt like it would split open. It was buckling under the strain of barricading her mind while using magic.

The fairies' magic shifted, their illusions saturating her pores. The pit flickered, fading into blotches of golden light. Magic wrapped around her in soft, soothing layers.

It tasted like buttermilk pancakes and warm summer mornings. She staggered sideways.

Something hard and heavy slammed into her. She rolled to her feet, shaking her head to clear it. The beast was gone, swallowed up by the thick golden fog that covered the pit from floor to ceiling. A shrill cry bounced around the arena, the echoes making the beast impossible to locate. She closed her worthless eyes and reached out with her magic.

She felt it—no, them. There were five of them. They were…diving. She snapped her eyes open and looked up, right into the red eyes of the griffins about to dive-bomb her. She threw up her hands. Forks of lightning erupted from her palms, skewering the beasts. Magic crackled and spat, and the light-woven griffins exploded.

The golden mist evaporated, revealing a dew-dripped meadow. It was morning here, the early sun painting the sky with light and color as it rose. Birds chirped and whistled. The mages stood on three tree stumps, their hands raised in the air. High above, something roared, rumbling the sky.

Bad. Really, really bad.

She'd no sooner had the thought when a dragon swooped down. Its jaws snapped at her. Sera punched out with her magic, and it shattered. Magic, tart and dry, scraped across her tongue. Salt burned her nose and stung her throat. Her stomach did a weak somersault. She had the overwhelming urge to retch.

Six dragons circled above her, their voices a chorus of beastly growls. Another one dove for her. She pushed out with her magic again, but her blast went right through it. Unharmed, the dragon continued to drop.

An illusion, she realized a moment before it passed

through her, scratching a layer off her mental shield.

More dragons appeared above. The sky was thick with them. Sera blinked down hard, trying to sift the illusions from the summoned beasts, to dissolve the fake dragons —but there were too many fairies. The illusions flickered for a moment, then came back stronger.

"Sera."

She pivoted around at Kai's voice, watching him step out of the forest. He smiled at her like she was the only person in the world. Her lips curled up to return the smile—but she stopped herself.

"You're an illusion," she told him, tapping his forehead.

He crumbled to dust before her. Her heart stuttered in protest, even though it wasn't real. None of this was real.

"Isn't it, though?"

Sera turned again, freezing when she came face to face with her sister.

"What's wrong?" Alex asked. "Aren't you happy to see me?"

"You're not really here." Sera flicked her in the arm, but the illusion refused to fade.

"Because I'm not an illusion. And let me prove it to you."

Alex swung a punch at her. Instead of going through her like the fake dragon had, the punch smashed into her stomach. Sera doubled over, pain blazing through her body. It sure felt like a real punch. Alex slammed two fists down on her head. Sera hit the ground, the ache of impact paling in comparison to the agony that erupted inside her skull.

"You're not real." Sera spit blood. "Just...an illusion."

"How wrong you are?" Alex sneered down at her.

The hard toe of her sister's boot slammed against her head, and Sera blacked out.

Wake up!

Sera groaned and rolled over. Or tried to, anyway. She couldn't feel her body.

Where am I? she asked. Her mouth as dry as sawdust, and her head felt like it had gone through a paper shredder. Some of the feeling to her body was returning—and now that it was, she was really wishing it hadn't.

You're mostly unconscious, and the fairies are whittling away at your mind. Your shield is about to crumble. You need to do something. Now!

Sera tried to push off the ground with her hands, but she didn't yet have the strength for that. Her fingers sank into the sand. She growled in frustration.

You need to fight it, the voice said.

I tried. Alex…she knocked me down.

It wasn't her. None of this is real.

Then why couldn't I shatter her like I did Kai? Why couldn't I make her disappear?

Because she is a part of you. You share a bond. That wasn't Alex. It was you. You were fighting yourself. That's why you couldn't shatter the illusion.

Do the fairies know about me and Alex? About our bond? Sera's pulse raced, pumping her blood faster. Her wounds throbbed, and her head spun. *Does Blackbrooke know?*

No, I'm blocking out those parts of your mind. But I

won't be able to block them forever. If your defenses fall…

Death, Sera said, the word hanging heavy in her mind.

Yes.

Alex told me to listen to the voice in my head. I guess she meant you.

A wise one, your sister. Yes, you should listen to me. Always.

But what are you? she asked. *Who are you?*

I'm your dragon.

My…dragon?

Your dragon side, dear. The part of you that is more than human. More than mage. You're Dragon Born.

I know that already.

Yes, you know the name, but you don't know what it means. The Dragon Born weren't named after the dragons. They are *the dragons. Two sides of one coin: dragon and mage. Together, we are strong. Strong enough to beat these Games.*

And Alex has a dragon too?

Yes, of course. The voice frowned inside Sera's head. *But she's rather brutish at times. You need to be careful around her. She's responsible for a lot of Alex's reckless behavior. I, on the other hand, am the sensible one. I'm a good influence on you. I don't play with fire.*

She snorted. *Really? You're going to stick to that story? Because I've done plenty of reckless things.*

Such as?

Jumped into bed with the dragon. The other *dragon. Kai.*

Yes, well, he's hot. And has nice dragon-like qualities. With our kind nearly extinct, he's as close as you're going to get to a real dragon mate.

Mate?

Don't give me that deer-in-headlights look, missy. We both know where this is headed. And I applaud your choice.

It sounds like you were the one to choose him, Sera commented.

He does taste like cinnamon-frosted euphoria, her dragon said with a smile. *But that's not the point. We're the same person, Sera. You can't go separating out me from you. We both chose him.*

Hmm.

We are linked to Alex and her dragon too. Linked by blood and magic. If we develop that bond, our power will grow.

In what way?

I'm not sure. I just know that it will.

This is quite possibly the strangest conversation I've ever had. Maybe she was losing her mind. What was left of it, anyway.

You are not losing your mind. But if you don't get up and fight, you soon will.

Her dragon was right about that. Sera could feel the layers of her shield being flayed off one by one. She had to get up. She had to fight this.

You said we have more magic together?

Yes, by combining our power. By allowing it to blend together, as it was always meant to do.

Ok. Sera pushed against gravity and pain, peeling herself up inch by painful inch. Finally standing again, she stomped her feet against the ground. *Let's do this.*

Magic surged through her veins. It poured across her skin, setting it ablaze with pink light. She thrust her hands out, tearing at the fairies' spell, unraveling the illusions. The dragons overhead exploded, their demise lighting up the sky. The tails of the fireworks dripped down, melting the walls of the meadow. The fairies collapsed like dominoes.

Sera's magic tore across the pit, cracking against the three mage summoners. They hung in the air for a moment, suspended, then dropped to the ground. Their spells puffed out.

The audience jumped to their feet and roared, but Sera didn't see them. She saw only Kai. He stood in the doorway of the pit, the biggest grin she'd ever seen on his face. Ignoring the protests from her bruised bones and the pulsing ache in her head, she ran toward his open arms.

She'd made it halfway there when her phone buzzed in her pocket. She must have forgotten to take it out. Wondering how it was still in one piece after all that, she opened the case. She knew it was probably Finn again, taunting her with another of his messages, but she just didn't give a damn anymore. She'd done the impossible. She'd made it through the Magic Games with her mind unbroken. She could track down one psychopath mage.

She glanced at the screen. It showed a view of her from above, taken just seconds ago. "Time's up, Sera," the caption said.

A portal opened beneath her feet, and she tumbled into oblivion.

CHAPTER TWENTY-FIVE

Darkness Falling

SINISTER MAGIC SWIRLED all around Sera, then spat her out. She lurched and hit the ground, barely managing to stay on her feet. It was dark here, wherever here was. Dim magical lights bobbed up and down overhead, like buoys on the ocean's surface. The air was stale and smelled of old sweat. A chorus of manic magic sang somewhere in the distance.

Sera reached out with her magic, trying to get a fix on where she was and what she was up against. Her magic bounced off the rocky, graffiti-drenched walls and slammed back into her. Iron. There was iron in those walls. Battling the emerging migraine—and the nausea building up inside of her—she inverted her magic, just like Kai had shown her in Alcatraz. The pressure in her head disappeared, and her stomach settled. Sera: 1, Sinister Underground Cavern: 0.

Of course, without her magic, she'd have a hard time finding the portal out of here. Assuming there even was one. She shook the thought from her head. Defeatist thinking wasn't going to get her out of here. And neither

267

was just standing around. There had to be a way out, whether magical or mundane.

We really need to learn to create portals, her dragon told her as she followed the rocky wall. *It's ridiculous how many times you've fallen through one.*

Agreed. Any ideas?

Some of the older mage dynasties know how to do it. Especially the European families. Any chance your lover boy can look through his family's library for information on portals?

Lover boy?

Do you think he'd prefer 'scrumptious eye candy' instead?

I think he'd prefer not knowing anything about this conversation.

Her dragon frowned in her mind, clearly disappointed. *Hmm.*

As to your question, I'm not sure the Drachenburg dynasty is so much into creating portals as they are into, well...

Scaring people shitless?

Sera nodded. *Something like that. Their specialty is highly destructive magic, usually elemental along with either shifting or summoning.*

And dragons.

There's that too, Sera agreed.

Someone's coming, her dragon told her. *A lot of someones. They feel like mages.*

How can you use magic with all that iron in the walls?

I can use magic just fine. The iron can't bounce it back to me. I don't have a body.

For someone who didn't have a body, she sure could shrug like a pro.

Glowing eyes peered out from the darkness. The

mages followed—dozens of them stepping into the light. They all had that same look about them. Eerie. Magic-drunk. Zombie-like, Sera decided. Just like the mages she and Kai had fought back at Alcatraz. So, she'd landed in Finn's secret lair, and those were his brainwashed minions. Great.

Magic crackled off the mage zombies like camp fire flames. Apparently, the iron in the walls wasn't giving the Crazy Pants Army any trouble. Maybe that was one of the perks of being completely nuts.

"Finn!" Sera shouted as the mages closed in on her from all sides. Their master couldn't be far away. "I know you're here. Come out, you coward! Or are you too scared to face me?"

"Careful, Sera," his voice echoed in warning from behind the mages. "I might take offense."

"You sent me sleazy SMSs from afar. Now you're hiding behind your mages. And you're offended that I'm calling you a coward?" She laughed. "Well, you are, and there are no two ways about it."

"Foolish woman," he growled.

The line of mages parted, revealing Finn. He strode down the aisle, power and confidence streaming off of him like a cloak flapping in the wind. His eyes, alight with manic magic, locked on hers. His aura was so strong that she could feel it through the veil of her inverted magic. Power—ancient and forgotten—pulsed around him, beating against her. His magic hadn't even felt this potent when he'd drained some of Kai's. The possibility that there could be a magic source stronger than Kai, the world's lightning rod of magical might, was almost unthinkable—and it scared her to her bones.

"We stopped you," Sera told him. The best coverup

for fear was to just talk your way past it. Preferably with generous helpings of sarcasm. She'd have to work on adding in the sarcasm. Some other time. When her head wasn't hurting so much. "The Priming Bangles are safe."

"Yes," he said with a sour frown. His voice was dry and rough. "We haven't been able to find the bangles. Kai has taken his paranoia to epic new levels. He didn't tell anyone where he's keeping them." Finn glanced back at his minions. "At least not anyone we could torture the information out of."

The crowd buzzed with whispered snickers. Madness clung to them, thick and sticky.

"So we've had to resort to other means for now," Finn finished,

"How are you draining power without the Priming Bangles?"

"The bangles just make it easier to drain, especially from strong, unwilling targets. Like Kai," he said, his magic flaring in anger when he said Kai's name. "But we have a purer source, one more powerful than even Kai. Our leader."

"Leader? I thought you were the one in charge of this one-way circus to hell."

A smirk slid across his lips, sweet and sour. "There's so much you don't know, Sera."

Magic smashed into her back. She fell, her face smacking the crumbled dirt ground.

"But you will soon see," Finn said as his boots came to a crunching halt beside her.

Laughter, panicked and unchecked, burst from her mouth, and her vision went fuzzy.

"What's so funny?" Finn growled.

She just kept laughing, even as darkness fell over her

eyes.

"What is it?!" Finn demanded, kicking her in the ribs.

Sera hiccuped in pain. "So much…you don't know too…spies in your…evil organization."

Then she passed out.

Consciousness, dull and throbbing, crept at the periphery of Sera's mind. She tried to ignore the unwanted visitor, but like a persistent rash, it just wouldn't go away. Something dripped nearby, slow and steady and sharp enough to cut straight through her eardrums. She tried to turn away from the sound, but her neck only creaked out in agony. When she tried her arms, they didn't move either. Instead, they sang out with as much jingling metal as a snowy sleigh ride.

She forced her eyes open, tearing the thick crust that had glued her lashes to her cheekbones. She was in what looked like an old abandoned tunnel, its rocky walls splattered with faded graffiti. Bright magic lights hovered overhead like a dozen tiny suns. As consciousness flared up, so did the pain in her head. She heaved forward as far as the chains holding her arms allowed and threw up.

"Oh, why did you have to go and do that, Sera?" Finn was leaning against the opposite wall, his arms folded over his chest in relaxed superiority. "Who's going to clean it up?"

She glared at him through hardened lashes. "Release these chains and give me a mop, and I'll show you what I can do."

His laugh could have chiseled stone. "Now, now. Don't be getting any ideas. You're our guest here."

"Right." She shook her wrists, and iron rattled. "Guest," she bit out the word, crisp as a piece of fire-blackened meat. In other words, basically what she was going to turn him into when she got free.

There's too much iron in those walls, her dragon reminded her. *You can't use magic as long as you're blocking it out.*

How about you? You said the iron didn't bother you. Could you shield me from it so I can use magic?

That's actually a good idea.

Try not to sound so surprised, Sera told her.

Her dragon snickered. *Ok, I'll work on it. You distract Mr. Brooding and Crazy.*

"Why am I here?" Sera asked Finn. "In this old... tunnel, is it?"

"We're beneath an old abandoned subway station." His words were smooth and confident, as though he wasn't the least bit worried that she could do anything with that information.

He was probably right. It's not like she could send a message to Kai. She didn't feel her phone in her pocket. Maybe the portal had crunched it into tiny bits—or maybe Finn's lackeys had. Phones could be tracked. Demolished phones—not so much. So it looked like she was on her own.

"What's wrong, Finn? Couldn't you afford a real building for your secret lair?" she taunted. Sarcasm was the next best weapon to magic. And right now, it was pretty much the only one that she had.

His eyes flared with fury and magic, but he choked them back. "There's iron in the rocks. It bounces magic, blocking out tracking spells. We wouldn't want to be interrupted." His smile returned, sick and languid as it washed over her.

Sera had the sudden and irresistible urge to shower.

"It doesn't have to be this way, Sera," Finn said, pushing off the wall. He took a cup from the table, then strode up to her like a king in his own castle. "Water?"

A dry film caked her tongue, screaming for his offering. "How long have I been here?"

She didn't expect an answer, so she was surprised when Finn replied, "It's been nearly a day. The magic Alden hit you with was pretty potent. We weren't sure we'd be able to knock you out otherwise. Your resistance to magic is troublesome."

"I've been called that once or twice before." Often by uptight members of the magical elite. "But I prefer charming."

"Yes." His tongue flicked out, sliding across the entire length of his upper lip.

Yuck.

He held the cup in front of her mouth. Since she didn't think he'd go through all the trouble of chaining her to the room only to poison her the second she regained consciousness, she took a drink. If she was wrong about the poison—if she choked on her own vomit—she vowed to throw up all over his shoes as she died.

"Who's Alden?" Sera asked when she'd emptied the whole cup without dying a painful and horrible death.

Surprise flashed across his face. "You don't know of the great Alden, the world's greatest mage?"

"Sorry, no."

"He was born millennia ago, at the height of magic."

"Like Gaelyn?" she asked.

"No, nothing like that pansy," Finn spat with disgust.

"Gaelyn is weak. The centuries have diminished his magic. But Alden is strong." Pure, undiluted adoration gleamed in his manic eyes. "He was so strong that the Magic Council feared him. They didn't have the power to kill him, so they had him entombed. He slept for centuries, waiting for someone to free him. Me."

Sera had heard this story before—all but the final bit where some idiot freed him. "You're speaking of the mage named the Grim Reaper."

"It was the sniveling fools on the Magic Council that gave Alden that name. He is so much more than death."

"More than death? Right," she said drily. "He was a monster who terrorized the world for centuries. He was put down because he was insane. He mass-murdered humans, draining their life force to increase his power and give himself immortality. He's no better than a vampire, except at least most vampires know when to stop. The Grim Reaper just drains them dead."

"Don't call him that!" Finn snarled, drawing back his hand. His fist collided with her jaw and bone creaked.

She spat blood at his feet. "You hit like a little girl."

He hit her again, harder this time. Yellow and purple lights danced in front of her eyes.

"You'll understand. Someday," he told her, his tone softening. His hand stroked down her face. "Or you'll die," he added with a crooked smirk.

Sera glared up at him through a veil of her own hair, wet with sweat and blood and who knew what else. It smelled like vomit. She sent a surge of magic across her skin, electrocuting him. The iron echoed her magic back at her, shooting her headache to new epic levels, but it was worth it to watch Finn flail like a fish on a hook.

"Stupid bitch!" he screamed, jumping back. His

fireball fizzled out. He clocked her hard against the temple.

She must have blacked out for a second because when she opened her eyes again, he was pacing in front of her, bouncing a new fireball between his hands.

"What do you see in him?" he snarled, rage quaking his body.

"Who?" she croaked. Her throat felt like it had been strangled then hung out to dry.

"Kai," he snapped out his cousin's name like it was poison. "Is it the way he blows things up?" The cup on the table behind Finn exploded. "Is it his dragon magic?" The fiery shape of a summoned dragon took shape behind him. Its tail uncurled, sliding up Sera's leg.

The fire of the dragon began to eat away at the fabric of her pants, turning it to ashes. Heat bathed her skin, searing it with pain. Sera shook her hands, pulling against the chains, but they were too strong.

Use magic to break them, her dragon said. *I've figured out how to shield you from the iron.*

Sera didn't have to be told twice. She slid her magic along the chains. As the metal weakened and moaned, Finn stepped back, his mouth flying open in shock. But it was taking too long with the chains. She poured water magic down her legs, putting out the dragon's fire. Steam hissing, her magic spread up the dragon's tail, her rage chomping away at the summoned beast. As the last piece of the dragon dissolved, she threw her hands forward, breaking through her chains. Tiny iron flakes crumbled to the ground.

"We're done here," she told Finn, her voice cold and flat.

Twin pillars of fire burst out of the ground, one on

either side of him. "Oh, no, Sera. We've only just begun." The ghost of a smile danced across his lips, his magic crackling in the orange-red light. He arched forward, primed to strike.

Liquid lightning slithering across her arms, Sera shot him her best demented grin. "Bring it."

Finn's arms lifted, quivering with magic. His eyes were a nonstop runaway train ride to hell.

"Stop," a voice boomed, the walls shaking with the force of the magic pounding beneath that single word. Overheard, two of the floating lights slammed into each other and crash-landed onto the table.

Finn's tense body went liquid, and he fell to his knees. "Alden," he said, his word kissing the ground as a cloaked man strode into the room.

"Serafina Dering," the Grim Reaper said, his voice burning as intensely as his fiery green eyes. "I've been waiting for you for a very long time."

CHAPTER TWENTY-SIX

The Grim Reaper

ALDEN'S MAGIC HUNG thick in the air, old and powerful. Like Kai-powerful—times a hundred. His magic tasted like death and dripped torment. Sera could see how he'd earned the name Grim Reaper. Her skin was drenched with the vile mist. The hairs on the back of her neck stood up like an army of rigid-backed soldiers.

Alden stepped into the light of the magic lanterns. He looked like a mage, and yet there was something eerie about him. Too perfect. Too fake. He didn't look a day over seventeen. It must have been all the life force he'd drained over the centuries. Power slid over him like a cloak of blood and tears. A cloak of death.

He looked down at Finn's groveling form with disdain. "This is no way to treat our guest," he said, his voice like crushed diamonds. "You were supposed to ask her about the traitor she mentioned in our midst, *not* force yourself on her. And most certainly not attack her," he added with a clinical glance down at Sera's burnt legs. The look in his eyes was so clean, so borderline bored, that you could have sterilized wounds with it.

Apologies and brittle excuses spluttered out of Finn's mouth. Alden raised a hand, and the words froze on his minion's tongue. Then he turned and glided toward Sera, fluid and graceful, his feet hardly touching the ground.

"Sera, I must apologize for his behavior," Alden said, primly sliding a handkerchief out of his cloak pocket. He dabbed it against the blood dripping from the corner of her mouth. "Young mages have so little control over their baser impulses."

With Alden's attention off of him, Finn decided it was safe to stand again. He hung back at a distance, his eyes darted nervously from the ancient mage to Sera.

"Welcome to my humble home," Alden told her. "It's not much. For now. This is what I've been reduced to, but it will change soon enough. Soon, I will reclaim my kingdom. Soon, I will rule over all. It will be a better world."

He stretched out his hand toward the doorway. She followed him through, hoping for a bigger room with more room to maneuver. She got her wish.

Magic flames burst to life, revealing a huge chamber. Mages lined each rocky wall, their magic standing at attention. The iron didn't seem to be bothering them any more than it had Finn or Alden. Besides the door she'd just stepped through, there were three other openings. Maybe they were exits, or maybe they were just passages into dead end rooms.

A centaur stood guard in front of every doorway, each one armed to the teeth and looking as mean as a harpy with PMS. One of them was Apollo, the centaur Sera had talked down from a fight in the Rich Witch section of Macy's. He held a sword twice as long as the one he'd had last time. As he met her stare across the room, his hand twitched on his hilt. Hand cramp or secret symbol? Sera was hoping for the latter. Chances were—well not good, but at least not impossible—that if Kamikaze Mage had weaseled himself inside of this evil organization, then someone else could have done it too. Apollo seemed like an upstanding, honorable sort of fellow. A little bloodthirsty maybe but definitely not crazy. She couldn't imagine that he would join a war campaign against the Magic Council.

"What do you think?" Alden asked, drawing her attention back to him.

Sera allowed her gaze to slide across the lines of magic-drunk mages, then turned to stare him down. "I am not your puppet." She could feel his magic skirting the perimeter of her defenses, trying to find a way inside her mind. She pushed back, snapping his magic back to him.

"No, you're not," he laughed, brushing his hands across the front of his cloak. "Your will is strong, your mind formidable. I am not surprised that you bested that spineless sap Blackbrooke at his own game."

"Did you have anything to do with the vampire attacks on the Magic Council?" she asked him.

"I?" Alden rested his hands before him, braiding his fingers together. "No."

"So it is just a coincidence that you and a mad mage just happen to both be gunning for the Magic Council?"

"Well, there are no true coincidences in the world, dear girl. Everything happens for a reason," he said, his magic ripe with amusement.

Whatever the joke that was tying his magic up into happy bows, she didn't get it—or want to.

"But, no, I didn't have anything to do with that," he

told her. "Those Convictionites are truly vile creatures. They were around even back in my time, and I was dismayed to learn that they hadn't died out in the centuries since. Especially given their utter lack of competence. Had they succeeded in their ploy against the Magic Council...well no matter." He clapped his hands together. "Let's not get caught up in pointless details. We will deal with those magic haters soon enough."

She arched a single eyebrow upward at him. "And everyone else who stands in your way?"

"There's no need to be melodramatic. I am not a psychopath."

Could have fooled me.

His eyes snapped at her, as though he'd heard the thought. "Let's speak not of the horrid necessities, but of more pleasant things." His smile returned with a vengeance. "You will have a place in my new world, Sera. A place by my side. You will be my sentinel, the white knight, the champion of might and righteousness. You will protect this new and better world. A world where you will be the hunter, not the hunted. But we will speak of that soon. First, tell me about this traitor in my midst."

Sera balked at the command in his voice, but she decided to tell him anyway. She needed to keep him talking. She had a feeling that as soon as he realized she wasn't going to join his creepy cult, he wouldn't waste time in disposing of her. Even if he'd been alone, she wouldn't have had a snowball's chance in hell of surviving a duel with him, let alone winning one. His magic was for the moment calm, but she could feel the power throbbing behind that cool facade. Bone-splintering, magic-shattering power. The man was a beast hidden inside of a teenage boy's body.

"Your traitor was the mage controlling the vampires. He was a Convictionite," she told Alden.

"How illogical," was Alden's cool response.

"I'll kill that traitor," Finn spat.

"No," Alden said. "That's a job for my new sentinel."

Sera laughed. "It's too late for that. Your traitor poisoned his own blood with magic. He's dead."

Alden folded his hands together calmly. "There will be others for you, my sentinel. You will uproot all those who threaten our noble cause."

Sera nibbled on her lower lip, pretending to consider his words. *Any idea how we're going to get out of here?* she asked her dragon.

Your centaur friend. Goldilocks.

Apollo? She tried to look at him, but the damn Grim Reaper was in the way.

He's subtly pointing at the doorway guarded by his tawny comrade.

Describe 'subtly pointing'.

Scratching his hindquarters with his middle finger pointed kind of in the direction of that doorway.

That's what you've got? For all we know, he's just flicking me off.

Her dragon shrugged. *That's a distinct possibility. You do tend to bring that out in people. And dragons.*

Hey!

Chuckles buzzed inside her mind and her dragon said, *I know it sucks, but Goldilocks and his middle finger are the best chance that we've got.*

Sera gave her a mental grunt. Her dragon was right. She began to pace, angling toward the questionable exit. Alden watched her, his eyes growing wary. Maybe he thought she'd try to pull something. Well, she wasn't one to disappoint.

"I am not your sentinel," she told him. "Not your lackey, your brain-dead worshipper, or whatever else the hell you want to make me."

His lips thinned. "How disappointing."

His magic pounded against hers—once, with the force of a great big hammer. He hit her again, harder. And again. Her mind was crinkling like an aluminum can beneath a battering ram. Fissures formed in her shield, and he slithered inside. She saw her house burning and her friends screaming in torment.

Keep him talking, her dragon said.

I don't think I can talk. She winced, buckling beneath the pain. She'd never felt anything like it before. Her brain felt like it was melting from the inside.

Toughen up and shoot off that smart mouth of yours! We need time to build up our power for a single concentrated burst.

Sera didn't think she could do anything more sophisticated with her magic right now than let it collapse to the ground like a deflated balloon, but she didn't think that to her dragon. Her head hurt too much to think, let alone talk.

"You don't know me at all," she croaked out, glaring out at Alden. Standing was getting difficult. So was staying conscious.

"Don't I?" His mouth quirked up. "I know what you are. Dragon Born."

The words echoes through the hollow chamber like a spell on the wind. Some of the mages began to mutter, their faces twisted in shock. They gaped at her, disgust rolling off of them. The word 'abomination' hummed over their heads. Even Finn looked shocked. He turned to

Alden like a confused child seeking comfort and answers from his father.

Alden pivoted, his cloak swirling around him. "She is not an abomination," he told his loyal followers.

The frightened whispers died down.

"No more than I am the Grim Reaper," he continued. "They are just vile names forced onto us by lesser mages. By the Magic Council." His eyes, alight with sweet, seductive magic, turned to Sera. "We are much alike. Both powerful, both feared for our power."

"We are nothing alike," she ground out. He hadn't lessened his attack on her mind, not even for a second. "You killed people. You wreaked havoc and devastation."

His laughter roared through the chamber, and the walls quaked. "And what do you think the Dragon Born did, my dear? Why they were sentenced to death?"

Dread crawled its way down her throat, choking her rebuttal.

"That's right." Victory sang in his eyes. "I was there. There the day the Dragon Born were sentenced to oblivion. I could tell you all about it. All you have to do is listen."

Lies!

How do you know? she asked her dragon. *Does your magic allows you to see back to that time?*

No, through my magic—our blood—a see fleeting glimpses of past days, but it's been too long. The history, the bonds of magic of the Dragon Born, are withered and old because any time one of us is discovered, we're killed. The mage dynasties with the right magic to produce Dragon Born twins have been all but destroyed. It's a rare condition of birth, the chance of a Dragon Born birth only one in millions. It requires the right combination of blood, magic, and luck.

"The others, the members of the Magic Council, are small-minded," Alden said, cutting into her thoughts. "They don't understand you, and they don't want to. I do. I alone am sympathetic to your plight, and I alone can help you. I can unlock your potential. You are special, Sera. You're worth more than the entire Magic Council put together."

She grimaced against the pain. Her skin felt like it was being slowly and methodically scraped off her back.

"I know what will happen if the rest of the world finds out about you. You will die. Your sister will die. Your brother will die. Everyone you care about will die. But that doesn't have to happen. You are a threat to their world, but you're an asset in mine." He extended his hand out to her. "Join me. Protect those you care about. And eliminate those who threaten you."

Temptation churned inside of her, his words like cool, liquid relief on a hot and sticky day, but she pushed it down and gave his hand a scathing look.

"Don't you want to know who sent the assassin after you and Alex? The assassin who killed your father," he added, his voice dropping to a scathing whisper.

"The assassin was working alone."

"How little you know, dear girl! A mage sent the assassin. This mage sent him running after rumors of Dragon Born sisters. The assassin tracked down these rumors, but he was never able to report back who you were to his employer because you killed him. And by the time the mage sent another, you and your family were long gone, your house burned to the ground, no evidence of your existence there remaining."

His smile was so vicious, so undeniably depraved—

and yet she couldn't look away.

"This mage is still alive. The person responsible for your father's death is alive," he told her. "It's someone powerful, someone on the Magic Council. I could tell you who it is. If…"

"If?"

"If you agree to join me."

Sera was so tired of being hunted and hated. His words sang to her soul, swaddling it like a warm, comforting blanket. Vengeance. It took every shred of willpower in Sera to shake her head in refusal.

"You are strong, Sera. Strong and far too stubborn for your own good. You allow yourself to be hunted. No, that is not the proper order of things. The strong should hunt the weak. Your first act as my sentinel and hunter will be to kill this mage who sent the assassin that killed your father. You will wipe away the old and bring in the new. They don't understand. The crime of even considering ending you is unforgivable. They are monsters. The members of the Magic Council are monsters."

He had a point, one that she'd made many times before. There were monsters on the Magic Council, but not every one of them was one.

"No," she said.

I'm Ready. My magic is synched with yours. It's time for us to blast out of here, her dragon told her.

Sera stepped forward, magic charging on her, building up. Her arms shook, her pulse pounding hard and heavy. She'd never felt so much magic inside of her, screaming to get out. She wanted to let loose. She wanted to burn them all.

Hold your horses there, cowgirl. We're strong, but we're not that strong. Mr. Death there has too much power. Plow a path through his flunkies and run like hell.

"You don't care about my pain or my family or even justice," Sera told Alden. "You only care about your power, your magic, your order. In other words, yourself. You want to use me like you've been using these poor people here." She swept her hand around, indicating the magic-drunk mages. "I won't make people stop thinking of me as a monster by acting like one."

"They will always see you as a monster."

"Maybe some," she allowed. "But not all."

"You are naive. Take your new boyfriend, the dragon."

Sera stiffened.

"If he found out what you are, he'd turn on you."

"That's not true."

"Isn't it?"

Magic flashed, and Sera shielded her eyes with her hands. When she opened them again, she wasn't in the cavern. She was standing opposite Kai.

"Abomination," he spat, igniting the air with his rage. "Vile creature." Dragon scales rolled across his arms.

"I thought you'd understand. You said I could tell you anything," she said, reaching for him.

He shrugged her hand off. "I thought you were dabbling in something benign. Like blood or demon magic. Not this." His eyes burned with hatred. "You are a monster. I don't know how you survived this long, but I will correct that mistake."

Magic pulsed out of him, blasting her across the room. Her back hit the wall in a crunch of agony. Tears and blood slid down her face, blurring her vision. Kai was stomping toward her, ready to finish what he'd started.

It's not real.

She wiped her face with the back of her hand, glaring

at him, willing herself to fight the illusion. Kai kept coming. He wasn't going anywhere. Not until she made him.

She pushed up from the ground, pain cutting across her body. She felt like she was being burned alive. Slowly —too slowly—she managed to get to her feet. Kai's fist pounded her against the wall. The back of her head was slick with blood. It gushed down her neck, staining her body red. He swung at her again. Ignoring the explosions going off inside her head, she caught his fist and slammed him against the wall. As he shattered, the illusion broke as well.

She was back in the cavern, Alden's forehead was pressed to hers, his fingers gripping the back of her head. She threw her head forward, butting him hard in the forehead. He stumbled back and fell on his ass.

"You're the real monster," she said, glaring down at him. "And I clean up monsters."

Then she blasted him with her magic. His head hit the ground, and she didn't stop to see how long it would take him to get up again. She ran hard for the doorway, hurling a second blast that sent mages and monsters flailing through the air. The centaur was down. She leapt over him, through the doorway.

"Get her!" Alden's voice roared from the hollow chamber.

Sera kept running, barreling down the long hallway as fast as her feet could carry her, praying that it led somewhere. She didn't dare look back to see what was following her, but she could hear them surely enough, a rumble of magic and brutality. Death's Army.

CHAPTER TWENTY-SEVEN
Death's Army

SERA'S STRENGTH WAS fading fast. That blast had pretty much sapped her magic dry, and sprinting down an endless hallway to who-knew-where with a band of mages doped up on Grim Reaper magic on her heels wasn't doing wonders for her stamina either. If she didn't find the exit soon, she'd have to do something drastic.

More drastic than knocking Alden onto his bony little butt? her dragon sniped.

That wasn't drastic. It was a calculated strategy. Too bad she hadn't calculated an exit plan into her strategy.

The air feels better up ahead.

Define better.

Her dragon shrugged into her mind. *Not as thick with cuckoo mage vibes. And maybe fresher. I think there's a shaft leading up to the surface.*

Sera pushed forward with renewed energy. If she could just get out of these tunnels, to where actual people were... Then what? Would Death's Army scuttle off, their tails between their legs, at the sight of a few humans? Unlikely. Humans meant nothing to them. Their lives meant nothing. Alden would murder every one of them in the city—all those millions—just to get at her, to warp her into his instrument of death. But why? Why her?

A piece of wall exploded nearby, pelleting her with razor-sharp shards of rock speckled with metal. Right, priorities. She could torture herself with these questions all she wanted later. First, she had to make it out of here. A second blast erupted from the wall. Sera shot the telekinetic behind her a nasty glare, the only retaliation she could muster. She didn't have enough magic to bathe the hallway in fire. Unfortunately. That telekinetic was none other than Olivia Sage. After the shit Olivia and her brother had put them through last month, Sera was salivating at the thought of payback.

But she had other things to worry about. Like the fireball that had just cruised over her head, singeing a few of her top hairs. Sera patted down her head. At this rate, she'd need to go buy a wig when she made it out of here. *If* she made it out of here.

A draft of cool air tickled her nose. The shaft! She could feel it. And, as she barreled around the corner, she could see it too. Magic and rock exploded at her heels, urging her to run faster. There was something else, something drawing her forward.

"Kai!"

Sera could feel his magic pounding out in hard, heavy beats. It poured down from the hole in the ceiling up ahead, searing the air with his scent. Hot and sweet and spicy—and most of all dragon. She burst forward with everything she had.

Behind her, Olivia's snickers echoed off the walls with wicked glee. "He's not here, little girl. Even he couldn't find you, not with all the iron in the walls."

Sera's step stuttered. Olivia was right. Kai had no way to find her here. Her mind was just playing tricks on her. Or Alden was playing tricks on her.

She'd reached the hole in the ceiling and peered up. The shaft dripped darkness. She couldn't see how far up it went—or whether it even led anywhere. One thing was for sure, though: there was no way she could climb up that thing. The mages would blast her right out of the ceiling. This was the end of the road. Sera spun around, drawing on every shred of magic left in her. A barrier of flames and lightning snapped up in front of her. Here she'd make her final stand.

"That won't keep you safe for long," Olivia snarled through the barrier. "Alden wants you, and Alden shall have you. But if you put away your magic and come quietly, I promise not to hurt you." A saccharine smile slid across her full lips. "Not until we get back to Alden."

A tendril of lightning-bound fire snapped out from the barrier like a whip, cracking the air in front of Olivia. The telekinetic jumped back, hurling curses.

"I think I'll pass," Sera told her.

"Fool," Olivia spat, waving the other mages forward.

They raised their hands and blasted the barrier with their collective magic.

"Not…good enough," Sera told them, wincing under the onslaught.

Satisfaction washed across Olivia's face. "Oh, but we're just getting started."

The mages beat at her barrier. Again. And again. And again. Sweat beaded Sera's brow, dripping down her neck. She wiped her slick palms on her pants.

"Sera."

She ignored the voice. It called to her again.

"Go away," she growled, keeping her focus on the barrier. It was all that stood between her and Alden's army. "I know you're not real."

"She's delusional. Probably dehydration coupled with severe exhaustion," Dal's voice said.

Sera licked her cracked lips. It felt like scraping sandpaper over an open wound.

"Have a look at that barrier!" exclaimed Callum. "It's eating their magic!"

"There have got to be at least fifty mages down there. She's holding off the magical onslaught of fifty mages," Tony said.

Since when had the commandos become figments of her imagination?

"Sera, I'm coming," Kai called out.

Another figment of her imagination. An illusion. But she wasn't falling for it, not this time.

"The drop is too big," Callum said. "We need to set up the ropes and rappel down there."

Sera stole a glance up into the hole. Flashlights beamed down, blinding her. She blinked and returned her attention to her barrier.

"No time," said Kai.

Wind howled out of the hole, and a second later, Kai dropped down on the wings of magic. Sera didn't even look at him. She didn't have time to talk to herself—or Alden, if that's who was really behind the illusion.

"Sera, we have to go."

A boulder exploded against her barrier. Tiny fissures split across its orange-pink surface. She poured magic over the barrier, trying to seal the cracks, but a second explosion fractured it again.

Can't hold it...any longer, her dragon said, then

winked out of her mind.

Sera fell to her knees, broken rock scraping her exposed skin. But the pain in her legs was nothing compared to the agony in her head. Spots danced in front of her eyes.

Arms, hard and rigid, grabbed her from behind, pulling her up. She struggled, her feet kicking uselessly against the ground.

"Stop…" Kai grunted. "…fighting me."

She clamped her hands down on his arms, shooting lightning through him. The bastard snarled but didn't budge an inch.

"What's the matter with you?" he growled.

"You're not real," she coughed, her tears burning her cheeks. She'd hit him with everything she had, but the illusion hadn't shattered. Her barrier, on the other hand, was on its last legs.

Kai shifted his grip so that he was only holding her with one arm. Magic had failed her, so she tried brute force. She pushed against his hold, but he had her arms pinned to her sides. She threw a wistful look at her dying barrier. As it whispered its final breath, a new barrier blazed up in its place, breathing fire at the mages. Sera looked down at her hands, then up at Kai. Her mind was trying to tell her something, but she couldn't make it work long enough to do that.

"You…" She coughed, blood splattering his cheek.

"It's ok. You're safe now."

She slumped against him, not even caring anymore that it wasn't real. His lips brushed against her forehead, his breath warm against her icy skin. She shivered. When had it gotten so cold?

"Let's get you out of here," he said. His arms wrapped

around her back, hugging her to him.

She nodded and nestled up to his chest, a stupid smile on her lips. She inhaled deeply, drinking in his thick, masculine scent. As far as illusions went, this one was pure rapture. A blanket of wind enveloped them, carrying them upward. They slid through the shaft and landed softly in what appeared to be an old abandoned subway station. The commandos were there, dressed in black and steel. Someone else was there too, standing back a ways and cloaked in shadow. She hoped it wasn't Alden.

"How many?" Tony asked.

Kai shook his head. "Too many…have to get her out of here."

The words echoed dully, as though spoken underwater. Sera's head spun, and her feet collapsed out from under her.

When she opened her eyes again, she was in Kai's arms, and he was carrying her toward the light.

"Just rest now," he said softly against her cheek.

Warmth embraced her, and she surrendered to the darkness.

CHAPTER TWENTY-EIGHT
Knight of the Occult

SWEET AND BLISSFUL dreams cushioned Sera's sleep like a bed of frothy clouds. She dreamed that she and Kai soared the skies on dragon wings. They dropped down to a field of giant yellow daisies, dragon scales fading to human flesh as they landed. Kai's eyes blazed with blue fire as they slid over her. Magic crackled on his skin. And when he touched her, it crawled up her arm and jumpstarted her heart.

Torn from sleep, Sera jumped up—and immediately tripped over something twisted around her ankles. A blanket? Heaving in labored breaths, she pushed herself off the floor. She was on a plane. Kai's plane. She looked around, finding him sitting on the sofa she'd just so gracefully fallen off of. His eyes were quiet, his magic withdrawn.

"Where the hell are we?" she croaked out. Her voice was dry and her throat raw.

"Somewhere over Wyoming."

He reached over to the side table and handed her a glass of water. She chugged it down and asked for more.

Then she hightailed to the bathroom. She couldn't even remember the last time she'd answered nature's call, but it had been a while. It was a miracle that she hadn't peed her pants during the whole Alden ordeal.

And now she was safe? A vague jumble of mismatched images—her running, fighting Alden's mages, her barrier falling, Kai sweeping her up—flashed through her mind. It had been real? *This* was all real? Her mind felt clear now. It didn't feel like she was trapped in an illusion. She splashed her face with water just to be sure.

Someone had cleaned and healed her wounds and dressed her in a snuggly sweatsuit. Cold. She'd been cold. And her dragon...

Are you there?

Yes, a voice said in her head, and Sera's heart leapt with joy. She didn't know when she'd become so attached to the snarky dragon, but she was glad her other half was all right.

Snarky, Miss-Pot-Calling-the-Kettle-Black? Indeed! Her dragon snorted. Then, her tone softening, she added, *I've become rather attached to you too, mage.*

Sera leaned her hands against the sink counter, slouching in relief. *We made it.*

Yes. Thanks to me. And maybe a little help from Sexy Shifter.

Are you going to stick with that name?

Her dragon smirked into her mind. *If you call him that, I bet he'll do that thing with his tongue you like so much...*

Sera jumped, her head smacking against the low ceiling. Damn airplanes. Her cheeks flushed, she hurried out of the bathroom, her dragon's snickers trailing her all the way back to the sofa. She plopped down and hastily threw her blanket over herself. She wasn't cold—not anymore—but she had the sudden and irresistible urge to hide under something. Unfortunately, she couldn't hide from herself, but after their delightful conversation in the bathroom, her dragon had gone silent again. She was probably still tired from their battle against Alden's people. Sera sure wished she could doze back off into oblivion. But first things first. She had to figure out everything that had happened.

"Kai." She turned toward him, trying not to blush at the magic lighting up his eyes. "I was a little out of it when you found me. I hope I didn't hurt you."

"Sera, you'd have to hit me a lot harder than that to hurt me."

"Still, I'm sorry. I thought you were an illusion. My mind wasn't all there. I didn't think it could be you, not there. You couldn't have found me."

Kai was watching her very closely, as though he thought she'd pop. "You disappeared in the fighting pit, right before my eyes. I saw you check your phone, then the portal swallowed you up. I knew Finn had you."

Alden actually, but Sera didn't interrupt him. She did, however, happily take the bowl of pretzels he was holding out to her.

"Sofia, one of the Magic Council mages we saved from the vampires, is an expert on portals, so I found her," he continued. "By the time we got back down to the pit, it was too late to follow you through. Sofia said the portal was a fast-fading one. Limited range, no matter how much magic you pour into it, but virtually untraceable."

"Then how did you find me?"

"The portal was virtually untraceable, but not

impossible. Sofia got a fix on a general location of where the portal had taken you, a section of a few city blocks."

"New York doesn't have the smallest blocks."

"It was a large area to search," he agreed. "But it was better than all of Manhattan. Or the whole city for that matter. The commandos and I went to the area to start our search, but I couldn't feel your magic anywhere."

"That's because of the iron in the walls bouncing magic like a house of mirrors."

"Yes," he said. "We had to search manually. We weren't making any progress. And then Cutler showed up."

"Cutler?" she gasped in surprise. "What was he doing there?"

"He said he was there to help."

"And you believed him?"

"No. Not at first. But then he showed us his phone. It showed your location, one block over and many levels down. He was tracking you."

"But…how?"

"He said he tagged you with an electronic tracker when you two spoke before your match."

A memory faded in. Cutler touching her arm. So that's what he'd been up to.

"So he's not evil?" she asked Kai.

"Apparently not. Nor as stupid as he seemed."

"Try not to sound so disappointed," Cutler said.

Sera looked across the room. The man that stood there, framed in the open doorway, had Cutler's face, but that's where the resemblance ended. His blond hair, always molded into architected disorder, was combed back with clean precision. Rather than his usual silk shirt and hip-hugging pants, he wore a suit. It was the sort of suit Kai, an executive at Drachenburg Industries, would have worn—if Kai hadn't had a scathing dislike for suits. Shutting the door behind him, Cutler crossed the room to stop in front of Sera.

"I'm happy that you're all right," he told her. There was none of the usual innuendo in his voice, and he wasn't looking at her like he was mentally undressing her. "And I must apologize for acting like such an ass to you all those times."

"Why were you…um, acting like an ass?"

The corner of his lip twitched. "I needed an excuse to be close to you, and playing the infatuated idiot was a good way to do that. Acting like a moron also throws people off. Keeps them from suspecting I'm a threat." He winked at her, a touch of the Cutler she knew in that gesture.

"But why? What were you hiding? And why did you want to be close to me?"

"So I could watch you, Sera, as my mother instructed me to do," he said. "You see, she is the commander of the Knights of the Occult."

"I haven't heard of them."

"They're a centuries' old society of mages," Kai told her. "Mages from many of the old dynasties are members."

Cutler nodded. "We have all sworn to protect the supernatural community from ancient threats. Demons mostly, but every so often, something else from our past jumps up and bares its ugly teeth."

"Alden," she said, her voice a whisper. "The Grim Reaper."

"After the recent fiasco with the Priming Bangles, we suspected something was amiss. We didn't believe Finn capable of such things. He's neither powerful nor devious enough to pull off something of that magnitude. And then mages broke him out of Atlantis."

"Alden's mages."

"A few of the Atlantis prison guards are in his pocket," Kai told her.

"We didn't know it was Alden at that point," said Cutler. "In fact, we didn't find that out until I went down into the tunnels with Kai and felt that old power for myself. All we knew was that someone from the past was planning something big and that he was using Finn to do it. I was trailing a mage we suspected to be involved. It turns out he was involved. He got Alden all the pictures of you."

"You were sitting close to him in the Magic Games audience?" she asked.

"Yes."

She shivered.

"We had a few ideas about who he was working for. It never crossed our minds that it could be Alden." Cutler paled. "In all the centuries, all the days of bloodshed and death, the Grim Reaper was the worst villain of them all. He was, as his name suggests, the personification of death itself."

"Yes," Sera agreed. The memory of her time in those nightmare tunnels was seared into her consciousness.

Kai squeezed her hand. Relaxing her clenched teeth, she turned her head and smiled at him. His eyes flashed, and one eyebrow cocked up at her.

"In any case, I'm glad you made it through," Cutler said briskly. Then he patted her shoulder and turned to leave.

"He's not what I thought," she said as Cutler slipped

out of the room, shutting the door behind him. Leaving her alone with Kai. Kai and those eyes as deep as the ocean itself.

"No, he's not."

Kai slid across the sofa toward her with liquid ease. He flipped her hand over. Lifting it to his lips, he kissed the underside of her wrist. Heat electrified her nerves, flushing her skin with heat.

"Bad dragon," she said, slapping his hand away.

A grin twisted across his lips, sexy and slow, like he was savoring every second. "I was worried about you."

"And you're not used to that?"

His smile faded, and his hand tightened with possessive unease around hers, like he expected an attack on her at any second. He looked ready to jump in and take a bullet for her. It was the most erotic thing she'd ever seen, and his next words were like dark chocolate icing on that devil cake.

"No, I'm not," he said.

Chuckling softly under her breath, she climbed into his lap and rested her head on his chest, hyperaware of the hard muscle pressed against her cheek. She reached up to trace a finger along his jaw. She was playing with fire and knew it, but she just didn't care. A deep groan rumbled in his chest, sending a wave of delicious vibrations down her neck.

"You are the most beautiful woman I have ever seen." His words brushed against her lips; his hands massaged her back in slow, deep circles.

She smirked at him. "You're just saying that because you want into my pants."

"Yes." His voice dipped lower—and his hands too. "But that doesn't mean it's not true."

"Mmm." She nipped at his lower lip. "You're not so bad yourself, dragon breath."

"I prefer Sexy Shifter."

Heat scorched her cheeks. She pulled back and met his eyes. "Where did you hear that?"

"You were muttering in your sleep."

Shit.

A sleepy chuckle buzzed in her mind.

We have got to talk about you putting ideas into my head. And words into my mouth.

Her dragon didn't respond, which was just as well. Kai was already giving her an odd look. She didn't need to add to his suspicions by having conversations inside her head right in front of him.

"Sera—" He dropped his hands. The heat in his eyes faded.

Was Cutler back? She turned, then froze. No, not Cutler. Riley and Naomi. Her fairy friend's eyes danced with delight. She was barely holding back a happy dance. Riley, on the other hand, looked like someone had just died. Guilt flooding her, Sera climbed off of Kai's lap and scooted as far away from him as she could. Oh dear God, she hadn't just been straddling him when her brother walked in. This was a dream, a far inferior one to their earlier rendezvous in the field of daisies. That one had been devoid of witnesses or humiliation.

"So glad you're awake, Sera!" Naomi said brightly.

She was the only person in the room who wasn't acting awkward. Well, maybe except Kai. Nothing ruffled his feathers—err, scales. He met Riley's narrow-eyed stare, a challenge in his eyes. Riley pulled something out of his pocket, something that looked like one of his magic bombs. If Sera didn't get between those two soon, they were going to blow the plane out of the sky. She rose, her bones popping in protest. Couldn't the boys have waited until they were back on the ground before having their shoot-out? She was too tired for this nonsense.

Naomi glided across the room with balletic grace. She caught Sera by the hand, pulling her back down to the sofa. Except Naomi was now between her and Kai. Riley relaxed noticeably. Kai shot Naomi an irate look but said nothing.

"How are you feeling?" Naomi asked Sera, wrapping an arm around her.

"Alive. Mostly," she added with an amused grunt.

"Kai told us about what happened. And Cutler. Wow. Didn't see that one coming." Her eyes twinkled with tiny golden lights, a perfect match to her glittery eyeshadow. "He looks hot in his Knight of the Occult suit, by the way."

"Don't tell me you hit on Cutler?"

Naomi grinned. "What can I say? I have a weakness for a man in uniform." Her gaze slid over to Kai. "Speaking of which, I'm curious to see your threads."

He arched a single eyebrow at her.

"I heard you were in the military. And played with tanks."

"By playing with tanks, he means tanks shot at him, and then he threw hissy fits and knocked them over in a fit of rage," Sera told her.

"Knocked them over? The soldiers?" Naomi asked.

Sera shook her head. "No, the tanks."

Naomi winked at Kai.

"So I don't think there's a uniform for that," Sera said. "He was in dragon form."

"Oh, honey, it's the military. There are always

uniforms," Naomi drawled, the words sliding off her tongue.

Kai glared back at her like he wanted to shoot *her* out of a tank. She winked at him again.

"So Cutler tracked me?" Sera said quickly, before she had to stop another shoot-out.

Riley had drifted over to Sera's side of the sofa. He was leaning against the window, giving Kai the stink eye, which Kai was pretending to ignore. Sera decided to ignore them both.

"Mmm-hmm," said Naomi, watching the drama show play out with a strange fascination that was bordering on excitement. "Cutler led them to the abandoned subway station. By then, they were close enough that Kai was able to hone in on your magic and find you."

Sera looked at Kai. "You could find me through all that iron?"

"Your magic has an entirely unique flavor."

Riley stiffened at the mention of 'flavor'.

"What about the Magic Games?" she asked Kai. "Since we're here and not still in New York, I hope that means Blackbrooke didn't insist that he keep testing me until I broke." She glanced out the window. "Or should I be worried that we're on the run and be very likely to be bombed out of the sky."

"*You* shouldn't be worrying about anything," Riley told her. "Between the Games, the vampires, and Alden, you've had enough on your plate. You need to let us take care of things for once."

"Agreed," said Kai.

Naomi bobbed her head. "Yep."

"I can't help but notice that you didn't actually answer

my question," Sera said. "If we're expecting an attack, I need to know about it."

"We're not," replied Kai. "Duncan wasn't happy that you withstood his tests, but you completed all your matches. And you fought monsters outside of the pit, to save him and other members of the Magic Council, no less. He agreed you've done enough fighting for him to complete your magic levels assessment."

Bullshit. She'd seen the look in his eyes when he'd promised her he would break her. That was a man who wouldn't simply back down.

"How much did you pay him to get me out of additional testing?"

"You followed all the rules," Kai said. "You completed all the matches. He can't just make you do more."

"He can do whatever he wants. The Council has given him a lot of power."

"Duncan was grateful to you for saving him from the vampires. The Council was grateful too."

Sera gave him a hard look.

"Fine. Ok. I might have bribed him a little."

Sera sighed. "I hope it wasn't too much."

"It's not anything I can't afford to pay." Evasive again. Kai owned a jumbo jet. He could afford a lot of things.

"So less than the cost of a skyscraper," she teased, thinking back to their battle in the Empire State Building.

His eyes flashed. "Yes."

"Ok." She looked at each of them in turn. "What about Alden? What is the Magic Council going to do about him?"

Riley picked up the remote, switching on the large television. He flicked to the Magic Channel. Bright text headlines played over a montage of images from the Games, the underground tunnels, and a few distinguished members of the Magic Council. 'The Grim Reaper Returns' was one of the juicier headlines. It sounded like a blockbuster movie sequel.

"The Council wanted to keep this all under wraps, but there were too many witnesses. Too much evidence," Kai said.

"They shouldn't want to hide this," replied Sera. "If people don't know about Alden, how can they defend themselves against him when he comes? Look at how easily he seduced all those mages, whispering sweet lies while hiding from the shadows. We need to shine a light on him, to remind people why he was entombed to begin with. Otherwise, he'll just keep corrupting and recruiting people."

"Is that what he tried to do to you?" Riley asked.

"Yes. He got inside my mind. Showed me things…" Her gaze drifted over to Kai. "Horrible things. He finds out your worst nightmares, twisting them into something a hundred times more awful. And then he uses them to break you."

"But not you?" Kai asked.

"I'm too stubborn," she joked, her smirk wobbling.

Riley snorted as Naomi's hand squeezed her shoulder. Kai just watched her, his face completely neutral.

"It hurts," she said in a soft whisper. "When he's in your head. You feel every punch. Every cut. Everything. Most of all, it's the fear. It gnaws at you from the inside. I think…I think he feeds on that fear. It makes his magic stronger."

"That's what the legends say," Kai said.

He stared at her, wonder in his eyes. They sang to her

in sinful promise. His magic caressed hers, ruthless and sensual. It was a bold move for him, even knowing that neither Riley nor Naomi could sense magic. He was essentially feeling her up in front of them. The man was wicked to the core.

"Yes, well…" Sera cleared her throat, batting his magic away, even though she wanted nothing more than to grab it and rub it all over her. She was so doomed.

Kai's eyes smirked, like he knew what he'd done to her and liked it. "We'll figure out how to deal with Alden. He was defeated before, and we'll do it again. But for now, Sera, you really need to rest. You've been fighting nonstop for weeks. We have a couple hours left in the air before we land in San Francisco. Take a nap."

"Ok," she agreed, spreading her blanket over herself.

Before she could even close her eyes, Riley had swung around the sofa. He was staring down at Kai. "We need to talk."

"Yes," Kai said, standing. He nodded toward the door that led to the next room. "There."

Sera sighed. "Wait."

They'd made it halfway to the door, but at that word, they stopped and turned to face her.

"Promise not to kill each other," she said.

"Really, Sera? Just what kind of people do you think we are?" Riley demanded with an impatient grunt.

"We're not barbarians," Kai told her.

She shot them a cool glare. "Just don't fight. Not up here." She fluffed up her pillow. "I'd hate to have to parachute out because the two of you blew a hole in the plane."

Riley glared at her. "Funny."

"I'm not going to blow a hole in my own plane, Sera,"

Kai said with strained patience.

She pulled the phone off the side table and dialed. "Dal?"

"Hey, Sera. Feeling better?"

"I'm fine. Thanks," she told him. "So, Kai and Riley are headed your way to 'talk'."

"I see," he said slowly. "And you want me to break it up if things come to blows?"

"Yeah, blast them with some of that compressed magic in the extinguisher on the wall."

He chuckled. "Sure thing."

"Thanks." She hung up the phone and glared at them both, daring them to challenge her.

They dared.

"Dal doesn't take orders from you," Kai told her, anger simmering just below the surface.

"Maybe not. But he's not going to let you blow up the plane."

"She's mental," Riley said to Kai.

"Why are you looking at me? She's *your* sister," replied Kai. "But, yes, she's crazy."

"Oh, good. You two have finally agreed on something," Sera said with a wry smile. "You're making progress already. Now, take your drama and get the hell out of this room so I can get some sleep."

They exchanged long-suffering glances, then left. Naomi scooted to the side of the sofa that Kai had left vacant.

"So, you want to talk about it?" she asked, balancing her chin on her knees.

"Those guys?" Sera snorted. "No. Not at all."

"I thought Riley wanted you to date Kai."

"Yeah," she said, closing her eyes. "But since when

have men ever made sense?"

She dozed off to the melodic jingle of Naomi's laughter.

CHAPTER TWENTY-NINE

Magic Games

IT WAS PIZZA night, and Riley was late. Sera glanced at the wall clock.

"What could be keeping him?" she wondered aloud.

Her stomach growled, voicing its concern as well.

It's not that Riley wasn't ever late—in fact, he often got so caught up in some magical experiment or another in the lab that he lost all track of time—but it was pizza night. It also just happened to be the night that Kai was back in San Francisco. Not that she was keeping tabs on his schedule. Nope. Not when he couldn't even be bothered to call her.

She wasn't upset about that either.

It had been just over a week since they'd returned from New York. Whatever had transpired between Kai and Riley in that other room on the plane, no one was talking. Kai because he'd flown back out that same day—and not bothered to call her since (nope, still not upset about that!). The commandos had gone with him, so she couldn't grill them. Cutler had been in the room too. Since she was still on leave from work, though, she hadn't had a chance to ask him. Sure, she could have walked into Mayhem on the pretense of using the gym, but she didn't feel ready to be around all those people again. To answer their questions about the Magic Games. And about Alden.

As for Riley... Well, she didn't know why her brother wasn't spilling the beans on what he and Kai had discussed. The plane had still been in one piece when she'd woken up, so she assumed that they hadn't been fighting—or at least that Dal had blasted them with the compressed magic in time.

All she knew right now was that Riley was late the same night Kai was back in town. She hoped they hadn't had a fight. It was unlikely Dal was tailing his boss 24/7 with a canister of compressed magic strapped to his back.

The doorbell rang. Sera's first thought was that Riley had finally arrived. Her second thought was the realization that Riley wouldn't have rung the doorbell. As she headed for the front door, she felt it. Him. His magic was simmering like a steaming teapot, rippling the air with subtle vibrations. It actually felt kind of nice—or at least it would have if she hadn't been too busy looking for her knives to enjoy it.

"I could have sworn they were..." she muttered, tossing a boot aside. "Oh, that's right. I put them in here." She dug two knives out of the potted plant in the entryway, took a deep breath, and opened the door.

"What have you done to Riley?" she blurted out before he could say anything.

Kai gave her knives a bored look. "May I come in?"

"Answer the question, and I might not stab you."

"To do that, you would have to abandon your position in front of the door. At which point, I would

310

breach your defenses."

Oh, he was challenging her, was he? A cool smile slid across her lips. "Not if I threw the knives at you."

He shook his head. "I'm too fast. In fact, I'm too strong for you to have any chance of drawing blood, let alone stabbing me. Why don't you just put those silly sticks away and talk to me like any reasonable person would?"

"I'm reasonable."

"You answered the door bearing weapons," he pointed out. "Albeit pitiful ones."

She crossed her arms against her chest, careful not to stab herself. That would have sure looked menacing. "You still haven't told me where Riley is."

He expelled a martyred sigh. "He got tied up."

Sera narrowed her eyes at him. "When you say 'tied up'..."

"No, I don't mean *literally*. Jeez, Sera! What kind of monster do you think I am? Riley told me he'll be late."

"You talked to him?"

"Yes."

Her body relaxed a bit. "In civil tones?"

"No, we snarled at each other like a pair of rapid dogs." His eyes hardened into blue diamonds. "Of course we spoke in civil tones. He invited me to come over for dinner. He said he'd be running late and asked me to pick up the pizza." Kai held up a stack of pizza boxes.

"Oh."

She hadn't even noticed the pizza boxes. That just went to show that rage was blind. Or was that love? Her heart thumped in her chest. She told it to be quiet, then tried to come up with something witty to cover the dull silence.

"Is Riley busy working late in his lab?" she asked. Ok, apparently witty wasn't on the menu today. She was too hungry for witty right now.

"No, he's busy flirting with a girl," Kai said, amusement flashing in his eyes.

Well, if they were talking about girls, then maybe they'd made up after all. What had they been fighting about anyway? She had a sinking feeling it had to do with her.

"Now may I come in?" he asked her.

"I'm still thinking about it."

"You said if I answered your question, you'd let me in."

"No, I said if you answered my question, I might not stab you. Big difference."

"Sera," he growled.

She chuckled.

"Your pizza is getting cold."

She lowered her knives and scrambled out of his path.

"Thank you," Kai said cooly as he passed, magic crackling off his lips. He walked over to the dining room table and set the boxes down. Then he turned and gave her an expectant look.

Oh, right. Manners. "How have you been?" she asked.

"Busy. I've spent the last week in Magic Council meetings, and it's made me downright cranky."

"Really?" She grinned. "I hadn't noticed."

"Cute, Sera. Real cute. But might I remind you that you're the one who answered the door armed."

"I knew it was you."

"I see." Kai leaned his arms back against the table, and didn't say anything more. He must have been waiting

312

for her to clarify her stupid comment.

"You just left. I... I don't know what I thought. And then you didn't call me." She shifted her weight uncomfortably. She was not *that* girl. "Whatever. Just forget it." She looked away.

"Sera."

She busied herself brushing down a wrinkle in her pants.

"Look at me."

She glanced up at him through lowered lashes.

"I have been doing nothing but sitting in meetings and sleeping—though there was precious little of that—for the past week while the Council hit their heads over the table trying to figure out what to do about Alden. A lot of ideas were thrown around but nothing workable. We would still be sitting there right now, going in circles. Do you know why we aren't?"

"Because you got fed up and killed them all in a fit of rage?"

"No." He licked his dry lips. "Though I did fantasize about doing just that once or twice during the week. The only reason we're not still sitting in that room is because I told them this was all pointless until we had more intelligence. Which we'd already sent our spies off to collect before the end of the first day. And then I got up and left. Others followed."

"I bet they were glad to be going home."

"*I* was glad to be going home." He took her hands, his thumbs tracing small circles across the insides of her wrists. "To see you."

She smirked over the furious pounding of her own heart. "You're addicted to my sarcasm, I tell you."

"I'm addicted to *you*." His fingers caressed her cheek.

"Do you even know what you've done to me?"

"Made you tell off stuck-up Magic Council members and recklessly storm out of meeting rooms?" She leaned into him, sliding her hands down the rigid muscles of his stomach. "Clearly I'm a fantastic influence."

His mouth brushed her cheek. "I'm not sure my colleagues on the Magic Council would agree," he growled into her ear. His hands traced burning rivers down her back.

"Screw the Council," she breathed, melting under his touch.

"I wanted to talk to you," he said, his lips caressing hers.

"Oh?" Desire scorched her body, piercing and pulsing through her. One word was all she could manage.

"Actually, you wanted to talk to me." His kisses slowed. "About yourself."

"Oh."

A memory tore through her. Kai's face was contorted with disgust as he spat insults at her. Abomination. Vile creature. She shook off Alden's illusion—his trick—but she couldn't shake the pain. And she couldn't shake the feeling that he was right. Kai had grown up believing that the Dragon Born were sin incarnated. Every supernatural had. To them, she was an abomination. And abominations were slaughtered.

Her body went limp, fear chasing out desire. "Well, I…"

"You've changed your mind." There was no emotion in his face. A blank slate. Or a slab of granite.

"I'm not ready." And might never be.

Magic swirled in his eyes, but his aura remained serene. "Take your time."

"Really?"

"Yes. I'm not going anywhere. And I have something to show you." He reached down, amusement tugging his brows when her breath caught in her throat. "Oh, but you do have a dirty mind, don't you?" Chuckling, he waved his phone in front of her face.

Sera gathered up the pieces of her shattered dignity and glanced at the phone. On the screen, there was an official-looking mail from Duncan Blackbrooke.

"It's your results from the Magic Games," Kai told her.

Odd, considering that she was the one who had survived the Games and she definitely hadn't gotten this mail.

"Results are sent to the coaches," he said, guessing her thought. Or maybe her eyes just screamed 'kill Duncan Blackbrooke!'. "It's antiquated, I know. But so are most traditions we have."

"Like wearing a suit?"

"I did away with that one many years ago. Except when I can't avoid it."

"Magic Council meetings?" she asked.

"No, I wear whatever the hell I want to those, and if anyone has a problem with me, we can take it outside. Or inside. I'm not particular."

She chuckled.

"It's not as though any of them could complain about my attire. The vampires wear two-hundred-year-old cloaks. And the fairies…well, they claim what they're wearing are dresses, but I think they've confused 'dress' with 'lingerie'."

"Kind of like your man Edwards and the fighting pit lingerie he bought me."

"Oh, no. Edwards's choices were downright modest compared to those fairies' dresses."

"Hmm. Maybe I should come with you next time you have a Magic Council meeting. You know, just to keep those naughty fairies in line." She draped her hands over his shoulders and leaned in to kiss him. "I can bring my sword. It will be fun. Like a field trip."

He snorted. "Do you want to see your results?"

"I guess." Sighing, she dropped her arms. "I'm going to find out eventually anyway. I need to show them to Simmons so he'll clear me for work again."

"Try not to sound too excited."

"I'm never excited to be called in to Simmons's office. Hey, maybe I'll send you instead. He likes you."

"Of course. I'll help you. We can go together."

"I was joking, Kai," she said. "But, um, thanks for offering."

"Bring him a muffin."

"Sorry?"

"A muffin," he repeated. "Simmons likes muffins. His favorite flavor is apple cinnamon."

Her mouth hung open in shock. "How do *you* know the head of Mayhem's favorite muffin flavor?"

He shrugged. "Research. Never go into battle unprepared."

"I wasn't aware you had ever battled Simmons."

"The battle of negotiation. Back when I wanted to hire you the first time."

"You mean, when you pretended to be Riley's friend so that you could spy on me to see what kind of weird funky magic I had?"

He sighed. "We've been over this, Sera. Riley and I already knew each other. That he was the brother of the mercenary I wanted to hire was just a lucky coincidence," he said. "But back to Simmons. I wanted to hire you, but I knew he'd try to push one of his top-tier mercenaries on me. I needed to soften him up first. So I had my guys research his weaknesses, and they came up with muffins."

"Did the muffin work?"

"Somewhat. He still tried to sway me toward some of his 'shooting stars', as he called them."

"Of course he did. He can charge more for mercenaries with high magic ratings. But none of them have my stellar sense of humor."

"Or your magic," Kai said, pointing at his phone screen.

"First tier mage," she read.

"No surprise there," Kai commented.

"First tier mage: Magic Breaker, Sniffer, Elemental. World rankings: Elemental #12, Magic Breaker...#1. Wow."

"You shouldn't be surprised. No one can break magic like you can."

Alex could, but Sera didn't mention that. She did not want her sister dragged through Blackbrooke's Games. "Sniffer: #1. Hey, I beat you in that one!"

Kai laughed. Or was that a grunt? A grunt-laugh?

Sera scrolled down, looking for more, but it was just a bunch of standard text about how her official results would be mailed to her...yada yada...more random bits. She got to the bottom. There was no reference to Dragon Born. In fact, there was no mention of anything weird whatsoever.

"You look relieved," Kai said.

She turned a smile on him. "Relieved that it's finally over. Well, that crisis anyway. We still have to deal with

Alden."

"And we will," he told her.

"Did the Council send a team to his underground hideout in New York?"

"Yes, but by the time they got there, Alden and his followers were gone."

Figured. "I saw the news," she told him. "There's a lot of speculation about the nameless mage who stumbled into Alden's lair and then escaped. Thanks for keeping me out of the headlines."

"I did that for purely selfish reasons. I didn't want to have to fight hundreds of reporters for your attention."

The look in his eyes scorched her from the inside out. She looked away, fussing with the bottom rim of her top.

"I missed you, Sera. Every moment I was there, in those stupid meetings, I was thinking about you."

She snickered. "I thought you were fantasizing about killing them all in a fit of rage."

"I can do both. And I'm not kidding," he told her, his voice as hard as granite. "I was thinking about you. Your lips. Your body." His hands slid down her sides, igniting her senses. "Our night together. How I want to have many more like it." He caught her hand as it scuttled to her hemline. "You've been trying to take off your clothes since I got here."

"That's not true." Her blush burned deeper—lower—as his hand brushed across her top.

Kai's phone chose that spectacular moment to ring. He answered it with one hand, keeping the other on her but sliding it lower, across her stomach, down to her hip.

"Ok," he spoke into the phone, even as his fingers traced the inside of her thigh.

Sera bit back a moan.

"Sounds good," Kai said, then hung up. His eyes met hers, wicked as sin. "Riley says hi."

"I can't believe you were touching me like *that* while talking to my brother!" She punched him in the arm. "Have you no shame?"

"Of course I have no shame. Don't you know that by now? Besides," he added, giving her a smoldering look. "I can't help myself around you. But I will." He smoothed down her top. "Riley will be back in a few minutes. I don't want to leave any evidence of my transgression."

"Oh? Am I finally going to hear about the fight you and Riley had?"

"I wouldn't call it a fight."

"What would you call it?"

He thought about that for a moment. "An understanding. He found out that we spent the night together."

"And he...understood?"

"No, he was pissed as hell."

"But I thought he wanted us to get together," she said.

"Not about the sex. He was pissed that I didn't tell him. Since we're friends and all."

"And I'm his sister. Are you supposed to tell your friend that you slept with his sister?"

"He thought I didn't trust him enough to tell him."

"Hmm." She nibbled on her thumb. "What else did Riley say? Did Dal have to use the compressed magic?"

"No, but you look like you wish he had."

She nodded enthusiastically.

"Riley told me that if I hurt you, he'd come up with a magical explosive that worked against dragons. And use it. I said I understood. That was the 'understanding' part."

"Wow."

"Precisely."

"I think it's easier to make jokes about your friend getting together with your sister when it hasn't happened yet," she said. "Once it happens…well, then you realize your friend is banging your sister."

His lips quirked. "The word 'banging' was not mentioned in the course of this conversation."

"Of course not." She grinned. "Because that would just be crude."

Kai looked at her, his hands clasped together behind his back, but his eyes burning. He cleared his throat.

"We should get the pizza ready," he said and swooped it off the table, carrying it to the coffee table in front of the television.

Sera followed him, her pulse still pounding. "Kai, what are we going to do about Alden?" she asked him as they sat down on the sofa.

"I don't know," he said, wrapping his arm around her in a protective embrace. "But we will find a way to end him. And this time, it will be permanent."

Author's Note

If you want to be notified when I have a new release, head on over to my website to sign up for my mailing list at http://www.ellasummers.com/newsletter. Your e-mail address will never be shared, and you can unsubscribe at any time.

If you enjoyed *Magic Games*, I'd really appreciate if you could spread the word. One of the best ways of doing that is by leaving a review wherever you purchased this book. Thank you for your invaluable support!

What's coming next in the series?

Blood Magic, the second book of *Dragon Born Alexandria*, and *Rival Magic*, the third book of *Dragon Born Serafina*, are coming early next year.

About the Author

Ella Summers has been writing stories for as long as she could read; she's been coming up with tall tales even longer than that. One of her early year masterpieces was a story about a pigtailed princess and her dragon sidekick. Nowadays, she still writes fantasy. She likes books with lots of action, adventure, and romance. When she is not busy writing or spending time with her two young children, she makes the world safe by fighting robots.

Originally from the U.S., Ella currently resides in Switzerland. She is the author of the urban fantasy series *Dragon Born* and the fantasy adventure series *Sorcery and Science*

www.ellasummers.com

.

CPSIA information can be obtained at www.ICGtesting.com
Printed in the USA
LVOW12s1147080316

478257LV00005B/338/P